EXTINCTION POINT: GENESIS

Also by PAUL ANTONY JONES:

EXTINCTION POINT:

GENESIS

PAUL ANTONY JONES

47NORTH

This is a work of fiction. Names, characters, organizations, places, events, and incidents are either products of the author's imagination or are used fictitiously.

Text copyright © 2015 Paul Antony Jones
All rights reserved.

No part of this book may be reproduced, or stored in a retrieval system, or transmitted in any form or by any means, electronic, mechanical, photocopying, recording, or otherwise, without express written permission of the publisher.

Published by 47North, Seattle

www.apub.com

Amazon, the Amazon logo, and 47North are trademarks of Amazon.com, Inc., or its affiliates.

ISBN-13: 9781503949690
ISBN-10: 1503949699

Cover design by Shasti O'Leary-Soudant/SOS CREATIVE LLC

Printed in the United States of America

For Samantha, my writing partner and constant companion.
We miss you.

CHAPTER 1

A single bead of perspiration ran down Emily Baxter's forehead, rolled across her flushed cheek, and dripped slowly off her chin.

"Relax, Em. Just ease forward on the stick," said MacAlister from the Black Hawk's copilot seat, his arms folded across his chest, well away from the duplicate set of flight controls. "That's it. Watch your altitude and air speed, don't want to stall her."

Far below, the canopy of the red jungle stretched out toward the horizon covering everything that had once been San Diego County and beyond. Not a single sign of humanity's dominance over the planet remained now; all had vanished beneath the creeping red plant life or succumbed to the alien fungus that devoured everything it touched. Everything, that was, except for the last remaining outpost of humanity: Point Loma, the former military base where some five hundred survivors now eked out an existence.

"Wine," Mac said, out of nowhere.

"What? What the hell are you babbling about?" Emily replied, trying to keep all of her attention focused on keeping the helicopter level.

"No more wine. Ever. Grapes are extinct. So that means there won't ever be any more wine."

It was something every survivor had experienced at some point: the sudden realization that something from their past life was gone, forever, irretrievably lost, thanks to the alien invasion. Mac had made a point over the past two years of vocalizing each of his as they came to him.

"I thought you told me you were a teetotaler?" Emily said this as she banked the helo hard left, moving it back in the direction of Point Loma.

"Well I am now, that's for sure. But I would have liked to have had the chance to try a bottle of the good stuff at least."

Emily's right hand, moist with sweat, pushed forward on the controls of the Black Hawk. She felt her stomach rise as the helo dipped down toward the ground, still a few hundred feet below them.

"I'm kind of busy here," she said.

"I know. Sorry . . . You're doing great, keep it steady . . . watch your yaw, we're drifting to the right a little too much . . . that's better."

Emily worked the foot paddles that adjusted the surprisingly agile machine's attitude, squaring it up with the yellow *H* of the landing pad she could see below, about two kilometers away. She had over eighty flight hours under her belt now thanks to Mac's tutelage. This particular flight was his final test before qualifying her to fly solo, the tail end of an intense training regimen leading up to this day.

Besides being her adorable husband, Mac was one of the biggest assets the survivors at Point Loma had: apart from his training as a special forces operative with the British Special Boat Service, he was also the only person still alive who knew how to pilot a helicopter. In this new world, skills had become the most prized asset, and the possibility of the world's last remaining pilot tripping on an untied shoelace and breaking his neck was apparently too great to allow. So Point Loma's council had asked if Mac would be willing to teach a select few how to fly, and he'd agreed, but only after he had insisted that Emily would be his first student.

"It's a smart move," he told her. "It'll strengthen your standing in the camp and give those idiots on the council something to think about."

Emily had agreed. There was an air of discontent within the camp these past few months that had both of them concerned, thanks in part to some of the new appointments on the council. Learning these unique skills from her husband would go a long way toward ensuring that both of them would remain indispensable assets.

For someone who just a couple of years earlier had not even been able to drive a car, Emily had quickly learned how to handle a wide range of vehicles after her predicament as the apparent sole survivor in New York; she had driven an SUV across the United States and Canada and then a snowcat over the desolate frozen wastes of Alaska, before piloting a boat to the Stockton Islands and the terrible disappointment she had found there. Since their arrival at Point Loma she had also learned how to ride one of several motorbikes the group had salvaged from the various parking lots around the camp. It was a lot of fun to ride the dirt bikes— "chicken chasers" Mac called them because of the *burrrrrk-buk-buk* sound the engines made—although she still found herself missing the freedom her bicycle had given her. Learning to fly a helicopter seemed the logical next step, especially as no one had been willing to teach her how to captain one of the four submarines docked at the base . . . at least, not yet.

The landing pad was growing closer too quickly, so Emily eased back on the throttle and gradually brought the Black Hawk to a hover before slowly descending until she felt the undercarriage touch the ground with a slight jolt.

She turned to look at Mac's grinning face.

"Perfect," he said.

Emily smiled back, resisting the urge to lean across and kiss him. Instead she went through the post-flight shutdown procedure and waited for the ground crew to secure the craft. When they were done she pulled off her headphones and unstrapped herself from the pilot's seat.

Outside the air was moist and sweet, the sky a flawless blue, accompanied by the sound of the ocean crashing against the beach less than a hundred meters or so away. If Emily closed her eyes she could almost imagine the world was normal. But when she opened them there would still be the vast hedge of the red jungle off in the distance to remind her that the world was a very different place from the one that had existed before the red rain.

"So, how's it feel to officially be the only other person in the world who knows how to fly this thing?" said Mac, as he walked around the front of the Black Hawk to join her.

"Pretty damn good, considering my husband was the one who taught me." Emily leaned in and kissed him deeply. "Thank you," she said when she pulled away.

Pleasure's all mine, his grin said.

They had a total of three working helicopters now: the Black Hawk they had used to fly on the mission to Las Vegas, and two others cobbled together from slightly damaged craft and spare parts Chief Engineer Parsons and his engineering crew had scavenged from around the base and the naval supply center, just across the bay on Coronado Island. "We'll need to set up a schedule to start training the other students as soon as possible . . ." Emily paused when she saw a look of indecision on Mac's face. "What's wrong?"

Mac's smile had faded, and he took on what Emily recognized as his professional soldier's demeanor, one she knew was usually reserved for delivering bad news. He took a deep breath, held it for a second, and then puffed it out. "The council's given the go-ahead for the mission to Svalbard Island."

Emily stopped folding her flight gloves and stared at Mac. "When did that happen?" As hard as she tried, she was unable to keep the note of disappointment from her voice.

"Last night. I didn't want to tell you the mission was on until we got through this flight. Besides, you were so damn tired, I just—"

Emily held up a solitary hand to silence the Scotsman. "How long until you leave?"

"Two days," MacAlister said, stepping in a little closer and taking her hand. "If all goes according to plan, we will be in and out again in about a month and a half . . . two, tops. It'll be a piece of cake."

Emily thought back to the last council meeting just a week earlier. The group of survivors—specifically the first group of scientists who had arrived on board the USS *Michigan* just a few months earlier—had been working on alternative sources to supplement the camp's resources. The survivors had managed to scavenge significant amounts of food from the cities surrounding Point Loma before they had vanished beneath the unrelenting onslaught of the red jungle, and the submarines had also been pretty well stocked. But those stores were finite and were dwindling rapidly.

One of the scientists, a food chemist named Franklin, had been studying the effects of the Antarctic's extreme cold on some kind of manufactured protein when the world ended. He managed some success creating a mostly edible dried food bar from the alien plant life surrounding Point Loma. His first few attempts had been pretty fucking awful according to . . . well, *everyone*. But his latest creation was almost tasteless, and with some decent nutritional value. The only problem was that the process of extracting and curing the alien weed was slow and laborious. Still, they were manufacturing enough to supplement everyone's daily rations.

But even with the current rationing there was simply not enough food left to allow them to survive much past the next year. So Mac had proposed that they take one of the subs and travel to Svalbard Island off the coast of Norway in the hope that the seed bank they knew was there would be untouched by the advance of the alien plant and animal life that now dominated the world. If they could recover sufficient stock from the Svalbard seed bank, then they could turn this little spit of land they called home into a sustainable farm. During her mission to Las Vegas, Emily had been captured by the aliens responsible for unleashing the red rain that had destroyed life across the planet, reforming Earth into the strange world the survivors now lived in. The Caretakers, as the aliens called themselves, gave Emily a message to take back to the survivors in Point Loma: stay where you are and you will be allowed to live; ignore this warning at your own peril.

In the months after her return to Point Loma, two submarines had made the fatal mistake of ignoring the warning Emily passed to them, choosing instead to try and settle in their home countries. Within days of the crew setting foot back on land, all radio communication with them had been lost.

Then of course there were those within the community—more than Emily was comfortable admitting to—who simply did not believe her story. There had been more than one occasion where she had been accused of outright lying about what she had experienced on board the alien craft after her capture by the Caretakers.

Emily's concern right now was for her husband's safety. She desperately wanted to go with him—and would have been prepared to argue her case until he gave in—but she had responsibilities here now, not least of all their son, Adam.

"How many of you are leaving?" she asked quietly as they walked back toward the encampment and the family quarters.

"Full crew of the *Vengeance* and the eight-man assault team I've been training. It's going to be a piece of cake, Em. Trust me."

"God! I really wish you'd stop saying that."

Mac paused and placed both hands on his wife's shoulders, turning her to face him. "This is what I do, Em. I'm the only one who's qualified, and if I don't do it, then one of these other Muppets will. And I can guarantee they will cock it up. We can't risk that . . . *I* can't risk it."

Emily knew he was the best man for the job, and she knew he was more than capable of taking care of himself. If she were being honest, her frustration stemmed more from not being able to go with him. Life during the two years since she and the other survivors had arrived at Point Loma, while certainly no bowl of cherries, was boring compared to the time she had spent travelling from New York to Alaska, and finally on to California. She felt . . . trapped, and she so wanted to go with him, to explore the world she knew lay beyond the reservation that had been assigned to the remains of humanity by the Caretakers. Humanity, what was left of it, lived on a dramatically changed planet now. And while all the continents remained the same, it was a world that, for all intents and purposes, might just as well be another planet altogether.

Mac and Emily walked the remaining distance back to their quarters in silence, Emily's frustration on a low simmer. She managed a smile when they reached their apartment as she spotted Thor, her Alaskan malamute, friend and rescuer, lying in a ray of sunlight on the front stoop. His eyes popped open at the sound of the couple's approach. He stretched and sat, tail sweeping back and forth as Emily and Mac climbed the steps to the porch.

"How you doing, boy?" Emily said, reaching down to caress

the dog's head. Thor licked her hand in return and wound his body around her legs like a cat, blocking her way until he had received the satisfactory amount of attention.

"We're home," Emily called out as they stepped through the front door.

Rhiannon appeared from her bedroom, her hair tied back in a bun. Every day she looked more and more like the beautiful young woman she was quickly becoming. *They grow up so fast,* Emily thought, with only a hint of irony. And that was going to bring trouble all of its own. Emily had seen the furtive—and, worryingly, some outright lecherous—glances the girl received whenever she stepped outside. With a disproportionately larger population of men to women, competition for Rhiannon's attention was going to become more and more intense. With the majority of the survivors being military there was still a fairly firm grip on authority, but who knew how long that would last? Thankfully Rhiannon seemed not to notice the attention; she was completely taken with helping care for little Adam. Of course, the fact that she carried her own pistol on her hip, and that everyone had seen how good of a shot she was, helped ease Emily's worries. The kid—she would not be able to call her that for much longer, she supposed—had proved more than once that she was capable of holding her own.

Speak of the devil, Emily thought playfully as Adam, now almost eight months old, crawled from behind Rhiannon's legs, a smile of pure joy lighting up his face.

"Gah!" he said and propelled himself toward his parents, his right hand tightly clutched around an object that he held out in front of him. "Gah!" he burbled again and slapped the object into Emily's outstretched hand. It was a beautifully carved wooden racing car, complete with moving wheels, and painted a bright green.

Emily looked at Rhiannon, puzzled.

"Parsons stopped by and dropped it off for him," said Rhiannon, smiling.

During the voyage from Alaska to California, the *Vengeance*'s chief engineer had cottoned to Rhiannon as though she was his own daughter. That loyalty had now expanded to include Adam, for which Emily and Mac were eternally grateful. An extra set of eyes on her family was a welcome addition, especially those of someone as loyal as Parsons.

And judging by the craftsmanship that had gone into the toy, Parsons had also become adept at working the wood harvested from the Titans—the name they had given to the enormous alien trees that now covered the planet—which the survivors used for repairs and building new structures. The detail of the toy was amazing; the Welshman was apparently an accomplished woodworker.

Emily reached down and plucked up her son with both hands, which brought an even wider toothless grin along with a cascade of giggles as she handed him back his new toy.

She stared: *My God, he is so beautiful.*

Adam was the first newborn child on the planet since the red rain had fallen, and, while at first glance he looked and behaved just like any other child his age would have before the coming of the rain, his eyes betrayed his heritage as firstborn on this alien world. Each was flecked with tiny specks of red that seemed to glow and scintillate in the light.

Although far less pronounced, Emily had noticed similar faint flecks of red in her own eyes. She was sure that they had not been there before her excursion to the alien ship, and, while they were only visible to anyone who got within kissing distance, she had resorted to wearing sunglasses whenever she was outside or not with her immediate circle of family and trusted friends.

A small but distinct and growing sense of paranoia existed

within the camp as the inevitable clash of cultures and beliefs of the survivors ground against each other on an almost daily basis, and Emily did not want to add any more fuel to that particular slow-burning fire.

Mac had seen her eyes, of course, but the only reason he could come up with was that they might be some kind of side effect of whatever process the Caretakers had used to transport Emily to their ship back in Las Vegas.

"Maybe there was some kind of malfunction in their transporter beam, you know, like in *Star Trek*," he had said, only half joking.

"That would make you Scotty, then?" she had said, nodding her agreement, but beneath the humor she knew better. She did not feel the same since her return; her nights had been plagued by odd dreams, strange voices echoing in her head and a sense that she was . . . fractured, splintered almost, and yet part of something larger, something unseen that was as elusive as trying to hold on to the past.

The dreams were not nightmares, exactly, but they were disconcerting enough to wake her on more than one occasion bathed in sweat. Instead of fear, she woke with a sense of longing, of missing something close to her that she simply could not figure out. And, of course, there was also the possibility that each of the twenty or so millimeter-sized red specks were a side effect of her being the only human to have survived direct contact with the red rain. Every other survivor had either been safely hidden away at the bottom of the ocean, protected by the extreme cold of the Arctic and the Antarctic, or hundreds of kilometers above her head in the International Space Station.

Before he died, Rhiannon's father had told Emily that the rain had stopped short of their hilltop home; they had been protected by the peculiar weather system of the area. So that left Emily as the sole witness to the metamorphic effect of the rain, how it had changed human life along with every other life-form on the planet, molding it to a preprogrammed plan that transformed the skin of the planet into what lay beyond the border of Point Loma. It wasn't difficult to imagine that the virus had had some kind of effect on her too, even if only as small as changing her eyes.

"You okay, love?" Mac's question tugged her mind back to reality.

"What? Oh yeah! I just zoned for a second."

Mac lifted the boy from his mother. "You wee rascal, you weigh a bloody ton already," he said. Adam gurgled his contentment and clung tightly to his father.

Rhiannon tickled the boy under his chin, which brought about another fit of giggles.

Emily wasn't really sure when it had happened, maybe that first day after they had buried Ben, but the truth was it did not matter: Rhiannon had become her surrogate daughter, and, eventually, once Mac came into their life, his too. And when Adam was born Emily had seen an almost instantaneous shift in Rhiannon; she had gone from being a child to a young woman, a big sister eager to take on whatever responsibilities Emily was willing to delegate to her. Emily was sure that the loss of Rhiannon's little brother, Ben, had played a huge part in the girl's almost obsessive dedication to Adam. And if Emily were being completely honest she had leaned on Rhiannon a little too much in these early months. But that was what families did, right? When things were tough, they stuck together and held each other up and helped when and wherever they were needed, each one shouldering whatever load was placed on them. It was sad to think that this little group of five entities was in all likelihood the only complete family left on the planet.

Emily sidled over to Rhiannon and placed an arm around her shoulder and squeezed.

"What's that for?"

"Just because."

"We've got a council meeting to go to. You okay looking after His Royal Highness for a little while longer?" Mac asked, nodding at his boy, who was now happily playing with his new toy car again.

"Sure thing," said Rhiannon.

"We'll only be a couple of hours," Emily said. She leaned in and gave Rhiannon a kiss on the head and the same to Adam. "You're a life saver."

"I know," said Rhiannon with an assured smile.

■ ■ ■

For some unknown reason Dr. Sylvia Valentine flat out did not like Emily.

From the second the woman stepped off the USS *Michigan* and stood on the dock squinting in the California afternoon sunshine, Emily had sensed a tension emanating from her—a disturbance in the Force, Mac would have described it—a sense of aloofness that Emily realized later, after everything that had happened, she had never expected to experience again. She *had* expected some humbleness. Every other survivor Emily had greeted in her capacity as Camp Loma's official welcoming party had looked tired from weeks or even months of travelling, but inevitably they had a smile on their faces when they felt the welcoming California sun on their skin and saw the crowd of smiling faces waiting to greet them.

But when Sylvia—"That's Doctor Valentine," the woman would insist later when Emily made the mistake of using her given name—stepped off the deck of the *Michigan*, refusing the outstretched hand of a sailor placed there to assist the debarkation, her face was cloaked in a scowl.

And right then Emily knew she was going to have a problem with this one.

The doctor was tall, easily five nine, maybe even five eleven. The woman's brunette hair was tied in a tight, neat knot behind her head. She was smartly dressed in a light-yellow blouse and dark-gray business pantsuit that showed off her trim figure. She carried a large suitcase in one hand. With her free hand Valentine had pulled a pair of sunglasses out of her breast pocket and placed them on her face, then slowly turned her head to survey the dock, as if she were looking over a piece of property she was going to buy. She did not look particularly happy with what she saw.

Fine, Emily thought, *you can catch the next boat back to McMurdo for all I care.* But she had to admit, the stranger looked damned good for a woman she guessed must be in her midfifties and had spent months locked away in a submarine.

Emily had met plenty of women like this during her time at the *New York Tribune*, back in Manhattan: professional, smart, capable, used to getting her own way. This was a woman who only ever at ease when she was in control. And that was just fine as far as Emily was concerned. Camp Loma was a big enough place for them both, and God knows women were in short enough supply around here. Emily was willing to overlook any potential character quirks if only for the sake of having an additional feminine mind in the same vicinity amid all the testosterone flooding the camp. They would warm to each other, given enough time, she was sure of it. The woman had been cooped up on a frozen island for the last year and a half or so. Emily could afford to cut her some slack.

But as Emily had stood on the quay watching the newcomers disembark, she remembered a warning from the McMurdo radio operator: "Don't trust Valentine."

The truth was, everything had been fine right up until the bitch had to go and confirm every Goddamn thing Emily had been worried about.

Thor, always riding shotgun with Emily and always happy to make a new friend, had immediately launched into his own welcome routine. Running from newcomer to newcomer as the *Michigan* disgorged them one by one, his tongue lolling out the side of his mouth, he happily accepted pats on the head and the inevitable "Oohs!" and "Ahhs!" that followed.

But Valentine . . . Valentine was different.

As Thor reached her, his head up, back end swinging like it was about to fly off from all the tail wagging, the woman barely even acknowledged his presence. The malamute continued to circle her for a few seconds, looking up expectantly, his tail gradually dropping as he lost some of his enthusiasm. Finally he sat at her feet and raised a single paw.

The kick was subtle; if Emily had not been looking directly at Valentine she would have missed it completely. It was aimed at the muscles of Thor's haunches, and exercised as casually as anyone else might swat away an annoying fly. Emily heard Thor yelp in pain and saw her friend flinch, his tail dropping between his legs as he scooted sideways while the woman stepped past him and onto the concrete quay.

Valentine's head tracked back and forth across the camp and the forest of red that lay off in the distance.

Emily felt her own smile falter. Her right hand instinctively dropped to the butt of the HK45T holstered on her hip as her anger boiled up . . . and for a second she forgot where she was. In that moment she was back on the road to the Stockton Islands, her instincts and sheer will to survive the only thing keeping her alive. And her instincts told her that this woman wasn't just a social threat, this woman was dangerous. Emily almost drew the pistol . . . almost.

Instead she forced her fingers to relax and dropped her hand to her hip. *Be civilized, now.* "Thor, come here, boy," she yelled out, her eyes remaining fixed squarely on Valentine. With those big sunglasses she looked like a giant bug: a praying mantis.

She needs to watch her step, Emily thought, *because I would be more than happy to step on the bitch if she gets out of line.*

The big malamute scampered to Emily's side, his tail back in the air and his tongue lolling again, but he was still occasionally looking back at the stranger as if he suspected she might deliver another swift kick when he wasn't looking.

"Sit, boy," Emily told him. Thor obeyed, and his mistress rested the flat of her hand on the dog's head.

For many of the new arrivals, this would be the first glimpse of the strange alien world they all now lived in. Most of them would have seen the original news reports when the red rain had first fallen, witnessed the sudden and final severance of all communication with the rest of the world. All of them would have experienced the great red storm that had changed the world so absolutely, and all of them had heard the stories of survival relayed to them via Point Loma's radio. But this first step into the world, this was reality, and seeing the changes for themselves was often the psychological equivalent of being cracked on the head by a hammer.

And given those mitigating circumstances, Emily would give Valentine a chance to change her first impression, she decided. This time.

Every developed nation from both the east and west had had a base on Antarctica before the red rain had fallen. Around fifty of the seventy bases were permanent, while others operated only during the summer months. On the day the rain came there were 1,722 souls on the continent. An American submarine, the USS *Michigan*, was in port for a routine visit, along with two large container ships, docked at McMurdo base to supply the islanders with both food and fuel. Counting the crew of these three vessels, the total number of humans present was just shy of two thousand.

As the alien rain swept across the world it left the deep-frozen Antarctica untouched. The rest of the world quickly disappeared, and the Antarctica survivors believed themselves to be all that was left. They were well stocked with both food and fuel thanks to the two resupply ships sitting in the port and waiting to be offloaded. They believed they had time to wait out the effects of the red rain.

They continued to believe that until the day of the great storm.

The world-spanning storm swept inland from every direction, erasing half of the continent with an ever-tightening noose around the survivors' necks . . . then it stopped, less than a couple of kilometers off McMurdo. The research station was not unscathed. By the time the storm died away and the survivors emerged out onto the ice, one of the two supply ships had been swept out to sea along with its crew and all its remaining supplies, presumed sunk. The other, the *Maria Consuela*, was taking on water and threatening to capsize along with all its precious cargo.

The human toll was even greater. Everyone who had not made it to McMurdo or hunkered down in their own base had perished. At least, the remaining survivors *presumed* they were dead, as not a trace could be found when rescue teams had been sent out. Of the original 2,000 or so to have survived the red rain, just 628 people were left alive on the island after the storm.

The USS *Michigan* had dived deep before the full force of the storm hit. By the time it surfaced again and headed back to McMurdo, it had suffered only the equivalent of a few minor bumps and bruises.

If there was an upside—and Emily had made a veritable habit of turning sows' ears into silk purses these days—roughly one third of the survivors were women, which greatly helped to reduce some of the tension the Point had been swimming in.

The days after the storm were bleak for the McMurdo survivors, but they pulled together enough to salvage the majority of the supplies still left on the *Maria Consuela*, before patching her up and making her seaworthy again.

It had taken months before the base's radio tower was repaired and the weather had settled enough that Point Loma's nightly radio signal, Emily at the microphone, found its way to McMurdo.

It was difficult for Emily to describe the swell of relief that swept through the Point Loma survivors at the announcement that they had found more people alive out there. It was as though the entire base had been holding its collective breath and, at the news, had released it. The air felt lighter afterward.

Still, not everyone at McMurdo had wanted to come to Point Loma. Some had decided to stay and eke out whatever existence they could in the freezing wastes of the South Pole. While Emily could understand the choice to stay behind, she did not think their chances of survival were going to be high once the food ran out. But the majority of McMurdo survivors, thank God, had decided that California sounded like a good idea after months of freezing their asses off.

It was just a shame that one of them had to be Sylvia Valentine.

Valentine, according to others from McMurdo, had been a vocal advocate for staying put. But her tune had changed once it became clear that the majority would be leaving, and that, with or without her consent, the supplies would be going with them.

There was no way the USS *Michigan* could accommodate all of the McMurdo residents, so straws had been drawn for the remaining spaces after essential personnel and supplies had been loaded aboard the submarine. The remaining survivors, those who had literally drawn the short straw, were to wait for the USS *Michigan* to reach Point Loma and sound the all clear and then set sail on the *Maria Consuela*. The cargo ship would make its way to the United States over the course of three months, but a problem with the engine had delayed the ship's departure.

The McMurdo survivors had arrived two months ago. And somehow, in that time, Valentine had gone from a newcomer on the fringe of the community to insinuating herself into every major aspect of the running of Point Loma. Emily had been convinced that the other survivors would eventually see her for what she was, but now Emily realized that view had been rather naïve, and it had been well and truly laid to rest when the two-faced bitch was elected as the chairperson of the Camp Council.

■ ■ ■

By the time Emily and Mac filed into the packed gymnasium designated as the town hall, the council meeting was already underway.

"'Scuse us . . . Sorry . . ." Mac said as he forged the way past several seated people Emily recognized only in passing. The place was packed, with the majority of the camp present. Point Loma now had so many survivors she could not recall everyone's name. She was going to have to work on that.

Within a couple of months of the Argentine sub *San Juan* and the French submarine *Le Terrible* arriving at Point Loma it had become obvious that some kind of government was needed. Between the growing number of newcomers and the varying nationalities, a common ground of law had to be established if the survivors were to coexist.

A three-person council had been appointed, comprised of each of the sub captains—no elections needed, apparently. When the military is in the majority, it tends to do things the way it knows works; at least, that is what they told Emily when she raised her objections. Not long after the USS *Michigan* arrived, the council had been expanded to seven, the four new places assigned to the captain of the *Michigan* and three civilians appointed by the council. Emily had not been considered.

She took her seat in the audience next to Mac. The plastic chairs were arranged in a horseshoe facing a raised stage with a table at the center of the gym.

Emily knew all of the councilors sitting behind the table: the French captain, Victor Séverin; Ignacio Vela, the captain of the Argentinian sub *San Juan*; Simon Patterson, the captain of the *Michigan*; Lynda Hanson, a botanist, and Deryck Maslanka, a structural engineer, both of whom arrived in the *Michigan*; Raoul Béringer, a French journalist who had somehow found himself aboard the *Le Terrible* when it set sail just as the red rain hit Europe, and, of course, Valentine. She had replaced Captain Constantine when he stepped down. Emily knew that Maslanka and Hanson were both in Valentine's pocket; they were going to vote any way Valentine told them to, and she suspected Vela might be enamored enough with the woman to be persuaded to vote with her—Emily had seen the way Valentine smiled and touched the man's elbow whenever they were within stroking distance of each other. She was on the fence about Béringer; in all Emily's dealings with him, he had struck her as a decent sort.

". . . so let's put that to a vote, shall we?" Valentine said from the podium in that annoying sickly sweet Southern drawl she used whenever she expected to completely get her way. And sure enough, whatever agenda item was being discussed before Emily and Mac's arrival got a five to two approval. Valentine, Hanson, Maslanka, and Vela. And, surprise, surprise, Béringer's hand was raised with the others, which got a disapproving stare from his fellow countryman, Captain Séverin.

"And on to item four on the agenda: the creation of an expeditionary force to investigate the potential for expansion outside the Point Loma peninsula."

Emily stiffened, unsure if she had heard correctly.

Maslanka took up the item, his deep sonorous voice filling the room: "As you are all aware, we are facing a looming crisis. Food, ladies and gentlemen. It is not going to last forever. And, yes, I know that Captain Constantine and his crew are about to set sail for Svalbard, but let's be real here, folks: there's no guarantee that they are going to get there in one piece, and, if they do, and they are able to find a viable seed crop, there's no guarantee that they are going to make it back alive either."

Emily felt her blood go from a low simmer to its boiling point in a few seconds flat. Did this asshole not know that the majority of the crew he was talking about were sitting right here? She started to stand up and say something.

Mac placed his hand lightly on her knee before she could even lift her butt two inches off the seat. She turned to look at him . . . and stopped. Jesus Christ! *How the fuck does he stay so damn calm?* she wondered as she saw him smiling back at her. She could feel the pink flush of anger on her own skin, but he was his usual Limey pale, his face betraying nothing but calm . . . except for his eyes. His eyebrows had furrowed just slightly, barely noticeable to anyone who did not know him, and his eyelids were half closed, not enough to be called a squint but sufficient for Emily to know that Mac was pissed, with a capital fucking *P. Relax,* Mac's expression said, *don't give them the pleasure; we'll deal with this when we have to.* Emily allowed herself to grudgingly drop back into her seat.

This had the stink of Valentine's manipulation all over it. Of course, there was no way she would bring forward an item like this herself. Instead she would get one of her minions to put it out there, thereby maintaining her distance until she was able to judge whether the plebs approved or not before jumping on board.

This woman put the "fuck" into poli-fucking-tician.

". . . so what we . . . what I am proposing, is that we create several small groups of military and science personnel. Each unit—I call them Pathfinders—will be tasked with exploring the remains of cities and towns in an attempt to locate stores of food and potentially to identify areas untouched by the invasive species."

"And what about the Caretakers?" someone shouted from the back of the room. It was followed by a smattering of giggles from the crowd. Emily twisted in her seat to try to see who had spoken, but all she saw was a few condescending grins and dismissive glances.

"I'd like to answer that, if I may," said Valentine. She stood and looked out across the sea of faces staring back at her. "We have only the word of a couple of sailors who admit that they saw 'something' and a woman who claims that she had some kind of communication with"—Valentine paused dramatically and Emily half expected the woman to make air quotes; instead, she coated the next word with a heavy tone of sarcasm usually reserved exclusively for the tinfoil hat brigade—"*aliens* . . . who told her we all needed to stay in our cozy reservation." Her tone changed to a patronizing sweetness and Emily found herself again bristling as

21

Valentine continued. "None of us are arguing that a cataclysmic event overtook our world; we have only to look beyond the borders of our camp. But the suggestion that it was *aliens*?" She let the last word hang in the air, long enough for another well-timed smile of concern. "We have all suffered losses, and we have all experienced untold grief, and most of us have managed to overcome those painful memories and move on, while the impact on others may have been greater, the emotional damage deeper . . . more damaging."

Did that bitch just call me crazy? Emily thought. *Seriously?* She almost laughed out loud. *Oh yeah, that would look great. The crazy lady giggling in the center row. They'll lock me up in a second.*

Mac's hand tightened on her knee. *Easy now,* it said.

Valentine continued, closing her argument, "Well, I'm sorry, ladies and gentlemen, but I for one think we need to do a little checking for ourselves. But, of course, that is entirely up to our esteemed council members."

"I should have fucking shot her when I had the chance," Emily mumbled a little too loudly, smiling innocently when Mac turned to give her a wide-eyed "use your inner voice" stare.

Valentine continued, her chin tilting upward slightly as though she were personally witnessing the second coming: "Now I know that our very bravest and finest are leaving soon to travel to Svalbard, but I suggest that when they return we organize the expeditionary force of our most trusted citizens to travel into the interior of the red jungle and confirm whether these"—Valentine paused again, as if she was having difficulty finding the right words—"whether these ghost stories are real . . . or not."

Emily stood up.

"Oh shit!" said Mac, quietly.

"And you'll be the first to volunteer, I suppose?" yelled Emily, sounding way too calm for anyone who knew her.

All heads turned to look at her.

"Mizz Baxter. I think that you—"

Emily talked right over her. "Oh, and you'd better come up with a plan on how to replace whoever it is you're going to send off on your little expedition, because I can tell you that those"—she did make air quotes—"*aliens* you are so fucking skeptical of will turn them into mincemeat, or worse."

"Mizz Baxter, there's really no need for such language. I am merely drawing attention to the fact that you are the only one to claim to have seen what you allege to have seen. No one besides you and the three men with you has witnessed these—what did you name them?—oh yes, these 'Caretakers' you say abducted you. And let's be honest, I'm sure most people here find it rather unbelievable that if these so-called aliens actually exist that they would choose *you* to pass on their warning. I'm sure you can understand our skepticism."

Our skepticism? At what point had it become the general consensus that she was a liar? Emily had to give Valentine her due; she was damn good at deflecting and co-opting. Every word she had spoken was delivered with not an ounce of animosity; instead, it had the tone of a patient mother reasoning with an unruly child.

This woman was *really* starting to piss her off now.

Emily retorted, "That's because while you were snuggled up all safe and warm in Antarctica, we were here. We were the ones who fought and who saw what the red rain did, what it changed. I mean, I know you were a politician, but, Jesus Christ, you can't be so stupid as to imagine that everything that happened was something other than alien? Can you?"

"Oh, I can think of several other possibilities, the least of which would involve some intergalactic species whose sole job is to roam around the galaxies looking for worlds to destroy. If these Caretakers really exist, then where are they? Why has nobody else but you seen them? I know that your husband and the two other sailors saw *something*, but it was just you that they chose to speak to, right? So we only have your word for it."

"Are you calling me a liar?" said Emily.

The room was silent.

"Oh no, no, not at all. I'm merely suggesting that you are at best mistaken and, at worst, deluded. I'm quite sure that you all encountered some kind of a phenomenon while you were out there, but you offer no proof. I mean, you say you were a reporter and yet you don't even bring back a single photograph . . . So I think it would be quite foolish of us to take the word of a girl as if it were gospel." Valentine terminated her words with the biggest condescending smile Emily could have imagined.

The thing was, she was right, of course. Why would anyone take her word for any of it? In fact, Emily knew there were more than a handful of people who had quietly expressed a similar opinion, but Mac's status within the community, the fact that he stood beside her on everything she had relayed to the survivors, lent enough gravitas to her story that it had kept the original group swayed in her favor. But that had all changed now, the pendulum of power was swinging away from the original group of survivors as the newcomers integrated into the community. They had no attachment to Emily, had seen none of the things she had seen, experienced none of the nightmares her little group of survivors had. They were just going to have to find out the hard way, but she would be damned if she was going to be complicit in helping to send men and women to a certain death.

Emily looked for some cutting remark to launch at Valentine in her defense. "Fuck you!" she said eventually, and walked out.

■ ■ ■

"Emily! Wait," Mac yelled, jogging to catch up with her. "Hang on a second." He took her elbow and slowed her to a full stop. "You alright?"

Emily took a deep breath and exhaled. "Fuck! There's something about that woman that just pisses me off." She took a deep breath and exhaled slowly. "I met people like her every day before the rain. They try to obfuscate their own agenda by couching it to look like it's for the greater good. Jesus, Mac. I thought we'd left all that bullshit behind us. She gets right under my skin."

Mac squeezed her shoulder. "She's just a politician, doing politician things, Em."

Emily shook her head vehemently. "No, that woman has something else up her sleeve. And besides, it's people like her that got us all into this mess in the first fucking place with their 'fuck everyone else's opinion, you'll do it my way' attitude." She took another deep breath, trying to calm the anger she heard in her voice. "She's making a power play, Mac. And we're standing in her way."

Mac gave Emily a look that bordered on concern, then placed both of his hands gently on his wife's shoulders. "I think you're imagining things, sweetheart. You've got a lot on your plate, and I think that's probably got more to do with how you're feeling than Valentine having some nefarious plan to take over the world." He pulled her to his chest and planted a kiss on the top of her head, then eased her back out to arm's length again and, in a pretty rotten imitation of Valentine's southern drawl, he said, "I love you, Mizz Baxter."

Emily couldn't help herself—she smiled even as she landed a punch on Mac's bicep. "Bastard," she said, trying not to laugh, then leaped into his arms, throwing her legs around his waist. "Take me to the beach, sailor. We only have a couple of days before you leave me. We'd better make the most of it."

■ ■ ■

"Nice to know some things never change," said Emily, shaking the sand out of her bra an hour later. "A little help here, please." She nodded for Mac to fasten the clip between her shoulders. When he was done she lay back against the warm dune and stared straight up at the darkening sky, all thoughts of the council meeting gone from her head. Mac pulled his shirt and pants back on and stretched out next to her.

With no light from the now-extinct metropolises of Southern California to pollute the oncoming darkness, the evening sky was already a pincushion of stars, the Milky Way a brushstroke of white across the sky.

Something twinkled like glitter far, far up and Emily squinted to try to make it out better, her mind still pleasantly distracted by their eager lovemaking.

In the time since their arrival at Point Loma, Emily had occasionally seen the sky lit by the light of a dying satellite as its orbit slowly decayed and gravity dragged it back to Earth. There were plenty still up there, Emily knew, carving their way through the darkness, but what she saw now was something quite different; it looked like sunlight flashing faintly off thousands of tiny pieces of broken mirror.

"Do you see that?" she asked Mac, lying next to her, his eyes closed, his breathing low.

"What?" he said without opening his eyes.

She nudged him gently in the ribs with her elbow. "Look!" When she was sure he was paying attention, she pointed with her index finger at the scintillations.

"I don't see . . . Oh!" Mac sat upright. "What the hell is that?"

Emily propped herself up on both elbows. As the evening sky shifted gradually toward night it revealed more and more of the tiny, shimmering dots of light as, over the next few minutes, the growing darkness exposed a parabolic spiderweb-thin line of tiny gleaming lights arcing across the California evening sky like a vapor trail. It curved from the distant northeast to the opposite side of the horizon where the Pacific Ocean met the sky.

"I don't think it's a satellite," Emily said. "The debris usually burns up in a few seconds. This looks more like sunlight reflecting off of something . . . thousands of 'somethings' way up there."

Mac stood up, as if the extra six feet or so might give him a clearer view of this new phenomenon. "I don't think it's even inside the atmosphere; maybe it's in a low Earth orbit, but that doesn't make much sense."

"What?"

"If it was in a low Earth orbit then it would decay rapidly and fall out of the sky, unless it was powered somehow. Has it moved since you noticed it?"

Emily shook her head.

"So that means it's in some kind of geostationary orbit. But what the hell is it doing up there?"

Emily found it mildly amusing that neither of them had to ask who was responsible for whatever this new light show was. It went without saying that this was the handiwork of the Caretakers. Darkness had almost swallowed all that remained of the day, and the beach was now nothing but a strange mix of shadows.

"We need to get back before it gets too dark," Mac said after a few more minutes of sky gazing. Emily continued to stare up at the laser-beam-thin parabolic arc of twinkling lights slicing across the sky.

"It's beautiful, like someone cracked the heavens open," she whispered.

"Em? Rhiannon's going to be expecting us. We need to get back, love."

She plucked her blouse from the dune, shook out the remaining sand, and quickly buttoned it around her shoulders. "Think we should tell anyone about it?"

Mac shook his head. "Not yet. No reason to worry people needlessly. Anyway, it'll probably turn out to be nothing. Besides, what can we do about it anyway?"

The two lovers walked hand in hand along the beach back toward Point Loma, both occasionally glancing up at the newest addition to Earth's night sky. Both wondering what this new sign so high above them meant for the survivors down here on the ground.

CHAPTER 2

The following morning Valentine lay in wait for Emily and Mac outside the entrance to what had once been Point Loma's reception building but which now served as the main administrative council building. All of the councilors had an office inside.

"I trust everything is in order for your trip," Valentine said with not even a pretense of a hello.

"Well good morning to you too," said Emily. Then, because she was still feeling kind of pissy, added with a fake smile, "Sylvia." She felt Mac tap her foot with the toe of his boot, and tried not to let her satisfaction show when she saw Valentine's cheek twitch at the obvious barb.

Valentine fixed Emily with what she assumed was supposed to be a withering stare. "And good morning to you, Mizz Baxter. I trust you are feeling better after your little ... outburst last night?" Without waiting for a reply, Valentine swung her attention back to Mac. The conversation carried on for several minutes, Valentine obviously ignoring Emily as they discussed the logistics of his upcoming expedition.

For her part, Emily stood silently by, a fake smile fixed to her face. She would be the good little girl and not speak until spoken to, she decided. There was no need to stir the pot and make things difficult or embarrassing for Mac, as tempting as it might be.

When the conversation finally wound down several minutes later, Valentine bid Mac good-bye and gave Emily another of her stares before smiling condescendingly and stalking off toward her office within the administration building.

"I think she has a thing for you, honey," Emily said as they walked back toward their apartment.

"You know you really shouldn't try so hard to antagonize her, love," Mac said, taking Emily's hand in his. "She's getting a lot of people behind her very quickly, and you don't want her to come back and bite you on the bum."

Emily looked disgusted at the idea. "Yeah, well, it's her particular brand of populism that I have a problem with. It should have gone extinct with the rest of humanity." She paused for a second, then added, "Besides, there's only one person who's going to be biting my bum around here." She gave Mac a playful nudge, and he made a grab for her. Emily squealed and started to run toward the door of their apartment, closely followed by Mac, his arms outstretched zombielike.

"Come here, ya wee monster, you," he cackled and chased after her.

She let him catch her at the front door. He wrapped his arm around her waist, turned her around, and pulled her close to him. "I love you, Emily."

"I love you too," she said.

■ ■ ■

Emily's little group waited on the dock, watching Mac as he and his crew helped load the last few supply containers onto the deck of the HMS *Vengeance*. An invisible black cloud hung over her head, despite the beautiful day. In her arms, Emily cradled a sleeping Adam while Rhiannon stood at her side, a look of utter despair on the young girl's face. A sizable crowd had gathered behind Mac's family to bid the crew good-bye, but Emily felt more alone in that moment than she had since leaving New York.

"Bloody hell! You look like a bulldog chewing a wasp," Mac said to Rhiannon, when he finally climbed the steps from the dock to join them. He pulled her close and planted a kiss on the top of the girl's head, then slipped in next to Emily, easing Adam from her arms.

"I don't want you to go," said Rhiannon, her voice full of sulk and sadness. Emily almost chimed in that she was with Rhiannon 110 percent, but she knew it would only serve to make Mac's leaving even harder on him. He knew her thoughts, knew exactly how she felt. They had gone over it endlessly in bed the night before, and the same conclusion had been reached: there was no one else with Mac's level of experience, and there was too much at stake for every survivor if he did not go. Still, Emily felt as though she was about to explode at any second at the thought of his imminent departure.

"I'll be back before you know it, kiddo," Mac told Rhiannon, cupping one tear-dampened cheek in a big hand. "Don't worry about me. Besides, you'll have plenty to keep you busy looking after this little one and his mum for me."

A shrill blast from the *Vengeance*'s klaxon shattered the air.

"Take care of them," Mac said to Rhiannon and, after planting a soft kiss on his son's forehead, handed him to the girl. He turned to Emily and took her into his arms. "I'm doing this for you," he said. "Not for the others. For you, for my family."

Emily hugged him as hard as she could, pressing her face into his neck, drawing in his scent, and binding it to her memory. "I love you," she whispered into his ear. "Come back to me."

"Always," Mac promised. He held her for a few more heart-beats, then pulled away, turned, and strode toward the gangplank. He waved once before he climbed down into the belly of the submarine, pulling the watertight hatch closed behind him, and then he was gone.

Within a matter of minutes all remaining hatches were sealed and the engines of the submarine began to stir the water as it eased away from the dock and headed out to sea.

Emily and her family watched until the *Vengeance* slipped beneath the waves, leaving nothing but a quickly dissipating wake to indicate it had ever been there at all.

CHAPTER 3

Emily walked across the beach, Adam cradled in the crook of her arm, Thor trotting happily ahead of her, his nose fixed to the ground. Her eyes stared out to sea, but they registered nothing. Her thoughts were entirely with her husband, deep beneath the rolling waves, travelling in what equated to little more than a glorified tin can, heading north on what would either be the beginning of a new dawn for mankind or a fool's errand that would put a hard and heavy full stop next to the final chapter of the human race. Thor eyed the waves smashing into the beach; a gray-white froth of foam pushed up from the ocean with each new swell, almost a mirror of the storm gathering to the west. The sun was already low on the horizon, slowly being devoured by the angry clouds.

She was not used to feeling this way, so . . . unfocused. Always the independent one, she knew she was more than capable of looking after herself, but now, in this moment, with Mac well on his way to Svalbard, she was feeling—what? Diluted, diminished? Yes, that was the best way to describe how she felt. It was as though a part of her, and a major part of her at that, had been lost, and she was less because of it. She was so used to having Mac chime in on her conversation, or share his opinion on one of the many problems she encountered on a daily basis. It was just too damn quiet without him around. And the worry—holy shit! The constant gnaw in her stomach made her want to vomit . . . all the time. It was worse than when she was pregnant.

"At least I still have you two boys to look out for me." She sat down on the sandy slope of a dune. Adam gurgled happily at her from between the folds of his bright-blue blanket. She placed her free arm around Thor's neck. The malamute turned his head and licked her cheek, then dropped to all fours and placed his head across her feet. He gave a soft huff of expelled air and closed his eyes.

The next couple of months were going to be hard, she knew that. She would just have to busy herself with as much work as possible to keep her mind off Mac and the rest of the *Vengeance* crew. But she had decided that she was going to allow herself one night of moping about like a lovesick teenager.

That's right, love, you just get it out of your system, she heard Mac's voice say in her head.

She smiled . . . and then came the tears.

"Alright, that's enough of that now," she said after a few minutes, sniffling back the tears and wiping her nose with the back of her hand. She canted her head back as far as she could and drew in a deep breath of the evening air. It held the promising smell of rain, but the clouds were still far enough out to sea that she did not have to worry about the three of them getting caught in a squall.

I hope it pours.

Although the submarine's desalination units met the survivors' drinking water needs, the Point Loma locals all liked to gather as much rainwater as they could. It was sweet and pure now, free of any pollutants. Might just as well have come straight from a spring.

Emily allowed her eyes to drift across the concavity of the sky above her.

There! She spotted the unmistakable arc of the glittering line she and Mac had seen only a couple of nights earlier. Except . . . now it was bigger, thicker. In fact, it looked as though it had tripled in width, maybe even quadrupled, and it seemed to be even brighter than she remembered. Before, it had been just an indistinct thread, now it was a solid slash of twinkling light stretching across the night sky, unmissable in the growing darkness.

Emily got to her feet and followed the line of light across the sky with her eyes. She was sure it was in exactly the same location she and Mac had first seen it, which meant her husband had been correct in his observation that, whatever this new phenomenon was, it was fixed in place many kilometers above the ground. It was only the equivalent of a couple of human hairs in breadth at this distance, and while Emily had never been into astronomy, she was certain it had not been there before Earth fell to the aliens. It seemed logical to assume it could only be the handiwork of the Caretakers.

"What the hell are you?" she wondered to the heavens.

In the rush and chaos to get Mac on his way, neither had brought up the strange new addition to the night sky. She wondered if anyone else had seen it yet. Doubtful, she decided, because at night few people—*and wisely so,* she thought—ventured outside the fences that surrounded the camp. The perimeter security lights that kicked on just before dusk each night outshone anything in the sky, so no one was going to be able to see it from inside the compound either.

Maybe she should drag Valentine out here and show her, but she doubted that even this would go far in convincing that woman. In fact, she was beginning to think that that woman was choosing *not* to be convinced. She felt a creeping suspicion that Valentine's apparent dislike for her was an attempt to strengthen her position within the community by targeting the one person she could use to distract the rest of the survivors away from her own agenda.

She was effectively pointing at Emily and yelling, "Witch!"

Well, as long as Emily did not end up tied to a stake, she would be able to handle herself. Valentine did not pose much more than an annoyance to her at this point. She was just going to have to steer clear of the conniving bitch until Mac got back and then they could figure out how to deal with her and her cronies, if the need arose.

She spent a few more minutes pondering the lights, but by the time she decided the air was becoming too chilled for little Adam, she was still none the wiser about what the implications of the Caretakers' latest pet project might be. She knew that they never did anything without a purpose. This meant *something*, of that she was absolutely sure. Although God only knew what that might be.

"Come on, guys," she said as a cold gust of wind cut through her jacket. "Let's go home."

■ ■ ■

It was quiet in the apartment without Mac. *Too bloody quiet,* to quote the man himself.

So for the first few days after he left, Emily busied herself with anything and everything to help take her mind off his absence, but she found herself pausing during everyday tasks or conversations with others around the camp, waiting for one of his typical Mac one-liners, or—on a rare occasion, at least—a surprisingly deep insight. By day six of his first week away, she realized she was just not the same person without him around.

The *Vengeance* was cruising deep and running silent. It would not surface until it reached Svalbard, and even then it would only be above the waves long enough to get Mac and his team off the boat before submerging again in the belief—or maybe it would be better described as hope, as no one had yet put the theory to the test—that the Caretakers would not or could not harm them as long as they stayed below the waves. So there would not even be the opportunity to speak to Mac on the satellite phone. She would know nothing about him until the submarine returned to Point Loma in eight to twelve weeks . . . if it returned.

"Goddamn it," she said to herself. "You have to stop thinking like that." All in all, she was doing a pretty damn good job of dealing with his absence. That feeling of unease from the first few days had finally dimmed to a small burning spot in her stomach, but it would occasionally flare up and scorch her. But at least she was getting better at containing those sudden outbreaks of melancholy.

Emily eased the door to Rhiannon's bedroom open and peeked around. "Knock, knock," she said. Rhiannon was sitting up in bed, reading an old hardback book that, if the tattered cover was anything to go by, had seen better days.

"What's the book?" Emily asked, sitting down on the edge of the creaking mattress.

Rhiannon flashed her the cover: *The Prisoner of Zenda*.

"Good choice," Emily said with a smile. "You okay?"

Rhiannon nodded, then after a second said, "They'll be okay, won't they? They'll come back, you promise?"

"Of course they will, hon," Emily said, surprised at how easily the half truth slipped off her tongue. "A few more weeks and they'll be home. Don't you worry." Emily reached down and eased the book out of Rhiannon's hands. "How about I read to you?"

Rhiannon nodded. Emily began to read.

Twenty minutes later and Rhiannon's soft snores told Emily the girl was deeply asleep. She placed the closed book on the nightstand and pulled the sheets gently up to the girl's chin, placed a light kiss on her forehead, then eased the door shut behind her as she stepped into the darkening corridor.

Emily opened the door to her own bedroom and stepped across to the cot where Adam lay, also soundly asleep, his lips parted slightly, the silky tip of his blanket damp from his teething.

"Good night, little man," she whispered.

She undressed quickly, leaving her clothes draped over the back of a chair, checked on her boy a final time, then climbed between the welcoming smoothness of the bedsheets.

A current of cool air blew in through the open window, and, as Emily allowed sleep to take her, she imagined her husband could smell the same briny scent of the ocean the evening breeze carried to her.

■ ■ ■

I am flying.

She swooped down through the canopy, dropping quickly past the twisted branches before pulling up level with the ground, moving through the forest on diaphanous mother-of-pearl wings, their deep thrum pulsating through every muscle of her body as she darted between tree and over bush. It was dark here, with just the faintest hint of light seeping through the western edge of the forest. Dusk was coming.

I am everything.

The thought did not strike her as being the least bit incongruous; instead, it perfectly summed up her existence. A part of her brain—the human part, the distant echo of who she was, the part named Emily Baxter, the part that could never really accept what she was experiencing—still knew the statement made no sense, but that part of her no longer mattered.

Her perception was a gradual expansion of her consciousness from the single point of her being outward into a sphere-filling bubble of awareness; she sensed the presence of billions of potential doorways, all just within reach. She felt . . . connected. She was a facet within a massive structure of world-spanning immensity—all she had to do was choose one and . . .

I am colossus.

It was bright daylight now. In the distance she saw an ocean, gray waves slowly swelling against a shoreline. She no longer saw with anything resembling human sight; instead, she felt the colors as though they were textures, sensed the tiny vibrations flowing through the air around her, caressing the outer skin of her monumental body as it rose inexorably skyward. And from this great height, towering over every entity within the rest of the red forest beneath her, she felt a warm, salty breeze moving past her, caressing her branches. Her roots were deep within the ground, seeking out the rivulets and pools of water that collected there, sourcing the nutrients that ensured she continued to grow, and thrive, and give back.

I am leviathan.

Frigid water washed over her now as she eased through the darkness of the deep ocean. Around her other creatures moved and swam, ever vigilant of her, careful not to move too close. Not afraid, but respectful of her power; they were aware of her position within the Grand Hierarchy at play around her.

I am insignificant.

Now she clung to a rock, her tiny red tendrils reaching out across the stark cold landscape, waiting for the sunlight to come again. She was small, inconsequential by human standards, but as aware of her irreplaceable position within the Grand Hierarchy of the world as any other part of the immense machine that was life on this small blue planet.

I am here.

And now she saw through almost human eyes again. An intense sense of inquisitiveness consumed her, flooding through every limb. She looked down at a tiny human figure sleeping peacefully beneath a blanket—a feeling of recognition pecked at her. She knew this being. The child moved, quietly repositioning itself within the crib. A powerful vitality flowed from the child, as though it was somehow able to amplify the natural energy surrounding it. An almost overwhelming mixture of desire, curiosity, and longing gripped her. It was an irresistible pull the likes of which she had never experienced before, not in the millennia of time she had existed. The tiny creature lying in the crib was fascinating.

Long slender arms reached down toward the child, a single nimble digit extended and caressed its cheek—as if from a great depth the human facet began to struggle for control again— *then the finger traced the outline of the infant's ear, lifting the thin blond hair. Contact only fueled the feeling of curiosity, the pleasure of newness. A second stick-thin arm reached down, the hands extended and gently grasped the child—*No! No! No! The human facet began to scream—*lifting him from within his blanket cocoon. The child's eyes opened and stared back at her—*"Let him go!" the human facet screamed, forcing itself to the front.

I am Emily Baxter.

■ ■ ■

"Adam!"

Emily crashed into consciousness covered in sweat, her son's name echoing in her ears, the dream—*No!* she corrected herself, *the nightmare*—still burning in her forebrain as her mind tried to grasp which reality she now found herself in. Her heartbeat a syncopated rhythm to the panic that gripped her. She was sitting upright, she realized, one leg swung out of the bed, the crumpled sweat-soaked covers thrown aside as though she had been about to run somewhere. The bedroom window was open and a full moon filled the room with corpse-gray light, casting long shadows across the floor and the bed.

She inhaled a deep breath of the now-cold night air, exhaling silently as she checked the time on her watch. It was just after two thirty in the morning.

Emily freed her other leg from the tangled sheet and sat on the edge of the bed listening, waiting for her eyes to adjust fully to the darkness. Beyond her window, the camp was silent, the apartment quieter still. Across the room, Adam slept peacefully, the raised outline of his blanket barely visible through the bars of the crib. On the floor at the end of the bed Thor stirred, looking up for a moment before easing on to his side and drifting back into sleep.

All was as it should be, but still . . .

Emily stood up, trying to shake the remnants of the nightmare from her mind, but it refused to leave her, clinging to her with taloned claws. It had seemed so real. Normally she was able to recognize even the most vivid dream for what it was, but this . . . this felt as though she had been there, as though she had just been dropped unceremoniously back into her body; it had the weight of memory, not fantasy. She could still taste the briny saltiness of the sea sweeping though her gills, the feel of the air washing across her body.

Emily exhaled a long sigh, trying to bring her thudding heart under control. There would be no rest for her until she checked on Adam, she knew. So, with a sigh of resignation, she stood and padded as quietly as possible across to the boy's crib.

There he was, sound asleep, outlined within the shadows of the crib's interior. She paused for a moment, listening for his breathing, just to be sure . . . and heard nothing. Not a sound.

"Adam?" she whispered, reaching toward the shape lying on the mattress. Pulling back the crumpled blanket revealed nothing but the mattress beneath it.

"Adam!" she called out again, panic beginning to rise now as she snatched the blanket from the crib and dumped it on the floor. The crib was empty.

"Oh shit!"

Thor lifted himself from his spot on the floor between the baby's crib and her bed and stretched, then trotted to her side. He cocked his head to the side and stared at Emily as if to say *What's wrong?*

Emily looked under the crib, then under her own bed. There was no sign of the child.

The panic was a twisting knot in her stomach now, pulling the breath from her lungs.

"Adam!" she said aloud. "Adam!"

Thor sat and stared at his mistress, then, recognizing the name of his other charge, pushed his nose through the bars of the crib and sniffed heavily. Then he sat again, with the same quizzical confused tilt to his head.

Emily registered all of this as if from a distance. Thor seemed not the least bit panicked. That meant she must be the one missing something. What was it?

A thought hit her mind, momentarily smothering the panic

with relief: Rhiannon had him. Of course that was the only possibility. Emily knew she had been deeply asleep; Adam must have cried out and Rhiannon, asleep in the room on the opposite side of the wall, ever the alert and attentive aunt, had come in and taken him to her room to let Emily sleep. That had been translated into her dream as someone . . . some *thing* taking her child. Yes, that was it, of course that had to be it. She used that thought to quash the swirling fear collecting in her stomach like lava and rushed out of her bedroom to Rhiannon's room next door. Easing open the door, she stepped inside. The room was pitch black, and she could hear Rhiannon's steady breathing coming from her bed.

She flicked the light on without hesitation.

"Wha-What? Emily? What do you want? What's going on?" Rhiannon's voice was sleepy and confused as her face appeared from beneath the sheets, squinting hard at the light.

Apart from Rhiannon this room, too, was empty.

"Adam, where is he?" Emily demanded.

Rhiannon sat upright. "He's with you, in your bedroom. Where else would he be?"

"Oh my God! Oh my God!" Emily felt the surge of panic and fear burst free now. It engulfed her and she found herself fighting back the urge to vomit. Her bones felt as if they had been hollowed out and filled with lead. She slumped hard against the frame of the door for support, drawing in several rapid deep panicky breaths before sliding slowly to the floor. Her panic was being consumed by fear now—gut-churning, vomit-inducing, pinned-to-the-floor-like-a-butterfly terror.

Rhiannon was out of bed and by her side in an instant, a hand placed firmly on Emily's back, the other taking her hand to steady her.

"He must be in the crib," the girl said. "There's no way he could get out. Wait here, I'll go take a look." Rhiannon disappeared into the master bedroom and Emily heard the sound of the light switch clicking on, her footsteps across the floor, and a pause, followed by a shocked "Oh!"

Emily took one last deep breath and forced herself away from the door, turning back toward her own bedroom just as Rhiannon reappeared in the doorway.

"Have you checked the rest of the apartment?" she asked, her voice high pitched and, Emily noted, both of her hands shaking.

"No, not yet. Come on, let's look together."

Their second-floor apartment was small, just two bedrooms, a living room, and a kitchen. There really was nowhere for her child to hide, even if he had managed to somehow climb over or through the bars of his crib. The front door was still locked and bolted from the inside and all windows were secure . . . except for her bedroom window, Emily suddenly realized.

"Oh no! No, no, no," she cried and rushed back to her room, Rhiannon on her heels.

The sill of the window reached Emily's waist, a difficult but not impossible height for a determined child to maybe pull himself up to and then topple out of. Emily tried to steel herself for the worst as she leaned over the window ledge, gulping in cold air, and looked down: two stories below a concrete path ran along the side of the apartment building; beyond that was a single-lane access road, and beyond that a red-grass verge. Emily released the breath she had been holding. There was no sign of Adam, no pool of drying blood either. He had not gone through the window, which meant he had to be in the apartment *somewhere* . . . or someone had come in and taken him. But there was no possibility that could have happened. Even if somehow an intruder had managed to get inside without waking Emily or Rhiannon, there was just no way in hell they could have gotten past Thor. He had been asleep in the space between her bed and Adam's cot. He would have torn them to shreds before Emily could have even grabbed her gun to finish the job.

As inconceivable as Emily thought it to be, there seemed to be only one totally illogical yet ultimately realistic answer: the dream, *her* dream, was not a dream. Something had taken her child—something not human.

Emily's hand slowly rose to cover her mouth as the first sob erupted from her. Her heart thumped uncontrollably and erratically against her breast, and her legs would no longer consent to hold her up. Her head seemed to be floating away from her body as she felt herself topple backward into the bedroom wall and slide slowly down until she hit the floor.

By the time Rhiannon noticed and rushed to her side, Emily was an unconscious heap on the floor.

CHAPTER 4

Emily sat slumped on the edge of her bed, staring at Adam's empty crib.

"Ms. Baxter . . . Emily. I need your help." The male voice was followed by a couple of finger snaps that dragged Emily's attention to the man standing over her. It wasn't clear to Emily if the camp provost had shown up minutes or hours after Rhiannon had summoned him via her personal radio. Not that it mattered, anyway; she knew there was nothing he could do to help.

Adam was gone.

Eric Fisher was a man about as vanilla as anyone could describe: medium height, medium build, medium looks, but he more than made up for his middle-of-the-roadness with a dedication to his job that was unsurpassed by any other member of the survivors' encampment. Emily had always thought of him as just a little too serious, just a little too much in the moment for her liking, but she suspected this was his way of dealing with the events that had led all of them to this base on the coast of what had once been California. If she were assessing the man for one of her news articles, then she would have privately classified him as being someone who threw himself at his work as a distraction from the terrible history that lay in all of their pasts.

Fisher arrived a few months earlier on the USS *Michigan*, where he had acted as the submarine's master-at-arms. A former

Chicago cop, he had joined the navy not long after the 2001 World Trade Center attack. Now he officiated over the Point Loma survivors, enforcing the common laws they had set. Everyone simply called him "Sheriff." The designation fit him well.

"Emily? Emily . . . can you look at me?" His voice was calm and unemotional. Flat.

Emily raised her eyes from her knees and looked up into Fisher's face, a professional smile creasing his lips. "That's it. That's good." He reached out and took her hand in his own, squeezed it gently.

Behind Fisher, Emily could see several other men and women who she recognized vaguely as they passed by her bedroom door. Fisher's deputies. They milled around her apartment, moving back and forth through the rooms, talking on their walkie-talkies.

Rhiannon stood in the doorway, still in her pajamas, talking to one of the female deputies who was busy scribbling into a notebook. The girl had obviously been crying, her eyes puffy and red. Emily wanted to comfort her, but her limbs refused to move her from the bed. She felt as though she were a guest in her own body.

No, she would just sit here for a second or so and wait until she woke up from this obvious nightmare.

"Emily, I need you to tell me what happened. Can you do that for me?"

She looked up again and somehow managed to speak. "They took him," she said.

"Who? Who took Adam, Emily?"

"The Caretakers. They came here and they took him."

Despite the haze of loss that occupied the space where her mind used to be, Emily could still recognize the look of incredulity as it crossed Fisher's face. It was there for a second before being replaced once again by his professional game face.

"You mean the aliens you talked about, right? They came and they abducted Adam. Is that right, Emily?"

She nodded.

"But how did they get inside the apartment, Emily? The doors are all locked and there's no sign of forced entry. My people have checked everywhere."

"I don't know," Emily said, her voice a low whisper, conspiratorial. "I don't know how they did it, but I saw them take him. They made sure I saw them take him."

"But if you saw them taking Adam, why didn't you try and stop them? You have a gun, don't you?"

"I saw it happening in a dream," she said, and even as she spoke the words she knew they were the wrong ones to say, that this man would simply not understand. But that was okay. It did not matter what they thought. She knew the truth.

Fisher stood up. "A dream? You were asleep when this happened?"

Emily nodded again.

Fisher exhaled a long sigh. "Okay, Emily. Well, my people are talking with Rhiannon, and I've got teams sweeping the compound. So, if he's here then we'll find him, okay?"

"You won't find him," Emily said. "I know you won't."

Fisher regarded Emily for a few moments, his expression noncommittal.

"We'll see," he said eventually, and walked out of the room.

Two men stepped into view as Fisher arrived at the doorway. Fisher said something to them Emily could not hear and they both nodded. One, a large blond man with a permanent scowl, stepped inside her room and leaned against the wall; the other positioned himself outside the room.

Before Fisher could leave, Emily saw the unmistakable profile of Sylvia Valentine step into view. She took him by the elbow and he turned to talk to her. Their exchange of words was too low for Emily to hear what was being discussed, but it was obvious from Valentine's occasional glance in her direction that Fisher was talking about her, probably relaying the conversation they had just had. Valentine nodded every few seconds, and when Fisher was done, she laid a hand on his shoulder and he turned and walked away.

Valentine lingered in the doorway of Emily's bedroom for a few moments, looking at her with those cold, emotionless eyes. Emily held her gaze with equal ferocity. A few seconds passed, then Valentine leaned in close and whispered something to the blond man standing in her room before she turned and headed toward the apartment's exit, but not before Emily saw a sly smile cross the woman's lips.

■ ■ ■

The camp doctor showed up about ten minutes later. Wallace Hubbard was a big man. He sported a full beard, completely gray, and had always reminded Emily of the captain of the ill-fated *Titanic*.

"Here, I want you to take these," he said, pressing two pills into Emily's right hand and a glass of water into the other.

Obediently she swallowed both pills in one gulp.

"Sedatives, they'll help you sleep." He rattled a brown prescription bottle. "Take another round this evening to get you through the night. They're long past their expiration date, but they should still work okay. If you don't need them, don't take them.

Medical resources are finite these days. I'm going to come back later and check on you, but right now I want you to get some rest."

"I don't need to sleep," Emily said. "I need to get out of here and help them look for my son." Her legs felt leaden, but she tried to stand anyway.

Hubbard pressed her gently back down onto the bed. "Rhiannon, can you come here, please?" he called over his shoulder. "Everyone else, please leave the bedroom." The blond man who had been standing around the room—suspiciously like he was making sure she stayed where she was supposed to, rather than watching over her, Emily's fogged mind suggested—grudgingly left as Rhiannon stepped into the bedroom.

"Close the door, please," Hubbard told Rhiannon as the blond man joined the other guard in the corridor, both glowering back into the room.

Hubbard pulled back the sheets to the bed and lifted Emily's legs under them and gently pushed her back until her head touched the pillow, pulling the sheets up to her chin as though he were tucking a child into bed.

"Rhiannon," he said, "I want you to stay here with Emily. If you need anything, you can contact me via the emergency channel on the radio. Can you do that?"

Emily saw Rhiannon nod, her mind already slowing as the pills kicked in, forcing her toward sleep.

"Make sure she rests, okay?" The doctor smiled once at her and then left, closing the door behind him.

The last thing Emily saw before a wave of sleep pulled her under was Rhiannon's worried face watching her from beside the bed.

■ ■ ■

Confusion.

That was the only feeling Emily's mind could discriminate from the mass of sensory input playing through her head. It felt as though a billion different thoughts were elbowing each other to be heard, an infinite number of synapses firing within her mind at once, pummeling her, clamoring over each other for attention that she simply was not wired to provide. Images flashed across the screen of her mind, faster than she could process them, an impossible blur of superimposed pictures one on top of the other.

This must be what it feels like to experience time all at once, *she thought, not even sure she understood what the thought meant.*

Every sensation possible played through her body at the same time: vertigo, love, indifference, repulsion, desire, death, fear, and some that she simply did not recognize, alien yet familiar in their strangeness. The feelings went on and on and on, burning through her body. Occasionally an image possessed enough power that it lingered long enough for her mind to register it: a strange, alien landscape, twin suns burning red in a purple sky; clouds, yellow and sulfurous floating below her; what could only be cities, but not the work of human hands; a blue world of mostly water seen from space, an archipelago of tiny islands cutting across it like a crescent moon. Millions of images flashed in front of her eyes every second, each one just a glimpse, a memory of some unknown mind, forgotten the instant they had been seen in the constant rush of new information, more information, information flooding through her as though she were at the very center of all existence.

A thread appeared; it began as a tiny blue dot, glowing within the mass of searing red confusion, then expanded and rose up through the chaos like a snake, elongating and moving, extending outward, a lifeline of coherence within chaos. The line began to expand outward and she focused on it, everything else fading to a blur around it.

Emily urged herself toward it, pushing through memories that were not hers, through times that could have been before or to come, the only sense of normalcy the steady pulse of the blue line.

She reached out with a hand, a paw, a claw, a twig, a cloud of light, for the oh, so beautiful blue line, inching over the infinite space that separated her from it . . . and touched it.

Abruptly, the cascade of metaexperience ceased, replaced by an infinitely loud silence. Pure white stretched outward all around her as a serenity unlike anything she had ever experienced descended over her. A sense of clarity and . . . love, unadulterated and redolent, as though she had somehow tapped into the very source of that purest of emotions. As overwhelming as the flood of experience had been for her, this single pure emotion destroyed her completely, disassembled her atom by atom, before reassembling her into a new form.

And when her reconstruction was finished she was left with a single thought that filled her mind, woven throughout her essence with that single blue thread: Mommy.

■ ■ ■

Emily sat bolt upright in bed, gasping for air.

Her muscles ached as though they had all been used at once, her skin was covered in a cold sheen of sweat, and she felt a spreading warm wetness between her legs. *I wet the bed?* She tried to pull back the covers, but her arms ached so badly it took several attempts to actually achieve that simple task, and when she tried to raise her head it felt like gravity had quadrupled. When she was finally upright she could see that she had indeed wet the bed; her bladder had simply let go. Thoughts still burned in her mind, but they were fading now, and the confusion she felt was beginning to subside as her neural processes returned to her control.

She looked around the room with rheumy eyes.

It was dark, the window blinds closed, but a thin line of sunlight peeked in through the gaps around the edges, illuminating the room enough that she could make out shapes of furniture.

She needed help.

"Rhiannon," Emily croaked, through lips dry and cracked. Nothing. "Rhiannon?" She managed to swivel her head around the room, her eyes grown accustomed to the gloom now, and she could see that Rhiannon was not there.

She sat on the edge of the bed, waiting as her faculties gradually returned to her. A slow-burning headache throbbed in her forehead, tributaries of pain arcing up over her skull to the back of her neck. But through the pain, like the long, slow beat of an oncoming locomotive, Emily felt something . . . something *new* within the miasma of confusion. Something . . . odd. Something . . . ? She could not quite identify the feeling, but it felt like . . . a tug. Like the unseen force when two magnets of opposite polarity were placed close together. It was small but as distinct as a laser beam. It pulled at her, pinging across her consciousness like a homing beacon.

In the darkness of her bedroom, Adam's empty cot just feet away, its bars casting shadows across the vacant interior, Emily examined what she was experiencing. That tiny dot of attraction, like a voice she almost recognized calling her name over a great, empty distance. When she allowed her mind to focus on that tiny pulse, she felt a thrill, like a friendly face recognized in a sea of strangers, of a connection to something meaningful. To something that was precious.

Someone was calling to her, she knew it. Summoning her.

Emily felt something open in her mind, a switch flip. And in that moment, as the connection was fully established, she understood: Adam was *alive*! She knew it with every cell within her body. Her child was alive, and he was calling her to him.

Adrenaline rushed through her body, obliterating the pain, washing away the weariness from her limbs, replacing it with an energy the likes of which she had never felt before. She had to get up. Had to shake off this malaise and tell someone, anyone, what she had seen, what she knew was the truth.

"Rhiannon!" she called again, this time with more force as her voice returned to her.

The door opened and Rhiannon appeared, freezing in the doorway, a look of disgust and confusion jostling for position with her face.

Emily ignored the fact that she looked like shit, and, if she smelled half as bad as she thought she did, she couldn't blame the kid for wrinkling her nose up at her.

"Help me up," she said.

Rhiannon collected herself and was at Emily's bedside in three steps, and, bless her, only glanced once at the stained bedsheets before offering Emily her hands and easing her up onto unsteady legs.

"I need to get cleaned up," Emily told her. "Can you help me?"

"Lean on me," said Rhiannon.

Emily swung an arm around Rhiannon's shoulder, both women almost toppling over as Emily's legs, still weak from the lingering effects of the medication, staggered for a moment before Rhiannon caught her balance.

"Just get me to the bathroom," Emily said.

Dutifully, Rhiannon supported Emily out of the room and across the corridor to the bathroom.

The two guards Fisher had posted to her apartment were sitting in Emily's living room, the fat one asleep on the couch, the blond one sitting in Mac's favorite armchair, his feet up on the coffee table, reading an old magazine. At the sight of Emily and Rhiannon staggering out of the bedroom, the blond tapped his sleeping partner hard on the head with the magazine. They watched Emily and Rhiannon silently as they limped across to the bathroom. Neither offered to help.

Thor had been asleep in the corridor outside Emily's room. He raised himself to a sitting position and wagged his tail fiercely.

"They haven't left. They told me Fisher told them to stay here for our protection," said Rhiannon, shooting the two men an unhappy look. "But all they've done is sit on their asses and eat all of our day's rations."

The two men disturbed Emily. The fat one looked stupid and bored, but there was something about the blond one that set her senses tingling. Something about the way he watched them, particularly Rhiannon, a half smile, cruel, not kind at all, parting one side of his lips. And then there was the way he had interacted with Valentine. They were obviously on close terms, and Emily could not see why she would bother with someone obviously so far down the food chain.

"Don't worry, I'm not going to make a run for it," she said to the two men, then to Rhiannon as she swung the door farther open, "This'll do. I can make it from here."

She actually felt better, the burst of adrenaline still coursing through her veins. She wasn't going to be running a marathon anytime soon, but the stiffness and aches she had woken with were already beginning to fade as the thrill of the knowledge that her son was alive worked its magic on her body, even if she had no idea how she knew. "Be a sweetheart and grab me a change of clothes, would you?" she asked Rhiannon and closed the door.

She paused for a second when she caught her reflection in the bathroom mirror. *Holy crap, I do look like shit.* Her hair was a disheveled mess, and there were dark rings under her eyes. Her face was pale, drawn.

She quickly stripped out of her soiled clothes and tossed them into the bathtub. She would deal with them later. She walked to the sink and turned on the faucets, and, miracle of miracles, there was some hot water left in the tank. She quickly washed herself in the sink, not trusting the shower would last long enough for her to clean up completely. As she was drying herself off, Rhiannon knocked on the door and extended an arm through the gap with the change of clothes she had asked for.

Emily threw them on, then took a minute to fix her hair. She had some makeup in the sink drawer—not much call for looking glamorous these days, but she wanted to make sure she didn't look like the zombie she saw in her reflection. She applied a judicious amount of foundation to alleviate her pallid skin, and a little lipstick to erase the crust of dried skin on her lips. For what she had to do next it was going to be important to be taken seriously, so looking like she was still a part of the human race was going to be important.

"Not bad," she told her reflection a few minutes later, leaning against the sink as she examined the results in the mirror. She inhaled deeply.

"Okay," she said, "let's do this."

CHAPTER 5

"I'm sorry, Emily, I still don't understand what you're trying to say. Can you explain it again?" said Victor Séverin, the French submarine captain. The other council members all nodded in agreement.

Emily gave a deep sigh, her patience wearing thin. "I've already explained it to you once," she said, "I think it's pretty clear—"

Valentine held up a hand to silence her. "Emily, we granted you this emergency council meeting because you led us to believe that you had new information on the disappearance of your son. Now, of course, we are all very sympathetic to your plight, but I think you can do us the courtesy of repeating your . . . *story* one more time. Just so we have all the facts."

The other council members nodded their agreement.

Besides the full council, only Emily and Fisher's two men from the apartment were in the council hall. It had taken over an hour to get them all together.

Well, actually it had taken everyone but Valentine ten minutes. Valentine had waltzed in fifty minutes later, apologizing for her delay. "Pressing business," she had told her colleagues as she took her seat. No apology. It was an hour that Emily could not afford to lose, but what could she do? She needed the council's approval for the plan she had laid out in her mind, so she was at their mercy.

Forcing a smile to her lips, Emily ran back over her story,

PAUL ANTONY JONES

starting with Adam's abduction by the Caretakers, skipping over her second dream, and ending with her certainty that he was alive.

"And how can you be so sure your boy is alive?" asked Vela when she was done.

Emily paused, knowing she was going to have to be careful with how she phrased this. *Keep it simple,* she told herself. "I feel him," she said.

"Feel him? I don't understand," said Vela, his eyebrows furrowed as he glanced at the council members seated to his left and right. They all looked equally confused.

"I suppose it's more like I can sense his presence," Emily added, aware that she sounded too eager to explain. "I know the direction he is in." Emily swiveled in her seat until she faced northeast, and pointed. "He's there, that way," she said.

"You mean like ESP?" Vela said.

The feeling Emily was experiencing was not linked to any of her regular five senses. What she felt was like a magnetic attraction, gently tugging at her. It was how she imagined a bird might feel when it sensed winter was approaching and it felt the pull to migrate to warmer climates. The longer she sat still, the more insistent that pull was becoming. So, if she were being honest, she supposed it was an extrasensory perception of sorts.

"Yes," she said and tried to smile as though what she had just said did not sound absurd.

Valentine spoke up. "So, you're telling us you know where he is, then?"

"No," said Emily, "I don't know *where* he is, I just know what direction the Caretakers took him." She could feel the pull in that direction even as she spoke, like a light pinch against her skin, urging her to get up and move in that direction. The sensation was almost irresistible, even now, as she tried to remain calm and explain to

58

this group of idiots what she needed from them; the urge to stand up and start moving toward her son plucked at her constantly.

"So, what exactly is it you think we can do, Emily?" Valentine asked, before anyone else could say a word. Apparently she had decided to act as the voice for the group.

"I want you to give me a helicopter and a security team so I can go and rescue my son," Emily said flatly.

Valentine began to laugh, caught herself, and turned it into a cough, but her eyes still betrayed her incredulity. A few smiles creased the lips of several of the other council members too, Emily noticed.

Valentine did not even attempt to hide her contempt when she spoke. "So let me make sure I understand what you're asking; you want us to hand over our helicopter to you along with a security team, so that you can run off and chase your son, who you say is in the hands of some imaginary alien overlords that kidnapped him from your room, leaving no trace whatsoever? Does that about sum up your request, Mizz Baxter?"

There was a smattering of laughter from the other councilors.

"Yes," said Emily, ignoring the obvious attempt to bait her.

"And what evidence other than your word do you have to convince us that we should commit these resources to this . . . this wild goose chase?"

Emily stayed silent. It was already obvious how this was all going to play out, and she knew that even if she had irrefutable evidence to back up her claims, there was no way Valentine was going to cut her any kind of slack. Jesus, she must have really pissed her off in some other life.

"No? Nothing? I didn't think so," said Valentine after Emily's silence had stretched into seconds. "Let's put this to a vote. All those in favor of granting Mizz Baxter's request?" No one said a thing. "All those against granting Mizz Baxter's request." There was a resounding chorus of "Nay" from the assembled council.

"While we appreciate your predicament, we cannot commit our scant resources to something we have no proof of," Valentine said. "Meeting adjourned."

"Fine," said Emily, abruptly standing and sending her chair skidding across the floor. She had managed to keep her growing anger from her voice, but now her words dripped with contempt. "If you bastards won't help me, then I'll do it myself."

■ ■ ■

Emily stormed out of the council building, her rage at Valentine and the rest of the worthless council quickly frozen away by an ice-cold resolve. If the council was not willing to listen to her, then she was going to have to take matters into her own hands. She had already made up her mind how she was going to do that before she had taken less than a handful of steps back toward her apartment.

Glancing over her shoulder, she saw she was alone, the two guards assigned to her still inside the building, waiting for their orders from Valentine, she guessed. Emily ducked to her right, putting a building between her and the council chambers. Valentine's mutts would be on her trail pretty fast once they discovered she hadn't gone straight back to the apartment. They might think she had gone to the beach to cool off, but she had to assume they would start looking for her, so she had better make this fast.

She began to jog up the path leading up to the helo pad.

No one thought to post a guard around the Black Hawk. Why would they? Besides herself, no one else knew how to fly the thing, and it wasn't like someone was going to walk in off the street. And apart from the ground crew who kept it oiled and fueled, no one paid it that much attention.

When the helo was not scheduled to fly, it was covered with a huge tarpaulin and secured by tie-downs to protect it from the elements. Emily slipped under the edge of the tarp, then let herself into the cockpit. A quick check of the instruments showed that the fuel tank was at optimal. The service log showed that the ground crew had done their job and run all the required maintenance after the last flight with Mac.

She was ready to rock and roll.

Emily stepped back outside, checked that no one would see her, then slipped out from under the tarp and made her way as nonchalantly as she could down the path toward her apartment.

She checked the time on her wristwatch. It was just after two. If she tried to take the helo now, the entire camp would be all over her before she could get the engines up to maximum speed. She was going to have to wait until it was dark. That should buy her enough extra time.

Her entire body ached, not from the weariness she had woken with, but from the slow-burning anxiety created by the constant pull she felt toward the northeast.

Take it easy, she told herself as she pushed open the door to the apartment block. *Everything is under control.*

She hoped that she was right.

■ ■ ■

"But I want to come with you," Rhiannon said for the third time in as many minutes. She sat on the edge of the bed as Emily moved around the room.

"Pouting doesn't look good on you, kiddo."

Rhiannon scowled. "I'm *not* pouting and I'm *not* a kid. Why can't I come with you?"

Emily continued to pull clothes from her closet and pack them into the backpack lying on the bed. "I've already told you why; I need to travel fast and light, and, I'm sorry, but you're just going to slow me down." An ember of the anger she felt at the council's decision still smoldered deep in her breast, and she regretted the harshness it brought to the words the second they left her mouth.

Rhiannon smarted as though she had been slapped.

Emily dropped a light rain jacket on the bed and stepped in close to the girl. "I'm sorry," she said, "I didn't mean it the way it sounded. It's just that I don't know exactly where it is I'm going, and, well, you *know* how dangerous it is out there. I don't want to have to worry about you. Besides, I need you to stay here and look after his lordship over there." She nodded toward Thor, who was asleep by Adam's empty cot.

"But . . . but . . . what if something happens to you?" Rhiannon blurted out. "What if you don't come back? I'll be all alone."

Emily stepped in closer to the girl. "No way. No way is that going to happen and no way would you be on your own. I'll make it back with Adam. And even if I don't, then Mac will, do you understand me?"

"But . . ."

Emily placed both hands on Rhiannon's shoulders. "No buts. We will all be okay . . . okay?" She smiled and then added a hug when she received a halfhearted, unsure smile in return. "Now, I need to finish packing." She released Rhiannon and moved to the closet, pulled down two boxes of ammunition for her .45 and the extra magazine she kept on the top shelf. She checked the boxes to make sure they were full and then tossed them on the bed too.

EXTINCTION POINT: GENESIS

"But you said that the council wouldn't give you permission to go find Adam," said Rhiannon.

"I know."

"So how are you going to get the helicopter?"

Emily stopped for a moment and looked at Rhiannon. "I'm just going to borrow it. That's all."

"You mean steal it, don't you?" Rhiannon said, deadpan.

Emily almost laughed. "No, I mean borrow it. I'll bring it back when I find Adam. Listen, these people refuse to believe me. They haven't seen any of the things that you and I have. They still think this is some kind of global pandemic or something, that everything will eventually go back to how it was. They're living with their heads shoved firmly up their own . . . heads buried in the sand. So the only way I'm going to get Adam back is if I do it my way. Besides, it's not like they're going to need it; no one else knows how to fly the thing apart from me."

"Can't we wait until Mac gets back?" Rhiannon asked, sitting down on the edge of the bed, next to Emily's backpack.

Emily continued packing. "By the time Mac gets here it'll be too late. I have to go now." She didn't want to add what she was thinking: that there was a high possibility that Mac might never make it back, but she forced her mind away from that thought. "Food," she said. "I need supplies. Where did Mac leave the MREs?" She was halfway to the cupboard where she remembered her husband had stored his surplus military Meals Ready to Eat when there were two loud thumps on the apartment's front door.

"Emily. This is Provost Fisher, please open up." Three more dull fist thuds against the door followed.

Thor started to bark.

"Stay here," Emily told Thor and Rhiannon as she slipped her .45 into its holster and stepped into the hall, closing the bedroom door behind her. A trio of thoughts manifested themselves unbidden in her mind as she walked toward the front door: *What if I'm crazy like Valentine seems to think? What if Fisher's here with news about Adam? What if they have found him?* Well then, this would be one occasion when she would be more than happy to apologize to Valentine. Her heart skipped a beat or three as she released the latch and opened the door.

Fisher stood in the doorway, his face stern, the two guards who had been in her apartment standing on either side of him, arms folded across their chests.

"What's going—" Emily began to say.

"Get her weapon," Fisher ordered. The two goons leapt at Emily, grabbing her and pushing her face-first into the wall. One twisted her arm up behind her back while the other grabbed the pistol from its holster on her hip.

"What the fuck are you doing?" Emily demanded through teeth gritted in pain. "Get your Goddamn hands off of me."

"Emily Baxter, on the orders of the Point Loma council, I am arresting you on suspicion of the murder of your son, Adam. Please don't resist."

The sound of the bedroom door opening was closely followed by a deep growl. Thor padded out of the bedroom, his teeth bared in a menacing growl, Rhiannon right behind him.

"Shoot the dog," Fisher ordered the man holding Emily's pistol, a hint of panic in his voice.

"No!" Rhiannon screamed and grabbed Thor's collar, pulling him back even as he lunged toward the man who had Emily's arm pinned up behind her back.

Emily felt the grip on her arm relax as the fat guard holding her reflexively backed away from the snarling malamute. This was her one chance. She slipped her arm out of his grip, twisted to face him, drew her head back, and drove her forehead as hard as she could into the man's nose. She felt the satisfying crack of his nose shattering like the shell of an egg and a spray of blood splatter across her face. The man screamed in pain, releasing her as both hands flew to his face. He staggered backward, moaning in shock.

"For Christ's sake, get her," Fisher yelled, pointing at Emily.

The blond guard, Emily's .45 still in his hand, looked stunned. He had her weapon raised and pointed down the corridor at Thor, but Rhiannon had positioned herself between the dog and Emily's attackers.

Emily grabbed his gun hand, twisted around until she had his wrist locked, the gun pointed at the far wall and his elbow moving in the opposite direction, then applied all her weight to his wrist. The man screamed in pain as his elbow hyperextended, ligaments stretching like pieces of rubber.

Her pistol clattered to the floor.

If she could just grab the gun, she'd have a chance to seize control of this mess. She released the man, expecting his reactions to be impaired by pain, but he had enough of his wits left to realize what she was attempting and kicked the .45, sending it skittering across the corridor carpet where it bounced against a skirting board and disappeared through Rhiannon's open bedroom door.

Emily shoulder-barged him while he was off balance and sent him face-first into the wall, before he tumbled to the floor.

"Get in the bedroom," Emily yelled at Rhiannon as she turned back to face her attackers.

She saw the pistol descending toward her and tried to dodge away, but it was too late, the butt of Fisher's pistol caught her square on her right temple.

The last thing Emily sensed was Rhiannon's high-pitched scream, then her universe disappeared into blackness.

■ ■ ■

Adam was five years old. Emily didn't know how she knew this, but she did. He was asleep on the bed, the blankets pulled up to his chin, his hair spread out around his head like a halo.

He was beautiful.

Emily leaned in and kissed his forehead. She placed the pillow over his face and pushed down hard.

■ ■ ■

"No!" Emily cried out, and instantly regretted it. The yell rang her head like a bell.

Where the fuck was she? She raised her head, looked around, but didn't recognize the room. Her mind was full of fog and confusion, her thoughts running from her each time she tried to focus on them. She remembered something about a fight, but the why of it eluded her.

Emily felt metal beneath her fingers. She was lying on some kind of a gurney, a hospital gurney with collapsible metal sidebars to stop patients from rolling out of them. A gray blanket lay crumpled below her knees. She sat up, reached to caress the throbbing spot on the side of her head, and almost dislocated her wrist, yelping at the sudden pain as her arm was abruptly stopped. Emily stared at the metal handcuffs securing her left arm to the gurney's railing.

What the hell?

And then it all came back to her: the knock at the door. The three men. The fight.

Those bastards!

"She's awake." Emily looked for where the voice had come from, but her eyes were still blurry, her head swimming. Each time she moved she felt as though she were going to throw up. God! She hoped she didn't have a concussion. She tried to ask who was there, but all that came out was a scratchy croak, her throat as dry as sand.

A shape began to materialize beyond the bars—bars? Where the hell was she? Her eyes gradually began to focus, and she could now make out the shape and features of Fisher.

Jesus! That motherfucker! Now she remembered everything. He was the one who had hit her. So much for being a stand-up guy.

Her eyes swept the room. She was in the brig, she realized now. They had knocked her out and brought her here while she was unconscious. Not only was she a big-enough threat that they had to throw her in the brig, they also needed to handcuff her to the gurney they had brought her in on too. Like she was Harry fucking Houdini or something.

A second shape appeared from beyond the edge of her cell. Valentine! The queen bitch herself.

"Hello, Emily. How are you feeling?"

"Fuck you," Emily tried to yell, but it came out as a mumbled mess, but by the dismissive smile on Valentine's face, Emily's sentiment had been made abundantly clear.

Emily sank back down onto the gurney, her chest heaving, her head throbbing.

"Why don't we get Mizz Baxter some water," Valentine said.

A key turned in the latch of the cell gate, and then a man was standing over her.

"Here," the voice said, shoving a red plastic cup of water under her nose. It was the blond guard who had come to arrest her earlier. Emily could see a bruise, purple and angry, on the side of his face where she had clocked him. But it was the look in his eyes that worried her. Cold. Angry. This was not a happy man.

She took the water from his hand and drank it down in two

deep gulps. It was warm but dear God it was *so* good. She could already feel the tightness in her head beginning to loosen.

"More," she said. The blond guard looked at Valentine, who nodded. Grudgingly he brought a second cup.

Emily looked at her feet. What the hell? The laces from both her sneakers were missing.

"Is this really necessary?" she said, rattling the handcuffs against the metal security bar of the gurney.

"You were unconscious when we took you to the infirmary," said Valentine. "Dr. Hubbard insisted that you be treated there. We wanted to make sure you wouldn't try to harm yourself . . . or anyone else."

Well, that explained where her laces had gone. Emily shook her head in disgust. "Right, because I have a history of that."

Fisher spoke next. "Emily, where is your son?"

"What do you mean? I've already told you where he is."

"You told us that an alien spirited him away from a locked room in the middle of a heavily armed camp. My men searched your apartment and found no indication of any kind of break-in or—"

"Because they're fucking aliens," Emily interjected.

"—any signs of a struggle. We searched the entire compound and the perimeter, and, again, my men found no sign of Adam."

"Well maybe you need to employ better men," Emily said, shifting her gaze to the guard leaning against the cell bars.

The blond guard pushed away from the bars, his fists balled.

"Curtis!" snapped Valentine. The man froze and stepped back to his position. *Interesting,* thought Emily, *that it is Valentine and not Fisher issuing commands here.*

"As I was saying, Emily, we have found no evidence that your son was abducted by any kind of exterior force. Which leads me to my final question: How did you dispose of your son's body?"

"*What?*" Emily gasped. "I didn't harm my son. You think I'd hurt him?"

"Here's what we think happened, Ms. Baxter," said Valentine, stepping closer to the bars of her cell. "We think that the last few years have finally caught up to you. That your delusions of an alien menace somehow being responsible for the devastation we see beyond the safety of Point Loma has slowly grown over the time since the red rain first fell. We think that your husband's willingness to leave you and your son behind was the final straw."

"You are out of your Goddamn minds."

"We think that in a fit of paranoia, you killed your boy, strangled him in his crib, and then took his body and dumped it in the ocean."

Emily was stunned almost into silence. "That's your story?" she said eventually. "And you think *I'm* the crazy one."

Valentine stepped closer, grasping the cell bars with both hands. "Why don't you just make it easy on yourself and your family—what there is left of it, of course—and admit it."

"You are out of your minds. Fisher, for God's sake, you don't believe any of this, do you?"

Fisher just stared back at her, his arms folded across his chest.

"You believe her? Jesus! She's making this shit up, because she wants to frame me. Can't you see that?" Even as she said the words, Emily realized how paranoid she sounded.

Valentine smiled, the bait she had laid for Emily taken. "Yes, of course that's what's happening. I'm setting you up, because . . . ?" She left the question hanging. "Because I don't like you? I see you as a threat to some plan I have schemed? Or . . . or maybe I'm working for the aliens? Yes, I'm sure that's it."

Curtis cackled to himself.

"That's enough!" Fisher snapped. He stepped closer to the bars, took a deep breath, and said, "Emily Baxter: I hereby charge you with the abduction, murder, and illegal disposal of your son, Adam Baxter-MacAlister. You will be held here until such time as a jury of your peers decides your fate."

Emily shook her head in disbelief. "And if I'm found guilty?"

"The punishment for murder is death, Mizz Baxter," said Valentine. "The punishment for murder has always been death."

Fisher nodded at Curtis. The guard pulled the metal gate closed behind him.

"Curtis will be standing guard. If there's anything you want, ask him," said Fisher, then both he and Valentine turned and vanished down the corridor.

The guard lingered for a second, watching Emily, then he smiled a dark, lascivious smile and he was gone too.

■ ■ ■

Dr. Hubbard showed up some time later. Emily couldn't tell how much later, since the cell, which measured only about six by ten feet, was windowless on all three of its reinforced-concrete walls. The bars that made up the fourth wall had a view of the narrow corridor beyond and a single tiny oblong window near the ceiling made with what she was sure was shatter-proof glass.

"How are you feeling, Emily?" Hubbard asked as he was ushered into the cell by Curtis. The guard leaned against the wall and watched Emily and the doctor as though they had already hatched some preemptive escape plan.

"Been better," said Emily, her free hand rising to the bump on her head where Fisher's pistol had connected with her skull.

Hubbard parted her hair around the wound and gave it a close examination. "You've got a nasty bump, and it's a bit bruised. No double vision? Do you feel nauseous?"

"Only over the way they're treating me," said Emily, rattling the chain of her handcuffs against the restraint of her bed like Jacob Marley's ghost.

Hubbard smiled apologetically and turned to speak his next words directly to Curtis. "Yes, hardly the most optimal of environments for one of my patients."

"Mrs. Valentine says she's a suicide risk," said Curtis. "It's for her own safety."

"Oh, and Mrs. Valentine's qualified to make that kind of clinical observation, is she?"

Curtis stepped up close enough that the two men were almost face to face. He was a good head taller than the doctor and must have had at least fifty pounds on him. "Just do your fucking job, doc," he spat.

"Do you have any pain pills?" Emily asked. "My head hurts from all the bullshit this idiot is spouting."

Curtis threw a meaty hand between them before the doctor could even reply. "No pills! Fisher's orders. And you," he poked a finger in Emily's direction, "better watch your mouth."

Hubbard raised both his eyebrows and shook his head. "Well, I suppose that answers that. I'm sorry, Emily."

Now Curtis shook his head. "This bitch murdered her own fucking kid, and you're apologizing? A headache's the last of her problems right now. Are you done?"

The doctor turned back to Emily. "I'll be back to check on you in the morning," he said, smiling bleakly. "Try to get some rest, okay?"

The doctor turned and walked out of the cell with his escort. Emily had turned her back on them and was staring at the blank wall as the cell door clanged shut.

CHAPTER 6

Emily woke to the sound of her cell door rattling open. She squinted hard against the overhead lights that seemed to be permanently on.

"Sit up." It was the guard, Curtis. He held a tray with a bowl of food and a glass of water.

Emily did as she was told, carefully swinging her legs over the side of the gurney so as not to wrench her wrist. Through the narrow window in the corridor beyond her cell she could see night had descended once again.

"Good girl," Curtis said, setting the tray to her right.

"How about you unlock my cuffs, so I can actually eat."

Emily tried to hide her surprise when the guard said, "Okay," and pulled the cuff keys from his pocket, dangling them from his fingers. "Turn around and put both hands on the gurney. I don't want you trying anything funny."

This didn't feel right, but what was she supposed to do? The guy was twice her size and she only had one free hand. Emily turned and leaned both hands on the cushion of the gurney. Besides, what was he—

The thought was cut short as she felt something slipped over her head and pulled tight around her throat. Instantly her air supply was cut short. Her hand flailed uselessly, knocking the tray off the bed, the plastic mug of water bouncing noisily across the floor. She started to push away with her one free hand, but the full weight of the guard's body was suddenly pushed against her, forcing her painfully into the gurney. Her free hand reached for whatever was around her throat. Her fingers clawing at it . . . it felt like laces . . . her sneaker's laces.

"Dr. Valentine told me to make this quick," Curtis whispered in her ear. "But I say why rush it, mmmm? No reason I can't have a little quality time first, right? I mean, why should that fucking Scotsman have all the fun?"

The lace was pulled just tight enough to cut off most of her air.

She tried not to vomit as she felt his hand slip between her legs, rubbing hard as he ground himself against her backside. "Oh yeah, you like that, don't you?"

This could not be happening. She gasped, flailing uselessly at him, her free hand arcing back over her shoulder in a vain attempt to find his face, but she just could not reach. What little breath she did have suddenly felt even thinner as she felt the buttons on her jeans popping open as Curtis undid them one after the other.

Emily tried to scream, but only a high-pitched hiss came out. She tried to mule kick him, but he had her bent too far over the gurney to be able to swing her leg hard enough. So she stomped down hard where she thought his toes should be and heard a satisfying grunt of pain. She didn't have time to gloat as she felt his fist smash into her kidneys and her world exploded into reds and blues of pain. All her strength left her, and she collapsed facedown onto the gurney, the guard's full weight pinning her.

"Bitch!" he yelled into her ear. "Now I'm gonna make it real fucking slow."

His hands found their way back to the waistband of her jeans. He tugged hard, popping the remaining two buttons as he pulled the jeans down over her right hip.

Emily tried again to scream but felt bile suddenly fill her throat. She was choking to death as this bastard tried to rape her. It was just unbelievable. Her eyes clouded with hot tears as the maniac groped to the other side of her jeans and began tugging them down.

"So sad, the little baby killer hangs herself. So, so sad." Curtis laughed, it was a maniacal cackle of utter delight. "Oh, and when I'm done with you, maybe I'm gonna go and pay that little bitch of yours a visit next. Mmmm! Mmmm! This is gonna be so mu—"

The pressure around Emily's neck relaxed suddenly, the guard's oppressive weight gone too. She tried to suck in air but instead vomited onto the gurney, her legs now made of Jell-O, her arms barely able to maintain her grip on the gurney. She stared at the pale-gray wall, waiting for the assault to start again as she gasped in giant gulps of air, her brain trying to think of a way out, but it kept being distracted, trying to rationalize why this was happening to her.

When Curtis next spoke, his voice was outlined by an edge of fear. "Okay, okay, don't do anything stupid, I was just having some fun," Curtis said.

Even through the haze of terror that still flooded her body, Emily could tell something had changed dramatically. She reached up and tried to slip her fingers between the noose and her throat, but it was embedded so deeply she couldn't get a grip until she pushed her nails in and pried it loose.

"Emily? Emily, are you okay?"

"Rhiannon?" Emily managed to gurgle, her throat feeling like she had swallowed acid. It took a couple of seconds, but finally her limbs decided to obey her and Emily pushed herself slowly to her feet, pulled her jeans up as best she could, and turned.

Curtis stood about three feet away, his hands above his head. Rhiannon was in the open doorway of the cell, her pistol pointed at the man's head.

The strangest feeling came over Emily, a swelling pride and love for this child, this young woman with whom she had shared so much. She had so much love for her. But she was mad at the girl too, angry that she would put herself in this situation.

"Emily, are you okay?" Rhiannon asked again, snapping Emily back to reality.

"Okay," she croaked. "Keys. Give her the cuff keys."

"Not happening," Curtis sneered. "This little bitch isn't going to shoot me. We can stay here all fucking night until my relief gets here. I don't give a shit." Curtis reached down and slowly zipped his pants back up, his eyes fixed on Rhiannon. He waited a beat then yelled, "Fuck you!" at the girl, spittle flying from his mouth.

Rhiannon flinched and took a step backward, and Emily realized the girl was terrified beyond all limits. She had to think of something fast.

"Okay," she said, finally finding her voice again. "Why don't we do that."

Curtis's head swiveled in Emily's direction, his smile faltering slightly.

"Then you can explain to Fisher exactly what you were doing to me. And maybe I'll tell him how you're in bed with Valentine. I'm pretty sure this will all be news to him, right? Asshole." It was a gamble. For all she knew Fisher was as much a part of this . . . this assassination attempt as the guard, or he might just try and call her bluff.

The guard's mask of cockiness started to falter, then crumbled altogether.

"Okay, okay," he said as he reached into his shirt pocket and produced the cuff key. "Here," he said to Rhiannon, smiling as he held it out to her.

Emily was too slow with her warning. Rhiannon had already taken a step forward and extended her own hand before Emily could even say no.

Curtis dropped the key to the floor and his now-empty hand flashed out, grabbed Rhiannon's outstretched arm by the wrist, and yanked hard.

Rhiannon, surprised, flew forward, stumbling as her feet tangled. Curtis's free hand grabbed the girl by the hair and pulled her close to him, then threw her to the floor, his right hand pulling back for a sledgehammer punch aimed directly at Rhiannon's face.

"No!" Emily yelled, helpless to do anything.

The back of Curtis's head exploded, sending brains and blood in a splatter across the ceiling and walls of the cell. His body collapsed to its knees, arms limp at his side, and his chin sagged to his chest, exposing the bloody hole in the back of his head. It remained in that position, as if in some final unholy act of contrition.

Emily tried to process everything that had happened in the past few seconds. The sound of the gunshot had not registered with her, but it *had* happened; she could see the smoke rising from the barrel of Rhiannon's pistol that she still held outright, and her ears sang with a high-pitched ringing.

Rhiannon's hand quivered, and then the pistol dropped to the floor.

The girl did not move.

"Rhiannon!" Emily said. "Rhiannon, sweetheart, you have to stand up. Can you stand up, baby?" While Emily could not remember hearing the sound of the gunshot that had killed Curtis—*Oh my God, so much blood. So much blood*—it did not mean that others nearby had not. Emily had no idea how thick these walls were, but in the darkness beyond the walls of the brig sound would carry much farther through the silence of the night. There could be others on their way to investigate even as she sat here trying to comprehend what was happening

At the sound of Emily's voice, Rhiannon seemed to fall back into her body. Her head turned to face Emily. "Hi, Emily," she said, and smiled, the shock of what had just happened visible in the teenager's wide, unblinking eyes.

Emily smiled back as best as she could. "Hi, baby. Listen, I need you to get the key to these handcuffs. It's right there, do you see it?" She pointed with her free hand to where the tiny silver key had fallen, about a foot or so from Rhiannon's right knee.

Rhiannon followed Emily's finger. She reached down and picked up the key.

"Now bring it to me, okay?"

Rhiannon pushed herself to her feet. A thin splatter of blood was visible across her forehead, as if she had spent the day innocently painting and had inadvertently flicked a paintbrush across her face. She dropped the key into Emily's outstretched hand.

"Thank you, sweetheart," Emily said, surprised at how steady her own fingers were. She released the handcuffs, rubbing her wrists to get the blood circulating again. She pulled her jeans the remaining way up and refastened all but one of the buttons, which now lay on the floor near the wall. At any moment she expected to hear the sound of the brig's main door opening, feet pounding down the corridor. Well, if that happened she would be ready, because she sure as hell wasn't going to end up back in cuffs again. She picked up Rhiannon's fallen pistol from the floor, dropped the magazine to check how many rounds were left, then slammed it home again. And if Valentine showed up, Emily knew with a coldness the likes of which she had never felt before that she would not hesitate to shoot her right between the eyes.

Emily turned to look at Rhiannon. She had not moved from the gurney, her eyes fixed on the body of the guard. A trickle of blood dripped from the corner of the dead man's mouth, collecting in a pool around his knees. Rhiannon seemed fixated by it.

Emily placed a hand against Rhiannon's cheek and slowly, ever so slowly, turned her head to face her.

"Hey!" she whispered—not like she had much choice, her throat felt like it had been sliced open—"We have to get out of here before the others come. We have to leave now, okay?"

Rhiannon's eyes drifted back to the corpse of the dead guard, then her head began to follow. Emily reached out again and drew her face back to hers.

"I know it's hard, but we have to go now . . . right now." Her voice was a hoarse whisper.

All light had vanished from Rhiannon's eyes, the muscles of her face slack, blank, and expressionless, as though the girl's personality had vacated her body at the same moment as the guard's life had left his.

Rhiannon blinked once, twice, as her eyes focused on her friend, and Emily saw recognition flicker there, and a moment later Rhiannon was once again present.

"Oh my God, Emily, look what he did to your neck." Rhiannon reached out and touched Emily's throat. Her fingers came back smeared with blood.

"It's just a scratch," Emily said, managing a smile. "Come on, let's get out of here."

Rhiannon stood silently.

"You go first," Emily urged, ushering the girl out of the cell. Once Rhiannon had disappeared down the corridor Emily aimed a kick at the lifeless body of the dead guard. She had turned and followed Rhiannon before his corpse even hit the floor.

■ ■ ■

Point Loma had gone insane.

It was the only conclusion Emily could come to as she and Rhiannon crept their way along the corridor toward the brig's front office. Or maybe it was just Valentine, who, Emily was quite sure, was certifiable. Either way, this was obviously no longer a safe place for either her or Rhiannon to be. Even if she threw herself at the mercy of the council, the chances were high that she would just end up back in a cell again. And as soon as the dead guard was discovered, it wouldn't matter how she tried to explain it, her time would be up, and Rhiannon's now too. And even if the rest of the council weren't colluding with whatever plan Valentine had, there was no way that bitch was going to let either of them live to implicate her in a conspiracy.

Emily had no idea how it had happened, or even why it had happened, but somehow Valentine had silently and completely taken control of this last enclave of humanity. And even with the future of her race on life support, she was willing to murder for her goal, whatever that might be. It was the same age-old crap that had plagued humans since Cain's jealous fit of rage started it all. Dear God, she was tired of it.

There was no way she was going to hang around here now. Her mind was made up. Valentine had changed the rules; now it was everyone for herself. She was taking what she wanted and finding her son. And anyone who got in her way had better be ready to pay the ultimate price.

"Rhiannon, hold up," Emily whispered. The brig's front office was lit by a single table lamp on a desk behind a security counter. Emily scanned the room; no one else was there. She ran at a crouch to the desk, keeping low so if anyone was outside the windows they would not see her.

She felt Rhiannon squeeze in next to her.

"Emily, please don't leave me alone."

The simple statement, delivered in such a plaintive voice, caught Emily completely off guard. She was so involved in her own experience, her own goals, that she had almost dismissed the fact that Rhiannon, this girl of barely sixteen, had risked everything to come here and rescue her. Had killed a man to save her. Whether it was planned or accidental was beside the point; Rhiannon was human to the core, and that was a commodity apparently in short supply, judging by the actions of some of the survivors over the past few days.

Emily turned to look at Rhiannon; her face was ghostly white in the paltry light of the room. She reached out and found the girl's hands with her own. "I will never leave you," she promised, squeezing both hands gently while trying not to notice how cold they were.

They hugged then, Rhiannon wrapping her arms around Emily's neck, warm tears soaking into her shoulder. Rhiannon let go and sat back, wiping away the tears from her cheek.

"We're going back to the apartment, grabbing Thor and our equipment," said Emily, "then we're going to head to the helicopter and get out of here."

Rhiannon shook her head. "Thor's not at the apartment."

Emily felt her heart sink. "Oh God, no," she whispered, expecting the very worst.

"No, no. It's okay, they locked him up."

She felt a burst of relief that her friend was alive. She didn't think she would have ever forgiven herself if she had caused the malamute's death at the hands of Valentine or her cronies.

"You know where they took him?" said Emily.

Rhiannon nodded that she did.

"Okay, show me. You ready?"

"Ready," was Rhiannon's reply.

■ ■ ■

Only blackness was visible beyond the brig window.

"Kill the light," Emily whispered to Rhiannon, nodding at the nearby desk lamp, instantly regretting her choice of words. Rhiannon flipped the switch, and the corridor was plunged into darkness.

"Wait a little until our eyes are accustomed to the darkness." The last thing they wanted to do was trip over some shadow-obscured obstacle as they made their escape.

"It's okay, I've got this," said Rhiannon, producing a small LED flashlight from her pocket.

"Good girl. But don't turn it on unless I tell you. It'll bring every guard in the area down on us." Emily marveled at the girl's resourcefulness as she counted off thirty seconds in her head. "Ready?"

Rhiannon nodded.

"Quiet as you can, follow me." Emily cracked the door open and waited, listening for any sound of the two guards she knew patrolled the interior of the camp each night. When she was sure they were not anywhere close by, she whispered, "Let's go."

Emily snuck through the door first and out onto the raised wooden porch, the boards creaking under her weight. She held the door ajar for Rhiannon to come through, then closed it slowly, the unoiled hinges sounding much louder than she knew they really were. A sliver of moon cracked an almost cloudless sky, the light from it faint, but enough for the two escapees to be able to navigate by.

The brig was the second building of a row of three located in the northern section of the camp. The survivors' sleeping quarters were far enough away that the chances of someone who wasn't a guard spotting them were pretty slim. Judging by the position of the moon, it was well past midnight. Everyone should be asleep.

"Where did they take Thor?" Emily whispered, crouching at the corner of the building.

"There's an empty storage building down by the dock. They said if I didn't take him they were going to shoot him. They took him inside and Fisher locked him up," Rhiannon explained.

"You lead the way," Emily said. "But keep low."

Rhiannon took a second to orient herself, then headed off east. They moved quickly, keeping to the edges of the buildings where the deepest shadows were, halting periodically to listen for the patrolling guards. Apart from the guards on foot patrol, there were another four manned security towers around the perimeter of the camp they would need to avoid. The guards in the security towers were equipped with night-vision goggles, but their attention should be focused beyond the camp's perimeter fence— *should* being the operative word, of course. They crossed a large parking lot, using the rusting remains of the few cars still there as cover. Emily could hear the waves lapping against the dock, just beyond the parking lot. A low corrugated-metal security fence ran around the perimeter of the lot, and they hunkered down next to it. A road separated the lot from several gray buildings that sat close to the edge of the dock. The buildings had been used for unloading and storing supplies for the navy before the red rain. They were all empty now, whatever supplies that had been in them liberated by the survivors.

"Which one?" Emily asked.

Rhiannon poked her head up over the fence and scanned the row of buildings.

"It looks different in the dark," she said, then, "That one . . . I think." She pointed at the second from the corner. The entrance to the building was off the street, facing the wall of the building adjacent to it, which gave some extra cover, but it resulted in a lane that was far too deeply shadowed to be able to negotiate safely.

"Let me have your flashlight," Emily said, holding out her hand. She popped her head up over the fence and gave the road another quick scan. "Let's go."

The two girls hopped the fence, jogged quickly across the open road, and melted into the shadows between the buildings.

"Stand next to me," Emily instructed Rhiannon, pulling the girl in close to her. She flicked the flashlight on for a second then off again, trusting that the buildings on either side of them would absorb the majority of the light, and that their bodies would block the rest. The brief flash was still enough for her to spot the door a few meters ahead of where they stood.

"Wait by the door. Give the building a tap with your knuckles if you hear anything. Just one, though," she told Rhiannon.

Emily reached into the darkness until she laid the flat of her hand against the building's warm siding, then followed it blindly until she found the cooler wood of the door. Emily tested the handle. The door was unlocked. Easing it open, she slipped inside.

It was even darker inside, but from somewhere ahead of her she heard Thor's inquisitive huff, followed by his nails on concrete and the unmistakable swish of his thick tail in the air. She might be blind, but he certainly was not.

She turned on the flashlight.

The building was all but empty, just three large, round oil drums scattered over the bare concrete floor. Thor was across from where Emily stood, behind a wire-mesh security cage that still held a couple of propane gas canisters.

He let out a loud "woo-woo-woo" of recognition when he saw her, jumped up, and landed both front paws loudly on the cage.

"*Shhhhhh*, baby boy," Emily said, hoping no one had heard his welcoming coo. She knelt down next to the cage and pushed her fingers through the gap, drawing Thor down. He nibbled and licked them, then pranced back and forth in the tiny space, eager to escape his cage.

"I know, I know. You're ready to get out, right, boy? Just give me a second."

She gave the cage a once-over. A rope noose was tied around Thor's neck, the other end attached to one of the propane tanks. The bastards hadn't even bothered to leave him any water. *What the fuck was wrong with these people?* A bolt secured the cage shut, a padlock attached to it. Emily gave it a halfhearted pull on the off chance it was left unlocked; it wasn't.

Not able to track down whomever had the key and force them to give it up, and damn certainly not content to leave Thor here to die at the hands of these assholes, she was going to have to risk busting the lock. It wasn't like she routinely carried a crowbar, and a quick sweep of the building with the flashlight brought nothing useful to light.

She tapped her fingers impatiently against her thighs. She could either shoot the lock away (and hope she didn't hit Thor or herself with a ricochet), which would alert the entire camp, or try and smash the lock with the pistol. She would shoot the lock if she had to, but it was probably a good idea to try hitting it first. She pulled the pistol from her pocket, raised it over her right shoulder, and brought the butt down. She completely missed the lock and instead grazed the knuckles of her hand.

"Son of a bitch," she hissed, before smiling through the pain at Thor and adding, "Present company excluded."

She brought the gun up again and this time held her arm a little firmer as she smashed it down onto the padlock. It rang with a sharp metallic ping that Emily's imagination was sure could be heard throughout the camp. She had better get a move on. The third time she brought the gun down she heard something shatter, and the lock's clasp sprung open, leaving it swinging from its latch. She pulled it off and tossed it aside, instantly regretting doing so as it clanged noisily into the corner. Hopefully if anyone was close enough to hear they would think it was just the wrecks in the harbor complaining to the rising tide.

Thor almost leaped into her arms, throwing his front two paws up onto her shoulders and covering her face in wet licks.

"I missed you too, but we need to get the hell out of here." She picked the knot of the rope noose apart and pulled it from his neck. "Come on, let's go."

She led Thor to the door and opened it slowly. A frightened-looking Rhiannon, her face glowing palely in the flashlight's beam, waited on the other side. Her eyes lit up when she spotted Thor, and she threw her arms around him.

Emily killed the flashlight and joined Rhiannon in the shadows.

They would have to get back to the apartment and pick up her backpack and supplies. Once that was done, they would head over to the helipad and liberate the copter. Emily had already decided it was probably a better idea to skirt around the back of the buildings rather than follow the same route they had come from; that way they would be able to keep the ocean to their left and reduce the possibility of being spotted. It was going to take longer to get back to the apartment that way, but the cover would be better; plus, it had the added advantage that they would stay out of sight of the western security towers.

She quietly explained the plan to Rhiannon, and they cut back toward the harbor wall before hanging right and crossing the road that led down to the berthing pier.

The moon was high overhead now, casting its pale illumination across the camp. It helped them make their way more safely, but it also meant they could be more easily spotted.

"We need to pick up the pace," Emily whispered, slipping into a jog. They rounded the corner of a three-story building and began to head north toward the apartment complex.

Emily didn't even see the guard until he stepped out of the shadows. He'd been taking a leak against the side of the building and was in the middle of zipping his pants up when he stepped back from the building.

"Hey! You should not be out here," he said. His highly accented English betrayed his heritage as one of the Argentinian sailors. "It's after curfew. You need to go back to your billets."

Emily smiled her most entrancing smile and quickly stepped toward him. His rifle was slung over his shoulder still, and he seemed more concerned with getting his fly up than realizing the two women and the dog were any kind of a threat.

"Hey," he said while she was well out of reach, "you're Emily Baxter, you're supposed to be—" The guard's eyes narrowed with recognition and he instantly began to sling his rifle from his shoulder.

Emily was still a meter or so from him. If he were fast enough it would be more than enough time for him to get his weapon off his shoulder and get off a shot. Even if he missed, the alarm would be raised and the chances of them getting to the Black Hawk would be dramatically reduced. Emily's mind made its decision before bothering to notify her, and she found herself barreling toward him, head down. She hit the guard hard in the stomach with her shoulder.

He let out an *"Uggff!"* and careened backward, his arms windmilling through the air, sending his rifle clattering away into the darkness as he fell. The unmistakable crunch of his head hitting something hard and the sudden silence that followed almost stopped Emily's heart.

Panting hard, Emily crouched in the shadows of the building, waiting for the man to move or at least moan. When he didn't she moved in closer to check on him. Pulling the flashlight from her jacket, she cupped the lens with her fingers until only a slit of light was visible.

Emily felt her stomach turn over. If she had eaten any food she would have thrown up; instead, she dry heaved into her hand.

The guard lay on his back about three feet in front of her. He had tripped over the raised curb along the edge of the road, toppled backward, and hit his head on the same curb. His sightless eyes stared skyward, an almost perfect reflection of the moon lighting the left orb, as a growing pool of blood spread across the road. One arm was bent crookedly toward Emily, his wrist limp, pointing accusingly toward her.

Rhiannon's sudden exclamation behind her brought Emily back to her senses. "Oh my God, is he dead? You killed him?" Rhiannon said.

"It was an accident," Emily insisted. She switched off the flashlight and pocketed it.

"But . . . but you killed him," Rhiannon insisted as darkness swallowed them.

"And there's not a Goddamn thing I can do about it. Now keep your voice down." Emily's heart thumped in her chest, the words she spoke more for her own tumbling mind than Rhiannon's reassurance. But even as they jogged the last few hundred meters back to the apartment building, Emily could not shake the image of the slack-jawed face of the guard, moonlight glinting from the pool of blood around his head. And she began to worry that she had finally stepped across an invisible boundary, a line that she would never be able to find again.

■ ■ ■

The rest of the way back to the apartment was spent in complete silence, and Emily was quite happy with that. While she felt no remorse for the death of Curtis, the death of the second guard had been a tragic accident. Either way, humanity was now two deaths closer to the point of extinction, and the knowledge that she had tipped the scales further toward their annihilation was even more terrifying, even if humanity was better off without Curtis. Of course the other problem was that the second guard would be expected to make regular check-ins with the watch commander in the northeast security tower. When the dead guard failed to respond to his radio calls, the rest of the security team would be alerted and sent out to investigate. It wouldn't be long before they found the body. They might think it was an accident, but if they also found Curtis's body in Emily's cell . . . well, then Point Loma would be on lockdown faster than a stripe-assed donkey. If Emily's plan was going to succeed, they had to get out of here right now.

And then of course there was Rhiannon. No way Emily could leave her behind now. It wouldn't take Fisher long to figure out that Emily had help getting out of jail, and once he put two and two together, Rhiannon would be right at the top of the list of suspects. She was going to have to come with her.

· · ·

The apartment building was a big black shadow. Emily, Rhiannon, and Thor eased into the foyer and silently climbed the stairs to the apartment, creeping through their front door.

Thor went straight to his water bowl and started lapping loudly.

"Your backpack is on your bed," Rhiannon said.

"Listen," said Emily, pausing at the door to her room, "I know I told you that you would have to stay behind, but that was before everyone lost their minds. I need you to grab some things as quickly as you can; you and Thor are coming with me."

"I know," said Rhiannon with a sad smile and disappeared into her own room.

Emily turned on her bedroom light, then, realizing that her window blinds were still up, she quickly dropped them and pulled across the curtains.

Sure enough, her backpack and the clothes she had been in the middle of packing lay exactly where she had left them; in the commotion following Emily's arrest Fisher had not thought to search her apartment. Why would he? She doubted the possibility of her making any kind of an escape would have even crossed his mind, which just went to show how much they were inclined to underestimating both her and the situation.

Rhiannon had been busy, apparently, because the MREs Emily had been about to grab when Fisher and his goons arrived were stacked next to her clothes on the bed.

And what was this? Her .45 also lay on the bed. Emily had a vague memory of the last time she had seen the pistol, skittering down the hallway.

"I found it in my bedroom," said Rhiannon, standing in the doorway.

Emily thanked her, then noticed the fully packed backpack sitting at Rhiannon's feet. She could not have had time to get ready so quickly.

"Well, you look prepared," she said.

"There was no way I was going to stay behind. Even if you hadn't been arrested, I would have snuck on board, whether you wanted me with you or not. Mac always says it never hurts to always be prepared." Rhiannon's voice had an air of finality to it, and Emily was reminded again that she should not underestimate the resourcefulness of the kid—young woman, she corrected herself. Or her dedication. Both were apparently quite formidable.

Emily quickly finished packing her clothes and supplies into her backpack. She fastened the watch Mac had given her to her wrist, pulled a Bowie knife and its scabbard from the bedside cabinet, and secured it just above her right ankle.

After a final check of the room Emily slung the backpack over one shoulder. She didn't bother fastening it; it'd be faster to stow that way, and every second was going to count.

"Let's go, Thor," she said as both women walked as quietly as they could to the front door.

As Emily closed the door to the apartment, she wondered if they would live to see it again.

■ ■ ■

In the darkness of the apartment corridor, Emily checked the time. The luminescent dial of her watch showed a little after 5:20 a.m. From the floor above came the unmistakable sound of creaking floorboards as someone walked across them. The day shift was stirring, and that meant they were quickly running out of time.

"We need to move faster," Emily said.

They jogged down the stairs and headed through the foyer, pausing to check that the coast was clear, then Emily, Thor, and Rhiannon slipped out of the apartment building and began to make their way toward the helicopter landing pad on the northwest side of the camp.

A faint line of white was already creasing the eastern horizon. Dawn was only an hour away at most and more of the camp would be beginning to stir soon. They had to hustle if they wanted to get to the helipad undetected.

Emily picked up the pace, slowing only when they reached the top of the path leading up to the landing pad.

"Unfasten those," Emily said, pointing to two of the four tiedowns securing the tarp that covered the helicopter.

They pulled the tarp off, bundled it up, and tossed it away.

In the slowly growing light of the fast-approaching morning, the Black Hawk looked like a huge black beetle.

"Toss your backpack inside," Emily said as she slid the side door open. She shrugged her own pack off and threw it in next to Rhiannon's. "Thor, up," she told the malamute, tapping the interior floor. The dog obeyed and she slid the door back into place when he was safely inside.

"You next," Emily said to Rhiannon, opening the copilot's door. Rhiannon pulled herself up into the seat. Emily quickly fastened the girl's safety harness, then placed a helmet that was far too large for Rhiannon on her head. "You'll have to make do," she told the girl as she connected the helmet's chin strap in place. "Once we're airborne this will be the only way we can communicate." She gave Rhiannon a reassuring smile, closed the door, and jogged around to the pilot's door. Pulling herself up into the seat, Emily closed the door behind her, then donned her own helmet.

The start-up procedure including preflight checks would normally take a good five minutes, but there was no way she was going to have that kind of time. Once the engine started up the entire camp would know exactly what was happening and where to find them. It would take about three minutes to get the rotors up to speed and get them off the ground. It wouldn't take a genius to figure out there was only one person who would be able to steal the helicopter. If she screwed anything up, or luck wasn't with them, there would be just enough time for Valentine to alert Fisher and have him here and pulling them out of the helicopter. If that happened then it was all over.

Emily disengaged the gust lock for the rotors and quickly went through the helicopter's start-up sequence. She held her breath as she fired up the engines.

The two massive engines rumbled to life and almost immediately she saw a light come on in one of the apartment buildings. Then another and another followed. It wasn't hard for her to imagine the radio conversations that were now surely happening.

She engaged the rotors and glanced upward through the glass canopy to check them. They were moving painfully slowly, but they *were* moving, gradually gaining speed. It was going to take about another minute or so before she could safely lift off.

The seconds seemed to stretch out. Emily had to force herself to run through the basic interior checks: Fuel was good, the tank almost entirely full. Oil pressure and engine temperature were all nominal.

She glanced down toward the camp.

Shit! Shit! Shit! A set of headlights was bouncing rapidly through the street toward the hill to their right, one of Fisher's security Humvees.

"Come on. Come on," she urged, as if her words would somehow encourage the rotors to spin faster.

"Emily?" Rhiannon's nervous voice came over the helmet's internal speakers. She had seen the oncoming Humvee too.

"It's all okay," Emily repeated, not sure if she was trying to reassure Rhiannon or herself. "Almost there."

The Humvee skidded to a halt about twenty meters away from the now rapidly rotating blades of the helicopter. The doors flew open and five figures exploded from inside, automatic rifles unslung and aimed at the canopy of the Black Hawk.

Valentine was the last to exit, unfolding from the back of the Hummer like a praying mantis, her face livid with anger.

Emily engaged the throttle hard and felt the Black Hawk lurch into the air. *Too Goddamn late,* she thought and smiled as the ground dropped quickly away.

The sound of something smacking into the fuselage snapped her attention back to the ground. Muzzle flashes sparkled and flashed in the morning half-light. *The fuckers were shooting at them.* Emily eased the throttle toward maximum and felt the Black Hawk respond accordingly, but not before several more rounds slammed into the fuselage. Then the only sound was of Rhiannon's panting breath over the comms.

"Are you hit?" Emily asked, fearing the worst. "Are you hit?"

"No," said Rhiannon after a long pause.

"Check on Thor."

Rhiannon unfastened her safety harness and twisted in her seat to look back into the rear passenger compartment.

"He's fine," she said as she buckled herself back up.

Emily let out a long sigh she felt she had been holding in since Rhiannon had first busted her out of the brig.

As she relaxed she felt the tingling attraction of her son's pull return, drawing her toward the northeast like a homing beacon. The nose of the Black Hawk was off course by about twenty degrees, and as she swung the helicopter, she felt the small hairs on her skin stand erect as the attraction shifted accordingly across her body.

"Too weird," she said.

"What?" said Rhiannon.

"Nothing. Why don't you get some rest for an hour? It's going to be a long flight."

"I'm okay," Rhiannon replied, but ten minutes later Emily heard the soft sound of Rhiannon's breathing in her headphones.

CHAPTER 7

The Black Hawk sped eastward, the grumble of the engines softened into melody by Rhiannon's light rhythmic snore as she lay curled up into an almost fetal position in the copilot's seat.

Emily estimated they were somewhere near the Arizona border. About a half hour earlier she had spotted what could only have been the Salton Sea in the distance, a huge forest of Titans sprouted up around its border.

The sun was almost above the horizon now, and in the early morning light the arc of Earth's new ring glinted and sparkled like a halo against the dark blue of the morning sky, majestic and heart-stoppingly beautiful. It had doubled in size since the last time she had seen it, and even as Emily marveled at its beauty, she still could not fathom what its purpose might be. It simply should not be there. It seemed like such an irrational thing to do, to expend so much energy to create something that served no purpose, at least to her mere Earth-born mind. Saturn had rings, and she had a vague memory that there might have been another planet within the solar system that had rings too. So why would the Caretakers go to so much trouble to create something that was, as far as she knew, a pretty common naturally occurring feature? The Caretakers were nothing if not inscrutable, but still . . . this seemed pointless.

The Black Hawk had drifted off course slightly as her mind considered the problem of the ring, and she instinctively piloted the helicopter's attitude back to better match her internal compass.

As she looked back, the first rays of morning sun hit the accretion ring, creating a light show that rivaled the aurora borealis. Waves of rainbow light played like fire across the canopy of the red forest as it rushed by beneath them, giving it the appearance of a vast ocean.

How did planetary rings get made, anyway? Wasn't it something to do with leftover material from when the planet was first formed? Or something like that. And would a planet that supported life also have a naturally occurring ring?

No idea, she told herself, but it sure did make for a beautiful sunrise.

This felt good. Like feeding a hunger, the urgent pull Emily felt across her skin had turned into a pleasurable tingle almost the second the helo had lifted off and she had begun directing it toward the source of the signal she was sure she was being directed to follow. With each passing kilometer, the intensity with which she felt the draw grew, as did the certainty that she was doing the right thing, that she was being called by and was answering her son. How did she know? Emily had absolutely no idea—it just, well, it felt *right*. And now she was fully committed. There was no way she was going to be able to go back, not now that Valentine had played her hand.

While it was easy to imagine Valentine giving the order to have her killed, she could not believe that Fisher would allow his men to open fire on her and Rhiannon. Fisher knew she was the only pilot qualified to fly the Black Hawk, and he knew that she would have no other choice but to come back to Point Loma at some point. Why would he risk shooting them down? Why kill her and Rhiannon? Emily had already decided Valentine was insane, but Fisher? He had never struck her as the type to react so violently. Perhaps he had lost control of his men?

Below the Black Hawk the red jungle zipped by. From this height, the canopy of the jungle looked almost cratered, the irregular span of the giant trees and tangled branches and limbs bound together to make a blood-red ocean. With the light show from the ring, the craters and dips looked like swells and waves washing across its surface. It looked almost serene, beautiful, even.

Emily's eyes kept up a periodic scan from outside the cockpit down to her instrument panel and as her eyes checked the fuel gauge she felt her heart skip a beat. She was 100 percent certain the tank had been close to full when they left Point Loma, but now it read just over the halfway mark. They had been in the air for a little over an hour, and taking a fairly leisurely pace, so there was no way it should be that low. Fuel pressure seemed okay, so unless she had simply misread the gauge or there was some kind of a fault with it, then there was really only one possibility: one of Valentine's goons had scored a lucky shot on a fuel line, and they were leaking fuel, slowly, but enough that it was going to impact the helo's range.

The possibilities of what could happen ran through Emily's mind: If the fuel came into contact with a hot engine part they could simply explode, right? Or maybe she had been watching too many movies. Did that happen in real life? She quickly decided that if it hadn't happened yet, she wasn't going to worry about it right now. Option two: she still had enough fuel left to turn back to Point Loma. But that would, at best, result in her being taken prisoner, but more probably, judging by the actions of Valentine, she would be tried in a kangaroo court and executed before the end of the day. And they had probably found the bodies of the two guards by now, she reminded herself. And what about Rhiannon and Thor? There was no way Valentine would let Rhiannon live and tell Mac and the crew of the HMS *Vengeance* what had happened when they finally returned. No, they would all meet with some kind of unfortunate accident. And it would also mean that Adam would be left in the hands of the Caretakers, and there was no way in Hell that she was going to let that happen.

So there was really only one choice at this stage, wasn't there: push on and hope the fuel lasted long enough to get them where they were going . . . wherever that might be.

■ ■ ■

Just over a quarter of the Black Hawk's fuel remained in its tank. That translated into about an hour's worth of flight, Emily estimated, if they were lucky. A slow-burning anxiety had begun in the pit of her stomach at the realization that, unless Adam was close by, they were not going to make it by air. While she was certain that the call of her child was a very real thing, there was no frame of reference that she could use to judge just how close she was to his location. It wasn't like there was some kind of a counter in her head that told her how far away he was, just this continual *need* to keep moving east. Adam could be just a few kilometers farther on, or somewhere back in New York. An even worse scenario, one she had not considered until now, suddenly reared up: What if he wasn't even on this continent? She knew the Caretakers had the ability to instantly transport themselves from one location to another—they had done it to her, after all—but over what kind of distance, she had no clue. What if he was in Europe: Spain or Britain or . . . or Russia? How would she reach him then?

Jesus! She felt sick at the very thought of it even being a possibility. No, she was going to have to simply rely on her belief that her son was still in the United States. Something about the pull just felt like he was close by, almost as though she could sense him in another room. She was just going to have to trust that sense.

As soon as Emily realized their fuel supply was shot, she had started to actively look for a place to put the Black Hawk down safely, but since fleeing Point Loma, the scenery had remained the same rolling canopy of the great red alien forest.

Rhiannon had slept for most of the journey and Emily had seen no reason to wake her until now; but now an extra pair of eyes might literally be the difference between life and death. They were both actively scanning the landscape for somewhere, anywhere, they could land.

Even after all of the years she had spent living in this reimagined world, the utter transformation of the American landscape—a land that once had held great tracts of homes, cities, businesses, and industries, and upward of three hundred million people—was still stupefying to Emily. Although she lived with the encroachment of the jungle on a daily basis at Point Loma, it was only from up here that she could truly appreciate just how complete the assimilation was. Apart from the occasional building that for some reason the rampaging alien vegetation had overlooked, there was no longer much to indicate that there had ever been a dominant race present on this planet. Here and there she might recognize the outline of a tower behind its mask of red foliage, maybe a signpost in a small clearing, a crumbling ruin, or a brief glimpse of road that disappeared as quickly as it came. If she had been flying to a specific location she would have been shit out of luck because, if it weren't for the occasional mountain range to break up the monotony, there would have been little to use as a visual gauge to show they were making any kind of headway. And if it hadn't been for the constant caress she felt pulling her onward, Emily knew she would have had no real idea where they were. If she had to make a guess, she would put them somewhere on the eastern side of Arizona, heading toward New Mexico, but there was no way to be absolutely certain.

But over the last twenty minutes Emily had noticed a distinct change in the scenery and her anxiety had begun to fade. The dense jungle was thinning. And as the kilometers rolled by, she began to spot more and more clearings within the alien trees, until the land finally opened up and the forest became a rarity, limited to clumps scattered here and there across the landscape. The topography of the land had changed too; it was flat, an unbroken plain. There was still the ever-present red vegetation, but this stuff seemed far smaller than the dense jungle they had left behind them. It was almost uniform in feature, like looking down on a field of corn or a plush red carpet.

"Hey, look, I can see a road," Rhiannon said, pointing down to her left.

Emily banked slightly left, dipping the nose of the chopper until she could see what Rhiannon saw. And yes, there below them, cutting a swath through the red plain like a scar across the landscape was the unmistakable gray of a freeway. It ran west to east, and here and there Emily could see the shape of a jackknifed tractor-trailer or a car.

She allowed the aircraft to continue its natural left turn until it was over the freeway, banked right, then began following the road east.

■ ■ ■

Emily descended until they were about twenty meters above the freeway. Every minute ate up another couple of kilometers, and she was determined to wring every last centimeter out of the

Black Hawk's dwindling fuel. That would mean leaving it until the very last second to land, a risk she felt she had to take. But at this height, Emily felt confident she could get them down fast when the time came. But this low to the ground, the sensation of speed was . . . alarming, to say the least. Her palms began to sweat. She resisted the urge to constantly adjust her grip on the cyclic stick. From the corner of her eye she saw Rhiannon's hands nervously searching for armrests that weren't there. She ended up stiffly grabbing both her knees instead.

Beyond the cockpit, the road stretched onward in an almost straight line to the horizon. Save for a few distant hills and even more distant mountains, there was nothing but featureless red plain on either side of the road. But beyond the hills, creeping toward them like a monster from some ancient B movie, Emily saw the unmistakable outline of storm clouds, gray and threatening against the backdrop of the sky. The storm collected along the eastern horizon in one large angry mass of swirling grays and blacks, hanging over the freeway like a beast. Thunderheads if ever she'd seen them. That was not good, and there was no way to tell which direction it was moving.

"Look," said Rhiannon. Emily's eyes followed where she was pointing and she could see a small black shape on the westbound side of the freeway, about fifteen kilometers or so away. It was the first and only building they had seen since leaving Point Loma. Apart from that there was no sign of anything that looked out of place, nothing that she could point at and say "There, that's where they're keeping my son."

An alarm suddenly filled the cockpit with its repetitive *whoop-whoop*, demanding her attention.

"What's that?" Rhiannon asked, her head snapping to look at the control panel.

"Low fuel warning," Emily said. Emily explained what she thought had happened to the fuel supply, that they were now out of it and would have to set the helicopter down.

"You mean we'll have to walk? Again!"

"'Fraid so," said Emily, trying not to laugh but failing despite the rising tension she felt as she guided the helicopter down. "At least until we can find a vehicle."

"But how far?"

"I don't know," Emily answered honestly. "I can't tell."

Rhiannon went silent.

Emily was tempted to push her luck for just a bit further, but she had the distinct feeling that her supply of that particular resource was pretty much linked directly to her supply of fuel, which meant she was almost out of both. The safest thing to do was to land the bird now.

She slowed her airspeed and allowed the Black Hawk to descend slowly.

A scattering of aluminum shells that had once been cars littered the westbound side of the freeway, scorch marks and melted tarmacadam from what must have been a pretty intense fire still visible around the derelict vehicles. Not safe to land there, so she aimed for the eastbound side of the freeway so she could get a clear view of the terrain ahead, her eyes peeled for any obstacles like overhead power cables or telephone lines that she might have missed.

"This will have to do," she said to herself.

She brought the Black Hawk to a hovering stop and dropped the final fifteen meters onto the eastbound center lane. The wheels bumped on the blacktop, and then the helo settled back onto its suspension.

Emily killed the engines. Silence quickly settled over them.

She peeled off her helmet, then helped Rhiannon with hers. Clambering out of the cockpit, Emily took a second to stretch her cramped legs and arms. It felt good to be back on the ground again. She gave a quick scan of the area she had chosen for their landing pad; it was a slightly undulating plain that reached out in all directions to the horizon, covered in a knee-high red plant that reminded her of the bull rushes that grew around some of the ponds back home. The reeds swayed back and forth in a gentle breeze, rustling like sand through a sieve.

A couple of kilometers to the northeast, a copse of alien trees stood silhouetted against the sky, a sky now painted with thick strokes of the gray clouds she had seen minutes earlier.

Emily unlatched the side door and beckoned Thor out. He leaped down and sniffed the ground inquisitively before peeing long and hard against the rear landing gear.

"This looks so different from California," said Rhiannon, joining Emily at the front of the Black Hawk, her hair a bird's nest of tangles from the helmet.

"I think the amount of plants and trees in an area reflects the environment, just like it did before the red rain came," Emily said, pulling first her backpack and then Rhiannon's from within the Black Hawk's hold. "And I think the amount of . . . biological material available in each location also has a lot to do with what developed there after the rain."

"You mean people, don't you."

Emily nodded. "And animals and plants. It all contributed. I think we're probably somewhere in eastern Arizona, and that's mostly desert. The cities are pretty spread out, so there was probably far less material for the red rain to transform." She fastened the belt buckle to secure the backpack and checked that there was nothing else in the helicopter that they might need.

The air was cool, made colder again by the gusts of wind that blew across them, and Emily grew even colder when she looked at the storm that now lay directly ahead of them. It was distant but growing. They had two choices: stay with the helo and ride out the storm or press on toward the building they had spotted from the air and hope that they got there before the storm did. Rhiannon looked at the thunderstorm but said nothing. Instead she opened the flap on her backpack and pulled out a thick waterproof jacket and put it on. Emily did the same.

"Think we can outrun it?" Rhiannon said.

"Of course. Come on, let's get a move on."

■ ■ ■

From the air, the freeway had looked like a flat, straight line cutting across the desert, but as Emily, Rhiannon, and Thor trudged their way east, they found the road at ground level cracked and broken from years of negligence and harsh weather. Large chunks of blacktop had broken away across the freeway's surface, cracked open by the same alien plants that covered the plains, pushing their way up through the openings and fissures. A light haze of what must be pollen floated above the top of the plants. It swirled and meandered through the air in clouds and streams.

Emily shifted her backpack to a more comfortable position. It was actually quite peaceful, walking wordlessly along this fractured road, Thor trotting out in front of them, nose to the ground, sniffing at the unfamiliar scents. The companions had reached a kind of walking rhythm that was almost tantric: one step after the other, the only sound their footfalls and breathing, a gentle rhythmic beat. The cool air was a welcome change from the almost constantly sunny days they had experienced throughout their years in California.

There were surprisingly few vehicles on the road. They had passed a couple of cars abandoned on a gravel easement that ran alongside the freeway, their doors left open as if the previous owners had simply pulled over, flung open the door, and run away, which perhaps was exactly what they had done. There was no sign of a body or even the shell of one of the alien spiders in any of the vehicles, but it would most likely have disintegrated long ago. They also passed the burned-out wreckage of a big rig, the blackened ribs of the trailer exposed like the old bones of some whale that had found itself dropped from the sky, the main cab nowhere in sight.

But ahead of them, the thunder clouds Emily had spotted earlier had grown closer, the storm clawing its way across the dome of sky almost directly over their heads, and joined now by the unmistakable haze of rain falling beneath it. A single flash of lightning burst silently through the body of the storm. Emily began counting out loud, "One one thousand. Two one thousand."

Rhiannon looked at her oddly. *What on Earth are you doing now?* the look said.

As if in answer, a peal of thunder rolled over them just as Emily reached a count of seven.

"It's a good way to figure out how far away the storm is," Emily explained. "Sound travels about a kilometer every three seconds, so that lightning struck about two and a half kilometers away from us. Which means the storm is moving our way fast." She was beginning to regret leaving the relative safety of the helicopter, but she estimated they were closer to the building than they were to the Black Hawk now. They would just have to keep on walking and hope that the rain held off long enough for them to reach it.

As if the storm were determined to prove her wrong on every count today, the first drops of rain started to hit the road ahead of them, fat drops splattering across the ground with audible *thwacks*, like a rolled-up newspaper slapped against a hand.

"Oh great," said Rhiannon, pulling the hood of her jacket over her head. Emily did the same and tilted her head down as a bitingly cold gust of wind drove the rain almost horizontally into her face. Within minutes, despite their jackets, the wind had helped the rain find its way through their jackets' sleeves and hoods, and both women were uncomfortably wet.

Shit! This was a mistake.

To reinforce her thought, a vicious slash of lightning flashed to the ground on their left flank, followed almost instantly by a crack of thunder that sounded like a bomb detonating, rattling Emily's fillings. Rhiannon and Emily screeched, and poor Thor, drenched and bedraggled, gave a yelp and ran to Emily's feet, shaking in fear.

"It's okay," Emily said, trying to overcome the thunderous drumming of the rain against the ground. "Come on, boy," she encouraged the malamute, who seemed rooted to the spot. The rain was a problem, but worse still was their exposed position. They were quite literally the tallest things for kilometers, which meant they made a perfect target for a lightning strike. They had no choice but to push on and hope that they either found some shelter or that the rain would ease up, but it was hard not to flinch every time lightning ripped across the sky.

She could pray, she supposed, but to what god? She had given up believing in any kind of benevolent being long before the red rain arrived, and the systematic destruction of humanity had put the final nail in that particular superstition's coffin for her (along with 99.9 percent of the rest of the world). Had to hand it to the Caretakers, they did not discriminate when it came to race, creed, or religion. They were willing to fuck up anybody's life, no matter their denomination or belief.

"We have to keep going," Emily yelled to Rhiannon. The rain was hitting the ground so hard it had created a mist of particles that hung in the air around their feet; that and a combination of the impenetrable cloud and driving rain had severely reduced the visibility down to maybe twenty meters. "Follow me." Emily abruptly shifted direction, heading toward the center median. She hopped over the center barrier, helped Rhiannon do the same, and then encouraged Thor to jump over.

"What are we doing?" Rhiannon asked; the rain against the metal of the guardrail sounded like ball bearings bouncing off glass.

"We need to find that building we saw from the air. The visibility is so bad, if we stay on that side of the freeway, we might walk right by it."

The rain was now a constant hammering against their bodies. And when the wind blew up, it beat directly against their exposed faces, stinging their skin and eyes.

The wind kicked up again as they trudged east, and this time it did not die down. Emily was frozen, and she was sure Rhiannon was faring no better. She tried to block the worst of the wind's force, but it seemed to be coming from all directions, staggering them each time it shifted direction. And the rain showed no sign of easing up either; if anything, it was growing even worse, battering them as the wind buffeted and knocked them about like a cat playing with a mouse. It was as if the God that Emily had so roundly denied had decided to finally put in an appearance, Old Testament style, and was going out of His way to say "And where do you think you are going, mortal?"

For the next hour or more, they fought against the wind and the lashing rain, Emily leading the way, trying to do her best to shield both Rhiannon and Thor from the main force of the storm. This had been a major mistake, she had decided many kilometers back, but now she thought she might have to recategorize it as a potentially fatal one.

There was no sign of the building. For all she knew they could have walked right past it already. About a kilometer back, they had passed the shell of a car, but it had been wrecked beyond recognition and offered no hope of shelter. There wasn't even a bush or a tree for them to shelter beneath. Emily could feel the continually dropping temperature beginning to creep into her bones through the thin layers of her Windbreaker. If they did not find some way out of this weather soon there was no question in her mind that they would die of exposure. Each step was now a labor, water having long ago permeated her boots and soaked into her socks. Every muscle ached, and she could not feel her lips. When she blindly led the group off the side of the road, Emily realized that it had grown so dark that she had actually lost her sense of direction. She managed to fumble her flashlight from her backpack and turned it on, illuminating the road ahead of them. She washed it over her companions: Thor looked as bedraggled as could be expected but seemed resolved to just put one paw in front of the other. He gave a slow wag of his tail in acknowledgment of his mistress's attention. Rhiannon's face was a pale moon in the artificial glow of the flashlight's LED bulbs. She looked as though she had been dropped in the deep end of the ocean, but there was still a determined sparkle in her eyes, and she smiled weakly. Emily managed her own wan smile in return; it was supposed to say *Don't worry*, but felt more like *It'll all be over soon. Just lie down and go to sleep.*

A second beam of light joined Emily's as Rhiannon fished her own flashlight from her pack, cutting through the wet, murky darkness as they continued on their way.

Once the torrential downpour had begun, the gullies alongside the road had quickly turned into streams and then rivers, carrying streamers of mud and dislodged flora back in the direction they had already come. A half-inch layer of water lay over the road surface too, dancing with the splash of each new raindrop.

All sense of time had evaporated. Emily was reduced to focusing on putting one soggy foot in front of the other, occasionally checking behind her to make sure that she had not lost her two companions. The only change marking the passage of time was the occasional flash of lightning and rumble of thunder. So it could have been a minute or it could have been an hour before Emily's foot-down/foot-up plod was broken by a tug at her jacket's elbow. She turned to see Rhiannon thrusting her flashlight forward like it were a dagger.

"There!" Rhiannon yelled.

Emily followed the beam of the girl's flashlight. It illuminated the shadow-shrouded fascia of a storefront, the paint flaking away from the clapboards.

"Let's go," Emily yelled back as the three half-drowned companions staggered as quickly as they could toward the building.

■ ■ ■

A boom of thunder rocked the travelers as they reached the building's entrance.

The building rattled like dice in a can.

Debris, fire-blackened pieces of wood—some the size of Emily's arm, others merely splinters—lay scattered over the ground in front of the entrance, as though an explosion had ripped through the structure. Putting aside the fact that the building had seen its last human over two years ago, the place was in surprisingly good shape. But as Emily played the beam of her flashlight to the right she saw a gaping hole and charred timbers in the center of the building. There had definitely been an explosion of some kind, judging by the ragged hole ripped in the fascia. That would account for the debris field they were walking through, but the fire must have been short-lived, because the rest of the structure on either side of the devastation looked to be in relatively good condition.

They climbed up a wide set of concrete steps to reach the wooden deck running along the front of the building. A slatted wooden awning also ran parallel to the deck, but it was pretty much wrecked, pieces hanging down from it like dead tree limbs. A glass-faced double door marked the entrance to the building. The glass had long ago shattered and lay in broken pieces around the foot of the door. Emily swiped it away with the toe of her boots. Rhiannon started to push the door open, but Emily dropped a heavy hand on her shoulder.

"Wait a second," she insisted. "Careful." She tried to reach down and take her pistol from its holster, but her hands would not comply. Hours of freezing rain had left her hands feeling as though they belonged to someone else, and they were shaking so much she might just drop the damn pistol anyway. They were all slowly freezing to death. If they didn't get out of this rain and warm up soon, they were going to die. She tried again to slip the .45 from its holster, but her hands just would not obey her. They were just going to have to chance it. If there was any kind of threat inside, she would deal with it when it needed to be dealt with.

Good luck with that, Emily thought. She would be lucky if she could even muster the energy to yell a few harsh words at anything that might be lurking beyond the rotted doors, let alone put up a fight.

Years of rain and wind had warped the doors until they no longer fitted the frame properly. Emily had to pull with all of her remaining strength to move them enough so that she could slip through. Rhiannon followed next, then Thor, who instantly shook a shower of rain water off his coat.

"Thanks for that," said Rhiannon, managing a half smile despite the new soaking.

Emily silenced her with an index finger to her lips. She swung her flashlight slowly through the inky darkness.

They were in a large room. A horseshoe-shaped glass counter occupied the majority of it, the counter's glass either broken into pieces or covered in too much dust and dirt to see what was beneath it. Shelves with what looked like figurines ran along the wall behind the counter. A doorway on the opposite wall read "Staff Only." To their right, hidden within shadows, the light revealed a shambles of broken and wrecked debris that Emily could not make out, but she could see the open gash of the room where the explosion had torn the building open. Waterfalls gushed off the exposed roof beams, collecting into a pool of water like a moat between the two still relatively intact halves of the building. Beyond that were the remains of the rest of the building, but Emily's light couldn't cut through the torrent of rain filling the open space to be sure what was in there. To their left were more glass display cases and shelves. This place had been some kind of a store aimed at tourists, Emily decided.

The rain hammered so hard on the roof of their shelter that it was impossible to hear if there was anything else sheltering in here with them. They were just going to have to be damn careful until they were sure. First things first: they needed to find somewhere dry so they could get out of these sodden clothes and, hopefully, light a fire.

"Let's try back there," she whispered to Rhiannon, pointing to the "Staff Only" sign over the door on the opposite side of the room.

Debris littered the floor between them and the room, mostly

broken pieces of ceramic and shattered glass. Emily did her best to kick it out of the way of Thor's paws as they made their way around the back of the counter. A cash register lay on its side on the floor in front of them, its tray open, coins and moldy bills scattered around it. An equally moldy-smelling curtain acted in lieu of a door to the staff area. Emily pulled it aside, turning her head in disgust as a cloud of dust and red spores cascaded into the air.

The room behind the curtain was small, only about four by four meters. Taking up most of the wall on her left was a set of ten lockers; the other walls were bare except for what might once have been a work roster but was now just tattered corners pinned to the wall. A small window sat in the north exterior wall. A wooden bench like Emily had seen in some gyms stood near on the right wall. At some point the bench had toppled over onto its side. Rhiannon righted it and sat down; actually, it was more like she collapsed down. In the light of their flashlights Emily could see that Rhiannon's hands were corpse pale, her body shivering violently.

Thor shook himself one more time, then headed to the far corner of the room, chased his tail in slow motion twice, then sank to the tiled floor, his head resting against his paws, his eyes closed.

Emily knelt down in front of the girl; Rhiannon's face was almost as pale as her hands. She unfastened the backpack's belt from around Rhiannon's waist, then slipped it off, setting it down next to the bench.

"Put your hands between your thighs," Emily ordered. "It'll keep them warm." Rhiannon did as she was told.

Emily's own hands were shaking too. Even out of the rain, it was still horribly cold in the building. She could feel her soaking-wet clothes wicking the heat away from her body. They needed a fire, and they needed one right now if they weren't both going to die of hypothermia or pneumonia.

She began looking around for something they could use as fuel. The bench was too thick, and, besides, she had nothing to break it apart with. The rain had ruined any chance of her using the debris lying outside the building, which meant she would have to find something dry inside. Her brain was sluggish with fatigue and the cold, but she remembered the wooden shelves she had seen in the main room of the store.

"I'll be right back," she said. Rhiannon barely acknowledged her as she disappeared back into the front of the room again.

Emily knocked the remaining figurines off the set of wooden shelves near the counter, then pulled five of the half-meter-long shelves from their fastenings. She didn't have time to worry about the noise the figurines made as they shattered on the floor; her energy was fading too fast.

She leaned the first of the shelves against the wall and the floor, lifted a foot that felt like it was made of lead, and aimed a swift side kick to the center of the shelf. It broke in two with a satisfying crack. She took each half and did the same until she was left with several long strips of wood that were small enough to burn easily. When she had finished doing the same to the remaining shelves, she gathered up the pieces and carried them into the back room.

Rhiannon lay on the bench, her hands tucked under her head, the bench vibrating against the tiles of the floor from her shivering body.

"Shit," said Emily. She dropped the sticks beneath the window, then moved to Rhiannon's side. "Sit up, come on," she ordered, sliding her complaining hands under the girl's arms and pulling until she was upright again. Emily began stripping the clothes from the girl layer by layer until she stood there in just her underwear, hands laced together beneath her chin, her pale body shivering in the cold light of the flashlight. Emily tossed the sodden clothes into a pile, then grabbed the girl's backpack and rummaged through the contents. It was just clothes and an ancient tube of Pringles potato chips, no blanket. She pulled a dry set of Rhiannon's clothing from the bag and set them down.

She was getting this all wrong, her frozen mind yelled at her. But this was the best she could do, her brain barely capable of processing thoughts in any semblance of order.

Emily pulled a blanket from her own backpack, placed it around the girl's shoulders, and began rubbing her as quickly as she could to try and bring some warmth back to her. She kept rubbing until the shivering had subsided, stimulating Rhiannon's circulatory process to pump warm blood around her body. The activity seemed to help her too, tapping a reserve of energy Emily did not know she still had.

When Rhiannon's skin started to take on a rosier hue, Emily quickly dressed the girl again in the dry set of clothes, then draped the blanket around her shoulders again and parked her butt back on the bench.

Rhiannon had said nothing through the entire process.

Seconds after stopping, Emily felt the old dull ache begin to creep over her again. It felt as though every joint within her body had begun to seize up. It was getting harder and harder to move, and her brain seemed to be finding itself incapable of holding on to any single thought for more than a few seconds. She stumbled back to the pieces of broken shelving and began to lean each stick against the other until she had built a pyramid.

She was missing something, though. Her sluggish mind dug for an answer. Kindling!

"Ah shit!" she mumbled and allowed herself to flop down next to the useless fire. Without tinder she had little chance of being able to get the fire going.

"What's wrong?" Rhiannon asked weakly from across the room.

Emily twisted around to face her. "No kindling," she said. "No kindling. No fire. Sorry." It was impossible to keep the feeling of utter despair out of her voice. But even without kindling she knew she was going to have to try, anyway, but it would just be wasting gas from her lighter. But first she had to get herself out of her own clothes. She went to stand, but Rhiannon spoke first.

"Potato chips," Rhiannon said, pointing to her backpack.

"What?"

"Potato chips, you can use them." Rhiannon leaned over and dragged her backpack to her. She rummaged around inside and brought out the tube of Pringles. "Here, I was keeping them for a special occasion." Rhiannon offered the tube to Emily. "They burn real good. Try it."

Emily took the tube; the cardboard was a little damp, but the chips inside seemed dry—and smelled delicious. "The cardboard's damp, it won't burn," Emily said flatly.

"Not the cardboard, the chips," Rhiannon repeated. "Just put them under the wood and light them."

Emily pulled out a handful of the chips, each an almost identical clone of the other, her cold, clumsy hands shattering half of them. She laid the intact chips around the base of the wood as though they were tinder. She had brought a box of matches but also a gas lighter, and she fished that out of her pack and pressed the igniter. She touched the orange flame to the edge of one of the chips. It instantly started to smolder, and then a tiny flame began to burn around the edge. She touched the flame to the other chips one by one.

"Wow!" she said a minute later as the chips burned like the wick of a candle, filling the room with the delicious scent of burning potatoes. "That's just . . . Wow!" Within a few minutes the flame had spread to the pieces of shelving, and they had a fire.

And they had smoke . . . a cloud had already collected at the ceiling. Emily forced herself to her feet and unlatched the window. It opened along a horizontal hinge at the top of the frame. The storm still raged outside, the rain hammering just as hard, but the window acted like a flue and began to suck the smoke outside.

Rhiannon had moved from the bench and now sat beside the fire, warming her hands, a smile of contentment on her face. Thor got up from his corner and sat next to her, the smell of wet dog almost as strong as the smell of burning wood.

Emily took a moment to warm her own hands beside the fire. When its warmth had permeated through her fingers and she could feel them again, she slowly stripped off her own clothing.

"Here, let me help you," said Rhiannon. She helped Emily slip from her clothes.

Even with the warmth of the fire, the cold air of the room against Emily's naked skin had her shivering again. Rhiannon offered her the blanket, but she refused.

"Keep it," Emily said.

She changed quickly into her dry clothes and sank down as close to the fire as she dared.

Ten more minutes beside the fire and she could feel sensation returning to her limbs and muscles. They ached and complained with every movement she made, and the fingers on both her hands tingled and twitched with pins and needles, but pain meant she was still alive. And with the return of feeling, Emily also felt the *tug-tug-tug* of her son pulling at her, a nagging sensation that she knew would only subside when she was moving toward him again. But even that siren call could not motivate her exhausted body to do anything other than sit in front of the fire for the next hour and feed it pieces of broken shelving.

The smoky aroma, life-giving warmth, and exhausted muscles

conspired to drag Emily toward sleep. Even though she fought it, she was no match and felt herself drift off.

■ ■ ■

When Emily awoke in the middle of the night, she was stiff from having sat too long in the same position. Rhiannon was asleep across from her, her knees pulled to her chest, the blanket beneath her. Thor had retreated back to the corner, and she could see him watching her, the light of the fire's flames reflected in his eyes.

She allowed herself the luxury of simply sitting there, her mind empty of almost all thoughts other than how wonderful it was to feel warm. Even the wet rumbling complaints of her stomach could do nothing to dampen the feeling.

Eventually Emily set about picking up their wet clothes from where she had dumped them. She hung them over the metal cabinets to dry by the warmth collecting within the room.

She had packed light, with only the second set of clothes she was now wearing and her soaked set, the rest of her backpack taken up with the MREs. Rhiannon, on the other hand, had taken a little more time and had an extra set of neatly folded clothes and shoes.

The fire was rapidly eating through the first batch of wood, so Emily made another trip back into the main room of the store and scrounged up enough wood to last through the night. By the time she returned to the back room, her arms laden with broken pieces of wood, Rhiannon was awake again, kneeling next to the fire, a saucepan full of food heating over it. Thor was already busy munching on his own dinner.

The two women devoured their meal in silence, occasionally smiling at each other across the fire, savoring the satisfying feeling in their stomachs.

When they were done Rhiannon climbed into her sleeping bag and was soon asleep. Emily vowed that she would remain awake to make sure the fire stayed alight, but the warmth of her own sleeping bag soon overwhelmed her; she felt her eyes begin to close, and soon she was gone too.

■ ■ ■

Emily awoke sometime later to an almost dead fire and a concerto of rainwater *splat-splat-splatting* off of hundreds of unseen leaks.

She poked around in the glowing ashes of the fire with a stick of firewood, blew gentle encouragement on the embers she found there, and gradually added more wood until the flames were established again. Her wristwatch said it was just after three in the morning. The rain had stopped at some point after she'd fallen asleep.

Rhiannon was curled up in a ball, her face the only thing visible above the caterpillar form of her sleeping bag. Thor lay next to her. The Malamute's eyes opened when he sensed Emily was awake, his tail giving three slow beats against the floor.

Other than the continual drip of water, the occasional creak of the building's rotting wooden bones, and the crackle of the fire, the world seemed to have ground to a complete stop.

Emily's body ached. The last twenty-four hours had been one of the most physically stressful days of her life. Each time she shifted position she found a new pain. But her pummeled body was nothing compared to the inner turmoil she felt.

It was almost as though Mac's announcement he was leaving for Norway had started a chain reaction of negative events. It escalated with Adam's abduction, her realization that he was alive, and then Valentine's attempt to murder her. She realized her mind was probably making connections where there really were none, but it was so much easier to link them all together as part of a single huge event than to simply allow for a confluence of multiple unrelated actions—a really, really shitty confluence.

Valentine. *That* woman. Emily understood, expected even, the Caretakers' murderous motivations, but Valentine? She was *human*. She understood how precarious the human race's position was right now, or *should*. They were all on life support, for Christ's sake, and here was Valentine making a bid to demolish the hospital and put up a set of condos. It was simple to Emily. The future of humanity teetered on the brink of extinction, so you put aside whatever petty differences you had and you worked together to ensure the survivors, well, survived. How blind did Valentine have to be to ignore that?

Pretty fucking blind, apparently, because she was more than willing to have Emily murdered to ensure that whatever fucked-up plan she had would become reality.

Emily had already concluded, if only halfheartedly, that Valentine was crazy, but she wondered now if that was actually the answer. A sociopath was someone who held no regard for people other than themselves, who had no conscience, right? That description would seem to fit Valentine perfectly. She had already cost two lives.

In the glow of the fire Emily thought back to the guard she had hit . . . and killed, albeit by accident. There was no doubt she had caused his death; she took full responsibility. That Valentine would use his death against her was a foregone conclusion, which kind of put a big speed bump in the way of any return back to Point Loma. Under any other circumstance she would have pleaded her case to the council and accepted whatever penalty was handed down to her. But the truth was, under any other circumstances, the events of the past couple of days wouldn't have ever happened. She was convinced that there was no way Valentine would give her a fair trial. The woman had already trumped up the charges against her to murder when she had seen the opportunity. The death of the guard would be all she needed to have her shot at dawn.

And she was still at a loss for how it had all happened. How it had escalated so incredibly quickly. Had Valentine been planning to get rid of her all along? If Adam had not been abducted, would she have met with some kind of unfortunate "accident" while she was out taking one of her strolls? Or had the woman simply taken advantage of the situation when it had presented itself? Jesus! The fact that people like her were willing to screw over a fellow survivor when the human race was hanging by a such a precarious thread was almost impossible for her to imagine. A week ago she would never have entertained the possibility that anyone would have been willing to kill to advance their own agenda. What was even worse was to find out that there were still men like the guard Curtis, sadistic bastard that he was, who were quite happy to work with Valentine. Emily wasn't sure whom she despised more: Valentine for coming up with the plan, or Curtis for being so fucking eager to carry it out.

Another thought suddenly came to her: What was going to happen to Mac when he arrived back from his mission? There was no way he would believe any of the story that Valentine would spin for him, and that bitch was smart enough to figure that out and plan accordingly. She would have Mac arrested on some equally trumped-up charge, and that would be that. *Jesus!* Valentine probably had enough of the council in her pocket that she could potentially take the whole crew of the HMS *Vengeance.* It would all hinge on how many of the survivors were willing to stand with Valentine, but, since she was so capable of spinning the most enticing lies, it might be easier for the survivors to believe them than to see the truth. And while she was on the subject of the "truth," all Valentine would have to do was make an example of a couple of the ranking officers and crew, and the rest of the camp would, understandably, cave.

"Shit!" she hissed under her breath.

Thor's head popped up and his brown eyes stared at her through the flames of the fire. He got up and walked over to her and lay down again. Emily reached out and stroked the dog's head, then down between his eyes, until he lowered his head again.

She was going to have to find some way to contact Mac and let her husband know what had happened, warn him that Valentine might be plotting against him and the crew. How she would do that she had no idea. There was no way for them to get back to Point Loma, no way to reach the submarine while they were radio silent, and no way to know if or when the *Vengeance* had made it back to California.

Of course, all of that was beside the point if she did not survive finding Adam. But Adam was the key to all of this. If she could locate him and take him back with her, she would have the proof she needed to fight Valentine, or at least cast some doubt on whatever story Valentine concocted. If there was some way to prove that the woman was the conniving murderous bitch Emily knew her to be, then maybe there was a chance.

Jesus!

Emily compartmentalized the negative thoughts. It would do no good to dwell on them right now. There was not a thing she could do about that particular problem, anyway—not right now. She would figure out how she was going to deal with Valentine after she had found Adam.

Emily lay her head back down and stared deep into the flames. She had fought so hard to survive, to ensure that the remnants of humanity had a chance, and had beaten the odds on more than one occasion. After all that, she would be damned if she was going to let another human being be her downfall.

CHAPTER 8

The next morning, the sun was a ghost haunting a leaden gray sky. While the clouds threatened to resume their downpour, the day was so far mercifully free of rain.

Emily shivered as she stepped out onto the wooden deck of their shelter. The morning air was just the wrong side of cool for her, but the mug of coffee she had brewed over the fire warmed her hands and insides. She had slept surprisingly well for the rest of the night. No dreams, thank God. She had left Rhiannon still sleeping in her bag, Thor ever watchful beside her.

The flat featureless landscape stretched off in all directions, giving Emily a clear 360-degree field of view for many kilometers, the open plain broken only by three distant clusters of Titan trees, nothing more than black silhouettes. Patches of early morning mist still lingered on the ground here and there, adding to the feeling of complete isolation. In the washed-out light of this new day, Emily could finally make out the building where they had spent the night. It had been some kind of tourist souvenir store. A sign, perpendicular to the roof, had been cut in half by the explosion that split the building in two, and now it read "Indian Supp." A rusting soft-drink machine sat just a little farther down the wooden deck from where she stood next to an equally rusted bench. She made a mental note to see if she could open the machine before they left; there might still be some goodies inside.

EXTINCTION POINT: GENESIS

Emily tested the bench to make sure it would not collapse and sat down. She took a deep swig of coffee and allowed herself to relax.

Since the night she had woken to discover Adam missing— What was it, three days ago now?—Emily's life had been spiraling out of control. This, she realized, was the first chance in all that time that she had had a second to simply sit, just sit.

She sipped at her coffee and allowed her eyes to wander over the scenery.

The freeway cut across the red skin of the world like a half-healed knife wound, east to west. Large pools of rainwater had collected on the freeway's surface, the channels running along the side of the freeway full to overflowing; she could hear the rush of water from where she sat. The building they had taken shelter in was on the west side of the freeway. The store's parking lot, veined with cracks and tufts of plant life, was surprisingly empty of any vehicles. Not a single car or truck. She supposed the building would have offered very little in the way of shelter back when the red rain had fallen. Travelers would have just wanted to get home to their families, and that would have included the staff. She had seen no evidence of the telltale circular holes that would have indicated humans had died here, been transformed into spider aliens, and then cut their way out in search of others like them. She shuddered at the memory of the *millions* of those same creatures she had witnessed swarming through the streets of Manhattan in the first days after the rain.

Still, *something* was out of place.

Emily could not put her finger on what it was exactly, but the scenery seemed different somehow, subtly altered just enough to alert her brain that *something* was not the same; it was like look-ing at one of those puzzles in a magazine that asks you to spot the difference between two seemingly identical pictures. Until you concentrate, you don't see the changes, but you know they are there. She stood up and began to slowly turn in place, taking in every detail that she could. While their arrival last night was hurried, to say the least, everything looked just as she remembered; the debris field of wood and broken glass in front of the store and their footprints through the mud-covered ground and then up to the doorway all looked as it should, but still . . . she could not shake this perception of change.

Emily stepped off the porch and walked a few feet across the concrete of the building's parking lot. Beyond the cracked tarmac, where once there had been green grass, there was now nothing but the ubiquitous red mosslike plant every survivor had long ago substituted the word "grass" for. It carpeted every inch of arable land.

Why was the building even still standing? Where was the voracious building-eating plant-animal they had encountered in Las Vegas—the all-you-can-eat bug, Mac had labeled it—that seemed so intent on reducing every building to dust? It had been just as prevalent in California, reducing the nearby cities and naval base to nothing but holes in the ground. Hell, Point Loma had a daily team dedicated to finding and eradicating any of the hybrid all-you-can-eat they found within the camp. Could it be as simple as localization of the species? Like certain plants or animals that could only be found in specific areas, before the red rain came?

Emily's pondering was broken by the sound of the door creaking open, followed by the clatter of Thor's paws across the porch and a not-so-bright "Morning" from Rhiannon.

"How are you feeling?" Emily asked, watching Rhiannon, the blanket thrown around her shoulders like a shawl, descend the steps into the forecourt.

"Okay. Better, I suppose. How about you?"

Emily smiled. "I'm good—a little tired, but okay."

"So, what do we do now?" Rhiannon asked.

Emily stood. She didn't even need to close her eyes; all she had to do was turn to the east and she could feel the warm glow of her son, burning like a pulsar, tingling her skin like tiny pinpricks of excitement.

"We head that way." Emily pointed toward the rising sun. "We just need to stay on the freeway; it'll get us all the way to the East Coast if we have to go that far."

Rhiannon looked pensive.

Emily watched her for a second. "What's on your mind?" she asked, trying to keep her tone as nonchalant as possible.

Rhiannon stopped, staring at her shoe for a moment, biting her lower lip. When she spoke it was almost apologetically. "Are you sure you know where we're going, Emily?"

Emily was not surprised by the question, but she was surprised by how long it had taken Rhiannon to ask it. It was one thing to tag along out of friendship and love, another altogether to believe in some kind of mystical compass that everyone else thought of as indicating that Emily had bought a first-class ticket on the Crazy Train Express.

"I don't know exactly where we're heading," Emily said, "but I know that we're closer now than we were before we left Point Loma."

There was no need for words; Rhiannon's conflicted expression of befuddlement was question enough: *How? How do you know?*

"It's like there's a thread, a connection, running from me to Adam. I can feel it tugging at me. And when I stop moving, it pulls even stronger, like he's telling me not to stop, to keep on moving."

Rhiannon continued to look at her with that same conflicted gaze.

"Look, it's okay. I'm not crazy . . . something weird is happening, I'll be the first to admit it, and I know it's hard for you to accept, but I also know beyond a shadow of a doubt that Adam is waiting for us. If we follow it, it's going to lead us to where he is."

"Or it's a trap," said Rhiannon. The words fled her mouth as though they had been released from chains.

"Yes, of course, I've thought about that. But it's not a trap; this is something . . . much deeper." Emily raised a hand to silence Rhiannon's objections. "Don't ask me how I know, because I won't be able to tell you. I just do. You *have* to trust me. It's a matter of faith, okay?"

Rhiannon was about to add something else but stopped, and her whole body seemed to relax, whether in resignation or acceptance of her explanation, Emily could not tell.

"Okay," the girl said finally, "let's go find him."

Emily smiled broadly, stepped closer, and threw her arms around Rhiannon.

"Thank you for your trust," Emily said as Rhiannon returned the hug.

They held the embrace for a minute, two humans just being.

■ ■ ■

The soda machine on the front stoop proved to be full of nothing but burst cans, the victims of so long an exposure to the elements, but they found a couple of candy bars in one of the lockers in the staff room and ate them as they continued their scavenger hunt around what was left of the remaining building. Emily gave the last half of hers to Rhiannon; the candy was way too sweet for her palate after so much time of no sugar or corn syrup.

"Oh! This will be useful," said Emily as they rooted through the front of the store, carefully trying to avoid the broken pieces of glass. She held up a tourist map of Arizona and New Mexico, protected by a clear plastic envelope, with only a few blotches of mildew near the corners.

Emily spread it out on the counter and followed the route she thought she had taken from California, guesstimating the distance they had travelled before setting down.

"I think we're somewhere around here," she said, poking an area on the map with her finger. If she were right, then they had lucked out and found the remains of the I-40, an interstate route that bisected most of the lower states from California on the West Coast across to the east of the country. They were somewhere in the middle of nowhere. There wasn't a major town or city for a good two hundred kilometers . . . assuming her guesstimate was correct, of course.

Emily folded the map up again and placed it in her back pocket.

She checked her watch. It was pushing toward eleven already. "Let's see if there's anything else of use in here, and then we need to get going."

They wandered deeper into the almost cavelike recess of the store, carefully picking their way through the debris of a lost age.

"I think this place must have been owned by one of the Native American tribes," Emily said when they found themselves standing in a room with the remains of scores of moccasins spilled across the floor, their boxes nothing but gray mulch, and the shoes all but disintegrated from exposure to the elements. Grime-covered statuary of wolves and cougars, bronco-riding cowboys and stalking warriors bearing mute witness to an extinct world, rested on glass shelves covered in splotches of red moss. The sparkle of broken glass glinted across the floor.

"Thor, sit," Emily commanded before the malamute could wander in and risk getting a paw sliced open. The whole building smelled of rot . . . and something else, something that smelled halfway between bad eggs and vomit.

"What *is* that?" asked Rhiannon, wrinkling her nose at the stink and switching on her flashlight to illuminate the heavily shadowed room ahead of them. In the far corner, beneath a glassless window, something had made a home from the desiccated shoes; it looked like a grossly oversized wasp's nest, about four feet tall and two wide, narrowing to a funnel at the top. A large opening halfway up the body of the nest was a pool of darkness.

"It looks like a—"

A pair of oval, luminescent green eyes flickered open in the entrance of the nest.

"Oh . . . shit!" Emily whispered, instinctively placing a protective arm across Rhiannon's chest.

A second set of eyes opened above the first. Then a third below.

Thor growled quietly and took a step backward.

Emily felt an odd sensation flicker over her; just for a second, she had the sense that she was looking at herself, Rhiannon, and Thor from the corner. It lasted for just a moment, like a subliminal frame in a movie, barely perceivable on a conscious level unless you were looking for it. But in that brief flash she saw herself staring at the corner, her hand still across Rhiannon's chest, Thor backing away. She sensed a mixture of fear and inquisitiveness at what she was . . . and, was that shock? Yes. There was an afterimage, an emotional imprint, if you like, of surprise.

"Just back up slowly," she whispered when she had recovered from her own shock. "Thor!" she hissed as the dog took another step forward.

The three companions edged back a few more steps, Emily's hand on the butt of her .45, before she turned and ushered Rhiannon back toward the room where they had spent the night.

"We slept here with . . . with whatever those *things* were right next door to us?" Rhiannon said, more a statement of doubt than a question.

"Come on," Emily said, grabbing the girl's backpack from the floor and handing it to her before shrugging her own over her shoulders. "Let's get the hell out of here."

■ ■ ■

A halfhearted drizzle had begun to fall by the time Emily and Rhiannon stepped outside.

"Oh great," said Rhiannon, pulling her hood up, the sky a forewarning of the desultory mood she was sure would mark the rest of the day.

"We need to make locating a working vehicle our top priority," Emily said, pulling the hood of her own jacket up, trying to give both her and Rhiannon a positive task to focus on. "If we have to walk we're either going to starve to death or die of exposure. We sure as hell don't need a repeat of last night." Of course, finding a vehicle out here was so much easier said than done.

A malaise as gray as the sky settled over the travelers and for the next few hours they followed the I-40 east in silence, the only sound the faint squelching of the soles of their shoes and the rustle of their waterproof jackets. Emily felt colder than she had in years; the balmy California weather had spoiled her, apparently. She pulled the hood of her jacket deeper over her head and turned to check on Rhiannon.

"You okay?"

"Cold and tired," Rhiannon said, trying her best to force a smile despite the constant gray that seemed to hang in the air around them. Even Thor's usual boundless enthusiasm and energy seemed to have been sucked dry by the dull dreariness of the weather.

"Well, at least it's not snowing."

"Yet," the girl replied without a hint of irony.

They plodded on.

"Cell phones," Rhiannon said about a kilometer later.

"What?"

"I really, really miss my cell phone."

Emily smiled. Of course, she was playing the what-I-miss game.

"I used to text my friends all the time," Rhiannon continued. "I had a lot of friends, and Dad was always telling me to turn my phone off, but I didn't." Rhiannon laughed like the little girl she had been, an innocent giggle of joy at the memory of her family. "At dinner I used to sneak it under the table, and I didn't even need to see the keyboard, I was that good at texting. Until Ben told Dad about it, because he always wanted to use my phone, and Dad said he wasn't old enough to have one yet . . . I wish I had let him, now," she said, her head dipping toward the road, shoulders slumping. "I miss them *so* much."

The pain in the girl's voice stabbed Emily straight through the heart. She had managed to store the memory of what she had done—what she had *had* to do—to Ben, Rhiannon's little brother, deep in the darkest corner of her mind, but sometimes the horror of it all, of what she was capable of doing, would surface, percolating up through the cracks of its prison like a poisonous gas, suffocating her mind and soul. This was her penance, her responsibility to Rhiannon and the grief of knowing that she could never share it with her, could never make her understand the horror she felt at having to lie to the girl for the rest of her life. It was *her* cross to carry.

"I know, sweetheart. I know." Emily reached a reassuring arm around Rhiannon's shoulders.

What a picture they must make, Emily thought: a pair of the last remaining humans standing on a road in the middle of a rain-soaked alien plain. Ludicrous, absolutely ludicrous. But the love she felt for the girl she held in her arms was overwhelming. *In spite of it all, everything I've done, everything I've seen, I am still human. I am still capable of love,* she told herself.

The desire to survive was almost the most astonishing to her. And what was even more surprising was that that desire to survive did not exist on just a personal level. If she spent the time to really think about it, the driving desire behind her emotion was not for her own survival, not even to ensure the safety of her immediate family and friends, but a need to ensure that the human race kept going. It was astounding, really, to think about how deep the connection she felt toward her fellow humans was, despite what Valentine and those like her had done. Only recently, standing on the brink of extinction, did Emily realize that she *loved* being human. Only after her son had vanished, taken by an invisible hand, did she understand what humanity truly meant to her. Only now that everything that had defined her before the rain was gone forever did she understand the connection, the honor she and every other man and woman had been handed by nature, the responsibility that had been given to them. Only now that it was all gone, did she understand what it truly meant to be human.

"It's all going to be okay," she told Rhiannon as rain dripped off the bridge of her nose. And strangely, she believed her words to be true.

■ ■ ■

The four lanes of the freeway—two heading east and two west—stretched out ahead of the companions for about two hundred meters before the rain, low clouds, and mist swallowed it. They had decided to walk along the eastbound lanes, near the center median. "If we hit any trouble, we can at least get the guardrails between us and it," Emily said. She did not need to elaborate on what the "it" might be. Both women knew the world held unknown terrors.

Since leaving the shelter earlier that morning, the only other building they had seen was the skeleton of a burned-out gas station, its blackened remains sticking out of the ground like a picked-clean carcass.

They had walked for kilometer after kilometer, and more than once, her feet aching from the constant step after step, Emily had wished for the trusty bicycle she had started her journey with.

For the last hour or so Emily had felt the incline of the road rising slightly in the back of her calf muscles. The drizzle had gradually grown heavier and now fell in a constant sheet of light, almost misty rain, nothing like the downpour they had experienced last night, thank God, but still dishearteningly uncomfortable enough to dampen the companions' spirits, all while limiting their visibility to under thirty meters.

Up until the world ended, the I-40 had been a major artery of the US supply chain, filled with trucks moving goods from east to west and back again. You could travel from California on the

West Coast to North Carolina and never leave it. Tens of thousands of vehicles a day passed along the freeway, the third longest in the United States. And that fact was what made it seem so strangely deserted. Of the few vehicles they had seen, most had been mere rust-covered carcasses, fossils of another time. And there had been so few of them, at least along the stretch of clear road that they had been travelling.

Maybe that was why the road was so clear, Emily thought, putting one foot in front of the other. Perhaps the majority of vehicles had made it to a city or to their homes, took one of the numerous spurs off to who knew where. Maybe.

"Can I ask you a question?" Rhiannon said a little while later.

"Shoot!"

"Why didn't the Caretakers just come and explain things to us? You know, rather than just destroy everything."

The question caught Emily off guard. Rhiannon had been quiet, contemplative even, for most of the journey since leaving their sanctuary that morning. Their conversations had been limited to whether she wanted to stop for water or a bathroom break. Emily was sure the kid was wading through the murk of what had happened over the past few days, but she was a different girl than the one she had found living with her brother and father so many years ago now. She was tougher, harder. If Rhiannon wanted help wrestling with the demons Emily was under no illusion the girl had, she would ask Emily for her help when she was good and ready.

"That's a good question," Emily said, buying herself some time to think about it.

The Caretakers. Emily had often thought about her experience with the aliens that had wrecked the world, trying to reason out just what their motivations were. They had told her that they were constructs of an even older race, tasked with ensuring that life, rare though it might be, thrived wherever they found it. When they did find it, they were the judge, jury, and executioner of any species that did not meet their level of worthiness. Humans, the Caretaker that had taken on the role of Jacob had explained to her, had all but guaranteed that life on Earth was close to being annihilated. They had stepped in and ensured, in the most brutal manner imaginable, that the planet would get a second chance.

"I guess they thought that if we were too dumb to not be able to see what was right in front of our eyes, then we probably weren't going to take their word for it either?" she said finally.

Rhiannon cocked her head inquisitively. "What do you mean?"

"We had years, decades and decades, to see what we were doing to the planet," Emily said, almost absentmindedly, "and I think that we had the chance to think, *really* think, about every barrel of oil we used, every doctor who overprescribed an antibiotic, every species we drove into extinction so we could make a profit, and every weak-kneed politician in the pocket of some big business more than happy to tell us what we wanted to hear rather than what we needed to hear, but we didn't. If we had *really* thought about it, we would have realized that all we were doing was driving another nail into our collective coffin. I think that if it had just been us humans that were threatened with extinction, then maybe the Caretakers would have just moved right along, but it wasn't, was it? We had become a threat to the entirety of life on this planet." Emily paused for a moment, her mind the clearest it had ever been. "So we did this to ourselves; well, *you* didn't, but my generation and everyone who came before us. We could have done . . . something to change it . . . something to make a difference. If we'd just had a couple more generations . . ."

Emily was astonished at the vehemence she heard in her own voice; a vein of bitterness ran through her that she had been totally unaware of, a begrudging acceptance of the logic that had been presented to her as *reason* by the Caretakers, and she was mad at them and the rest of humanity because they were right, Goddamn them, they were *right* in their justification. But that had not given the Caretakers the right to do what they did, not by a long shot. It had been the humans' problem to solve, and Emily was sure, deep down, that they could have succeeded. She had had faith in humanity; she just had not seen it back when she could have done something about it.

Rhiannon thought about what Emily had said for thirty paces. "But doesn't it seem, I don't know, like, really, really wasteful? I mean, why would the Caretakers want to change *all* life?"

"It never made any sense to me," said Emily, "but then they're not people. On my best day I had problems understanding the human race, so I'm not sure that I'd have much of a chance trying to comprehend the thought process of an alien race."

It was another full minute before Rhiannon spoke again. "You said they told you they've been doing this for, like, forever, right? So that means there are more aliens out there. More species like us, or kinda like us. If this was a movie, we'd all get together and kick their asses."

"If this was a movie," said Emily, with a smile, "we would have won already."

Rhiannon laughed too. Not a bitter laugh but an honest chuckle at the thought.

"But what they're saying, though, is that sometimes it's okay to take life if it means more life will be saved, right?"

Emily suddenly realized what the discussion was really about.

Rhiannon was rationalizing her own trauma. She was trying to grasp any meaning that might provide a life preserver for her innocence, to justify what she had had to do to the guard to get Emily out of that cell. And who was she to deny that rationale to her?

"Yes," said Emily, smiling at her companion, "I think that's exactly what they meant."

■ ■ ■

"What is that?" Rhiannon said, stopping suddenly and pointing off to the right side of the road.

The travelers were approaching a low concrete bridge over a wide but shallow arroyo that ran perpendicular to the freeway. The rain had not stopped its constant dreary drizzle, and a steady stream of brown water, just a few inches deep, Emily estimated, ran through the wash beneath the bridge, broken apart by four-meter-high concrete piers that acted as both support and breakwater. The space between the piers was clogged with debris and mud, leaving only a half meter or so gap at the top. The runoff had created a pool that was a meter or so deep already.

Emily stopped, shrugging her backpack into a more comfortable position while she tried to see what Rhiannon was pointing at through the strained light. She followed the stream from the bridge uphill toward the south. A few kilometers away, she saw the outline of a mountain; the range's upper half was gradually being devoured by black-and-gray clouds, and the occasional flash of lightning showed it was in the grip of yet another powerful storm.

"It's pretty far away," Emily said after a few seconds.

The storm was centered directly over the range. The slope of the mountains looked like it was taking a hammering, barely visible behind diaphanous sheets of rain. There wasn't much of a breeze, and the clouds looked to barely be moving—plus, the storm was far enough away that Emily was confident it wouldn't be heading in their direction anytime soon. A distant peal of thunder, barely audible, finally reached Emily's ears.

"I don't think it's anything we need to worry about," she concluded.

"No," said Rhiannon, "not the storm . . . that!" She jerked her hand again in the direction of the base of the mountain, and this time Emily saw what she was pointing at: a brown wave twenty, maybe thirty, meters across was sweeping down the scar of the arroyo from the base of the mountains. The water had already overflowed the narrow walls of the gully and was flooding outward. A few scattered smaller trees lay in its path, and, as Emily watched, the wave reached the first of them and it disappeared.

"What the . . . ah crap. We need to move . . . now!"

"What *is* it?" Rhiannon insisted.

"Flash flood," Emily said. It was heading down the arroyo toward them. And it was moving fast. "It's only going to take a couple of minutes for it to get here."

It was easily two hundred meters to the other side of the bridge, she judged.

"Come on," Emily said, nudging Rhiannon's elbow into motion. "We need to get across the bridge as fast as we can." She jogged out onto the bridge, stealing glances at the oncoming wall of water every couple of seconds.

They had made it as far as the midpoint when the leading wave rounded a bend in the arroyo about a quarter of a kilometer upstream. The wave barreled into the corner, splashing ten meters up into the air, raining down mud, water, and pieces of debris, before the main body of the flood caught up and began surging toward them.

"Keep your eyes on the ground," Emily yelled to Rhiannon, who kept slowing to look at the approaching water. Emily also slowed for a second to try and gauge the speed of the wall of water rushing at them. The corner had sucked away some of its power, but the river of ugly brown water continued to thunder their way. At that second, she saw another wave of muddy water thunder up over the bend and obliterate what was left of the corner, smashing away huge chunks of mud, sending them spinning into the air like meteors, and cutting a new channel directly through to the last section of the gully leading to the bridge.

Emily finally understood just how much danger they were in: that water was going to hit the bridge and have nowhere to go but up and over.

"Run! Run, faster!" Emily yelled as she took off after Rhiannon and Thor. The water was speeding toward them now, its thunderous roar filling the air, the surge powerful enough that it would sweep right over the bridge and take them with it, she was sure.

Rhiannon picked up her pace, sprinting at full speed for the opposite side of the bridge, easily outrunning Emily's older, tired legs and heavier backpack. Emily saw the girl's head flick to the right, and even over the growing din of the oncoming water she heard the girl yell out in fear, before she turned back, found an extra well of speed, and started to pull away from Emily even faster.

Thor had taken up a position in the space separating the two women, and Emily could tell he was holding back to stay close to her.

"Go, Thor, go to Rhiannon," she yelled, but her voice was drowned out by the thundering approach of the flood. From the corner of her eye, Emily saw the swell of water barreling toward the bridge, clumps of mud and foam bubbling in the frothing wave. She focused on Rhiannon's back, willing her onward as she forced her own feet to just keep moving, hoping that she did not trip.

Rhiannon had pulled ahead by a good ten meters when the wall of water finally reached them, smacking into the debris-clogged runoff below their feet. A five-meter-tall wave of mountain-cold water exploded over the side of the bridge with a hiss like sizzling bacon and rained down onto the road. Emily gasped as the dirty freezing water hit her, blinding her momentarily before she wiped it from her eyes. Within seconds, coffee-colored water tipped with white foam gushed between the gaps of the safety barrier running along the side of the bridge, spreading out over the road as though someone had turned on a thousand fire hoses at once.

Ahead of her she saw Rhiannon through a haze of water, her feet already splashing through several centimeters of water. But she was okay; there were only a few meters between the girl and the safety of the opposite side of the bridge.

The main body of water was still below the top of the bridge, Emily could hear it thundering against the concrete siding, hissing and spitting. The debris caught between the stanchions was acting as a dam, and the water, with no way to escape, was being forced up and over the edge of the bridge. All along the safety barrier was what looked like a stationary wave of raging, bubbling mud. The overflowing water was spreading tens of thousands of gallons out over the bridge every second. The road was completely awash, water already reaching to Emily's ankles.

Thor stopped, standing several meters away from Rhiannon, the water up to his knees, looking back toward Emily. His tail wagged slowly; he wasn't sure if this was a game or not. Emily began to yell at the dog to move, but her words were drowned out by an even louder roar. She thought she caught the sound of Rhiannon screaming *"Look out!"* and glanced to the right in time to see a boulder of clay as big as a VW Beetle pushed along by a second surge of raging water crash into the side of the bridge ahead of her. The boulder exploded on impact, smashing part of the bridge away with it and sending smaller pieces of concrete and metal and mud through the air to splash all around her like shrapnel. Now the right lane of the bridge looked as though a giant had taken a bite out of it. This new entrance and the force of the extra water was all that was needed for the flood to fully breach the top of the bridge, sending a wave of powerful sludge across the road. It bubbled up through the new hole like a geyser and reached Emily, hitting her just below the knees. She almost buckled but managed to steady herself as it washed against her. Before it had been like walking through a stream, but now Emily was wading across a fast-flowing river.

Thor! Where is Thor? Emily's head pivoted left, then right. The malamute had been following behind Rhiannon until the wave hit, but he had vanished, carried away by the force of the flood. She scanned the frothing lake that had been a bridge just a minute earlier, looking for her dog.

There! There he is. Emily could see his body pinned against the beam of the metal guardrail separating the central median of the east- and westbound lanes. The guardrail was acting in much the same way as the debris below the bridge had, slowing the spread of the water and creating a wall of angry bubbling water. Thor was caught by it, and Emily could see his body buffeted and pummeled as he tried to keep his head above the rushing water, his paws frantically trying to find purchase where there was none.

Emily started to move in his direction just as another surge of water pushed over the edge of the bridge, hitting her calves. She stumbled and fell to one knee, a hand dropping into the frighteningly cold mountain water. The wave covered the distance between her and Thor in a second, and she watched in horror as the malamute disappeared beneath the muddy water.

No, no, no!

Emily pushed herself up onto unsteady feet, fighting the pull and push of the sucking water, and started toward where she had last seen Thor. She wasn't going to make it to him in time. She could see him bobbing up and then back under the water. A dirty-looking gray scum of froth collecting on the surface made it even harder to spot him.

Rhiannon had made it to the opposite side and was standing on dry land, bent at the waist, panting from the exertion as the water rushed by her toes.

"Rhiannon!" Emily yelled as loud as she could, not sure she would be heard over the cacophonous roar of the river as she continued to try to cover the distance between her and Thor.

The girl looked up, her face contorted with fear and exhaustion.

Emily stabbed her left hand to where Thor had disappeared under another wave, just as his head broke the surface again.

Rhiannon turned in the direction Emily pointed. The second her eyes found Thor and she realized what was happening, Rhiannon sprinted toward him along the edge of the river. When she was parallel to his position she splashed back into the water, using the guardrail as a support, hurdling with exaggerated steps through the twelve meters of water that separated her and the struggling malamute.

The water was just below Emily's butt now as she zagged toward Rhiannon and the malamute, but the weight of her pack and her fight against the constant pressure of the water had sucked the strength right out of her.

Rhiannon reached Thor and grabbed his collar just as he was dragged under again. She pulled the dog to the surface and started edging her way back toward dry land, one hand grabbing at the submerged guardrail, the other towing Thor behind her like a dinghy. Seconds later they were both back on dry land and Thor was shaking himself dry while smothering Rhiannon with licks, before he sat then lay down on all fours, obviously exhausted. Rhiannon, her face pale with exhaustion, was starting to head back into the water as she saw Emily struggling toward her.

Emily waved her off. Rhiannon's energy was obviously close to empty; all it would take would be another surge of flood water to hit them and they would both end up being swept away.

The water was now more like a thick soup, a brown sludge of mud and debris that sucked at her feet, slowing her to a crawl. There was less than ten meters between her and safety, but it might just as well have been a kilometer.

This is finally it, she thought with a pang of sadness as the water beat at her stomach and her exhausted muscles. *I'm not going to make it.*

In her mind Emily saw Mac standing at the edge of the torrent next to Rhiannon and Thor. Rhiannon was holding on to Thor's collar to stop the dog from racing back into the water, the girl's face a mask of fear and confusion. Mac was yelling at her, telling her to *Move your bloody arse.* She managed another step, the water so thick with New Mexico clay it was more a river of slowly setting concrete now, but she was exhausted. Her legs were lead, lead surrounded by a pool of liquid lead that wanted to keep her for itself, the weight of her backpack pushing her down. *Dump the Goddamn backpack,* she heard Mac yell silently at her, then more quietly, *Just drop it, love. It'll be okay.*

She reached down and struggled to find the belt clip fastener at her waist, found it, squeezed with fingers that did not want to obey her, and felt the clip disengage. In the same instant she shrugged the pack from her shoulders and caught a fleeting glimpse of it as it was sucked away from her, disappearing into the roiling, frothing waves of scummy water. Free of its extra weight, Emily forced herself toward dry land.

"Come on," Rhiannon yelled urgently.

One more step, that's my girl, said imaginary Mac, standing behind Rhiannon, smiling. *You can make it.*

With just a few meters left, Rhiannon ignored Emily's weak protestation to stay back and rushed out into the water. She grabbed an exhausted Emily around the waist, and the two staggered the final distance to the flood's edge, where they both collapsed onto the road with barely enough energy left to even breathe.

CHAPTER 9

Emily lay facedown on the side of the road. Like a fish pulled from the turbulent flood water raging just meters away, she gasped silently for breath, occasionally coughing and spitting up muddy water.

She could see Rhiannon's boots a few centimeters away from her head, a cake of mud around the soles, the sodden bottoms of her jeans a darker blue than the rest. Then Rhiannon's butt as the girl flopped down on the wet tarmac, pulled her knees up to her chest, and leaned her head against them, panting deeply, more from the stress of what had just happened than the actual exertion, Emily thought. Even the normally ebullient Thor was stretched out on all fours, his tongue half out of his mouth, panting so heavily his chest about lifted him off the ground. His normally pristine coat was matted with streaks of dirt and clumps of mud, the rest of his fur sodden.

"Oh my God!" Rhiannon said when she was finally able to speak. "When the fuck will this planet stop trying to kill us?"

Under any other circumstances, Emily would have chided the girl for the profanity, but at this moment, she was right there with her. It was so much fucking trouble just to keep going, just to keep trying.

The rush of water from the mountains was now a horrendous roar, louder than anything Emily had heard before, terrifying in its raw nature. A sudden crack, like the sharp report of a rifle, drew her curiosity enough that she managed to roll over onto her back and sit up. The sound was followed by the snap of a small explosion, then another as the air was rent by an ungodly shrieking that ended just as suddenly with a *pop* like a giant balloon bursting, as the bridge they had just made it across began to break apart. The water ate through the deck of the bridge like it was made of papier-mâché, chunks of it dropping away, disappearing from her view as they were consumed by the river. On the plus side, the new opening relieved the pressure and allowed the corralled water to burst through and rumble on down the arroyo and out into the desert beyond.

Somewhere out there, floating away on the tidal wave, was her backpack, along with all her supplies and clothes—everything she had. Gone.

As if it had flown in from above or maybe been swept down from the mountains with the flood, a sudden and intense despair grasped Emily in its talons and refused to let go, overwhelming even the molecular call of her son with a hopelessness that slipped over her like a second skin. It tore at her inner resolve, shredding it almost instantly.

Oh, let me list the ways that my life is oh, so fucked up, she mused, her eyes staring up at the ugly gray sky.

Let's see: I've lost my son; my husband is thousands of kilometers away and probably won't be coming back alive; the place that I called home is slowly and systematically being dissolved by a woman almost as evil as the fucking aliens who had annihilated the planet, a woman who plotted to have me murdered. Oh yeah, and let's not forget the fucker who tried to rape me before carrying out Valentine's request. Can't miss the guard I killed either. And who could overlook the freezing weather and a planet that turned from being home to a world that could easily have passed for one of Dante's levels of hell?

Shit! That's what it had all turned to . . . shit!

"I can't do this anymore," Emily said matter-of-factly, the words slipping from her mouth so easily and feeling *so* good on her lips, like she was finally dislodging something that had been caught in her throat. It was *such* a relief.

"What?" said Rhiannon.

Another chunk of the bridge fell away with a rumble and a splash. A bit like her own life, really; chunks of it had methodically been eaten away by fate and the zombie corpse of what had once called itself humanity, until there was so little of it left it was hardly worth fighting for anymore.

"I said, I can't do this anymore. I'm done. It's over. I give up." *I'm just going to sit here,* she decided, *sit here and wait for everything to just stop and go away.* It wouldn't take long—she was already freezing from the waist down.

Rhiannon reacted as if Emily had slapped her across the face.

"But . . . but you can't, you have to get up. You can't just stop."

Oh yeah? Emily thought. *You just watch me.*

Rhiannon stood and waited for Emily to get up. When she didn't, Rhiannon bent over and grabbed her right arm with both hands and began pulling. "Get up," she demanded. "Get up now," she yelled when Emily resisted. Now she was tugging at Emily's arm, tears of anger and frustration percolating in her eyes.

"Would you just leave me alone, for fuck's sake? Just leave me alone." Emily wrenched her arm free of Rhiannon's grip.

Thor whined and crawled toward her.

"No," said Rhiannon. "You have to get up. Now!"

"I don't want to."

A tone of desperation had begun to creep into Rhiannon's voice. "What about me and Thor? What are we supposed to do now? Where are we supposed to go?"

Emily stared at her feet; her head was thumping, her legs felt like two icicles. God, she was miserable. Rhiannon did not seem to care how she felt, she just kept talking.

"You're all we have. You and Mac, you . . . you're my Mom and Dad. And Adam . . . what about Adam? Who's going to help Adam?"

Emily thought about that for a few slow heartbeats. If it hadn't have been for the constant tingling over her skin, she might have dismissed even Adam as being dead, and the journey they were on as pointless, but she couldn't. That connection she felt, that pull, acted as a lifeline, something that she had to hold on to, a life preserver that would not allow the terrible despair she felt to carry her any farther away toward the abyss that threatened to swallow her. But she was *so, so* tired. All she wanted was some peace.

"You can't just think about yourself," Rhiannon was saying, unaware of the struggle consuming Emily, "you have to get up and you have to fight for us. Like we would for you."

The kid was right, Emily knew it, and she was trying to care, but it was so hard. Maybe if she could just hang on to that feeling of connectedness, focus on it and allow it to fill her. She felt the sensation grow, like a tiny light in a dark room beginning to brighten and fill the dark space—slowly, gradually, but unstoppably. Emily held on to the thread of her love for her boy, for her husband, her surrogate daughter, and the dog who had saved her, and by default saved all of them. And like the room, she gradually filled her own darkness with light again.

"And who's going to stop Valentine?" Rhiannon was asking, "If you don't get up right now, then she's going to win. Valentine and that guard who wanted to . . . who was going to . . ." She could not get the words out. "The one that I *killed* for *you*. They'll both win, and then we lose. The good guys will lose, Emily."

Emily opened her eyes. The sky was still the same dull, dead, leaden gray, but she thought she could see a few patches of blue just above them, a hint that this momentary darkness was not an omen for the future of their world, but that there *was* hope.

"Okay," said Emily.

Rhiannon stopped midsentence. "Okay, what?"

"You're right. Here, help me up." She extended a hand, and Rhiannon helped her to her feet, then threw her arms around Emily and hugged her so hard Emily thought she was going to break something within her aching, fragile body.

"I thought you were going to leave me," Rhiannon mumbled into the material of Emily's jacket.

Emily held the girl for three heartbeats, then gently pushed her out to arms' length.

"Like I said already, I'm never going to leave you."

Rhiannon lunged forward again and held Emily tight.

■ ■ ■

The bleak mood, so intent on swallowing Emily, was gradually evaporating, replaced by an optimism that lasted until they took an inventory of what was left of their supplies. All Emily had was the soaked clothes she was wearing, her .45, a single magazine of ten rounds—the spare magazine and all her ammo were in the backpack—and the knife on her ankle. She found a couple of energy bars in a zipper pocket of her jacket sleeve, and a half-full canteen of water on her belt. Emily had taken back the blanket she had given Rhiannon and tied it around her waist like a sarong to ease the chill until her jeans dried out.

Rhiannon had her own clothes, none of which would fit Emily, enough MREs to last them all another day—two, if they stretched it out—a handful of energy bars, a flashlight, a full canteen of water, and her pistol. And that was it.

EXTINCTION POINT: GENESIS

"Well, that's better than losing all our supplies," said Rhiannon, trying to sound optimistic.

Emily tried to smile. She still had no idea how far away Adam was, which meant she also had no idea whether the supplies they had would be enough to get them to him. And even if they found him before their supplies ran out, they would still need to restock and figure out how they were going to get back to Point Loma, or if they even could.

"We have to find food," Emily said, "and that's going to be much easier if we can find a vehicle."

"Fat chance," said Rhiannon as she looked up and down the freeway. They couldn't go back the way they had come from; the bridge was no longer there, and there was nothing back there anyway. Ahead of them the road reached toward a set of hills, about fifteen kilometers in the distance, stark against the gray-white clouds that obscured the sky.

"Well, look at it this way," said Emily. "We know there's nothing back the way we came, so if we weigh the odds, seems to me the probability is that we'll find some kind of town or city ahead of us, right?"

"I suppose so," said Rhiannon, pausing, "maybe." She did not sound convinced.

"Well, if we can find a town or even a store, then maybe we'll find food there."

"But what if we don't?"

"We will," said Emily. "I know we will."

■ ■ ■

"Can you hear that?" Rhiannon asked, surprising Emily. They were a couple of hours farther on from the bridge. The conversation had petered off and for the last hour or so they had walked in companionable silence toward the slowly approaching hills.

Emily stopped and cocked her head to listen. "I can't hear a thing," she said after several beats had passed. "Are you sure it's not the wind?"

"It's like some high-pitched squeak," Rhiannon said. "I've heard it for the last ten minutes or so. It gets louder and then fades away."

Emily listened again, then shook her head. Rhiannon was a good seventeen years younger, so it didn't come as a surprise that the girl would pick up on a sound faster than she could. Emily raised her hand to shade her eyes against the diffused light pushing through the overcast cloud. Ahead of them, the road cut between the range of hills that effectively blocked the eastern horizon, but to their left, right, and behind was the ubiquitous flat plain of red that had become synonymous with their travels over this terrain.

"Well, we can't stop just because of some random sound, and I really don't hear it, so let's keep going, but keep your eyes open." Emily's hand instinctively dropped to caress the butt of her pistol. She was still kicking herself for not grabbing her trusty shotgun. She'd left it in the cupboard back at the apartment in Point Loma and in the confusion of their escape had simply forgotten about it.

They set off again, both Rhiannon and Emily walking just that little bit closer to one another as their eyes played over the red flora, watching for any threat it might hold. Thor seemed completely oblivious to whatever sound Rhiannon was hearing; he trotted along quite happily next to them. Emily placed a lot of trust in his far more acutely tuned senses, but, still, it would be foolish to only rely on the malamute for any kind of early warning of an approaching threat.

Almost ten minutes later, the twin humps of the hills now only a kilometer or so away, Emily stopped suddenly.

"Okay, I hear it now too," she said.

A *See, I told you* look was Rhiannon's answer.

It was a rasping, dry screech that rose in pitch and volume, then slowed and died away again. Emily listened for a good thirty seconds without speaking, but she could not isolate a pattern; it seemed completely random. It was almost like listening to something in pain, but she was sure there was a definite metallic sound to it; it didn't sound the least bit organic. Again the screech resonated through the hills, fading in and out as if carried on the gusts of the wind that kicked up the debris of the I-40 at their feet.

They continued to trace the road upward, the sound bouncing off the hills on either side of them, filling the air, sometimes a slow drawn-out screech, sometimes a short raspy moan. It was the silence in between that was the most nerve stretching. Drawing the .45 from its holster, Emily found the weight of it in her hand less reassuring than she had hoped, but there was no way she was going to be caught off guard.

The wind picked up again and brought with it a prolonged ululation that lasted for well over a minute. If whales were made of metal, Emily thought, *this* would be the song they made. It was so eerie, she half expected to see a line of ghosts rising from the ground and marching down the hill toward them.

"Come on, let's keep going," she said to Rhiannon, who seemed more annoyed than scared. The sound grew louder the closer they got to the summit where the road cleaved the two hills.

"Jeez!" said Rhiannon as they reached the top of the incline and looked out over the stretch of land ahead of them, the source of the eerie, otherworldly sound now obvious.

Emily simply stared, an echo of the melancholy she had felt earlier returning.

Strung out in lines along the northern skyline like sentinels watching over the landscape stood row after row of wind turbines reaching back into the distance, each one probably a hundred meters tall. Emily thought she remembered the ones she had seen in photographs being white, but that, of course, would have been before the red rain. These were varying shades of red and black. Some were motionless, their rotors locked in place, others were nothing but reeds missing their blades, while still others' rotors were bent and misshapen. But the majority still worked, in a fashion, at least, pushed by the constant breeze of the plain, singing a song of misery, a lamentation for a purpose now lost. Their rotors and bearings shot after two years of no maintenance, the turbines squealed and groaned like lost souls haunting the landscape, a sad aural testament to humanity lost. And for a moment Emily again wondered whether it was all worth it: the constant fight for survival, the need to try, to fight for some kind of a future for the remnants of the human race. Perhaps the paltry few humans left on the planet were like these turbines, outliving their usefulness, purposely striving to continue to be relevant in a world where their time was up and they should just lie down and die.

"That's actually pretty cool," said Rhiannon, staring at the distant turbines, genuinely smiling for the first time in a very long time.

Emily turned to look at her companion, momentarily taken aback by how differently Rhiannon saw the same scene. She turned back and looked again at the rows of distant mechanical monsters. *Maybe* they weren't the tombstones of a dead civilization. *Maybe* they were monuments to what could still be achieved, with a little perseverance.

"Yeah, you know what? It really is pretty damn cool," said Emily with a nod.

And they continued on their way.

CHAPTER 10

Rhiannon was the one who spotted the car.

About fifteen meters off the road, its roof was just visible above the tall red grass and, surprisingly, from where they stood, it looked like it might be relatively well preserved.

"Let's take a look," said Emily. They cut off the road and began to make their way toward the car, pushing the grass aside like they were Lewis and Clark. The vegetation seemed to have sprouted up over the last few days, almost doubling in height. *Maybe because of the rain*, Emily hypothesized as she tried to keep the vehicle in sight while not stumbling over the tangle of roots and new shoots sprouting up from the muddy ground. The growth was so thick it was hard to actually see more than an arm's length ahead.

"There it is," said Rhiannon, pointing at a patch of silver shining through the grass, just a couple of meters ahead of them.

It was a minivan; one of those vehicles they used to call "people movers" back in the nineties. The grass had grown up around it, and there were obvious signs that it had been here for quite some time. The tires had all but rotted away to little more than shreds, spots of orange rust over its silver paintwork gave it a leopardlike camouflage, and red lichen spores had spread over parts of the windows. Other than that, it looked to be in pretty good shape.

"The doors are all closed," said Rhiannon as they approached, then stopped and pointed at the perfectly round hole drilled in the windshield. There had been at least one occupant inside, apparently. Red strands had grown up and over the hood and found the spider hole. They had wormed their way inside and inched down over the dashboard, winding their way around the steering column.

"I'll check the inside," said Emily, "you keep an eye open."

Emily stepped up to the driver's side window and wiped away some of the lichen, leaned in close, and scanned the inside. Keys were still in the ignition, and the crumbling paper-thin remains of an alien pupae lay across the driver's seat and center console. A bottle of water sat in the holder of the driver's side door. Emily gave a little gasp when she saw the two kiddie seats in the backseat, the safety straps still in place, a pink pacifier on the seat of one, a blue blanket on the other.

A tug of the door handle proved it was locked, so Emily made her way to the back passenger door, but that was locked too. Wiping away more crap from the back window allowed her to see into the rear storage space and spot the two leather suitcases there.

"Bingo!" Emily said, allowing herself a smile. Maybe she'd have better luck with the rear—

Thor stopped midstep, his muzzle raised, sniffing the air around them, his head moving from left to right as if he were unsure that what he sensed was really there. If a dog could ever be described as looking suspicious, Emily thought, this would be what it would look like.

"Rhiannon," Emily called out as quietly as she could.

Rhiannon turned and looked at Emily, her face asking: *What?*

Emily nodded at Thor. She didn't even have to ask Rhiannon to come back. The girl was at her side in three steps, her hand on her pistol, eyes moving left and right, scanning the tall grass for any sign of movement.

Nothing seemed out of the ordinary to Emily. Drizzle still fell silently from the ubiquitous gray clouds, the red grass hushed and shushed as their reeds rubbed together, swaying back and forth in a breeze that never seemed to go away, rippling over the plants' surface as though it were a lake.

Thor turned and followed the scent for a pace or two around the flank of the minivan, then stopped again, staring into the wall of red. He let out a deep-throated growl, his head dipping low between his front shoulder blades.

Emily and Rhiannon simultaneously drew their weapons.

"See anything at all?" Emily whispered as she edged nearer to Thor.

Rhiannon shook her head.

Thor was frozen to the spot, his muscles tensed, ready to spring, his snarl constant now, like the low growl of an idling engine.

"Thor, get over here," Emily ordered, then to Rhiannon, "We need to get back to the freeway."

Rhiannon began to push her way through the grass back in the direction of the road.

"Thor! Get your ass over here now." This time Thor complied, backing up until he was close to Emily before turning toward her.

Emily had taken her first step after Rhiannon when she spotted movement in the field. It reminded her of the wake of a shark moving through water, the tops of the vegetation shifting aside in a *V* shape as something moved toward them.

Rhill-tik-tik-tik-tikkkkkk!

The sound momentarily froze Emily in her tracks. It had come from her left. She turned in time to see another wake moving through the grass, this one headed toward Rhiannon.

Rhill-tik-tik-tik-tikkkkkk!

Whatever these things were, they were coordinating their attack, and they had the upper hand. They had to get out of the long grass and back into the open to have a fighting chance.

"Run!" Emily yelled and began to sprint as quickly as she could back toward the freeway.

The call came again: *rhill-tik-tik-tik-tikkkkkk!* This time it was in stereo as both creatures called out at the same time.

An image of another time loomed up in Emily's mind: a forest, creatures intent on killing their prey. No way was she going to make the same mistakes this time. She sprinted as fast as her legs could carry her, more of a lope than a run, bouncing from one foot to another over the tangles of roots and sprouts of grass, like she was eight years old, and they were cracks in the pavement that went straight to Hell.

Rhiannon was ahead of her, using both hands to push the grass aside as she brute-forced her way to the road.

The second wake was angling toward Rhiannon, and Emily knew there was no way she was going to make it to the road in time. Halting, she leveled her pistol just ahead of the disturbance and pulled the trigger twice in quick succession. Two things happened next: Rhiannon reflexively screamed and ducked, stumbled, then fell to her knees. Whatever the creature in the grass was, it hesitated momentarily, then leaped, a black shadow cutting through the space above Rhiannon. Emily aimed her pistol again, expecting the creature to take its advantage and head back toward the prostrate girl, but instead it whirled around to Emily's right and met with the second creature, the two wakes merging into one.

Emily caught up with Rhiannon just as she made it to her feet. She grabbed the girl by the backpack and pulled her upright, pushing her ahead as she tried to keep her eyes on the creatures and not stumble herself.

Rhill-tik-tik-tik-tikkkkkk!

The creatures were headed toward them again, this time at breakneck speed, the red grass parting like a whirlwind was blowing through it.

"Move it," Emily yelled. Blacktop ahead, just a few more meters. She was in front of Rhiannon now, placing herself between the girl and the onrushing creatures, simultaneously pulling Rhiannon along. Then her feet were on the freeway and she had traction again, doubling her speed.

"Get to the median," she ordered Rhiannon, pushing her in the direction of the guardrail running down both sides of the median. Emily hoped it would provide some kind of a barrier if either of the things in the long grass decided they wanted to come out and play.

Halfway into the center lane, Emily slowed, turned to face the grass, backing up as she did. She glanced over her shoulder in time to see Rhiannon hopping over the metal guardrail, kneeling and leveling her own pistol to cover Emily.

Rhill-tik-tik-tik-tikkkkkk!

The creatures milled around the border between the grass and the hardtop of the freeway, as though they were uncomfortable or unsure about coming out into the open space, and that was just fine as far as Emily was concerned. She had eight rounds left in her .45 and would prefer not to use them unless she absolutely had to. If they could simply get away from—

The edge rustled violently as the creatures moved closer.

Emily caught a glimpse of Thor moving past her left side, barking insanely as he rushed toward the edge of the field.

"No, Thor!" Emily yelled. "No!"

Thor skidded to a stop but did not come to her. Instead he stood his ground growling and barking just a few meters shy of the grass.

"Here, come here," Emily yelled, edging forward, trying to identify exactly where the threat would come from.

"Get your ass over here, right now, mister," Rhiannon yelled, suddenly at Emily's side, and in a voice that commanded more authority than Emily had ever heard before. Thor, instantly cowed, stopped his barking, dropped his ears and head down, and ran toward Rhiannon . . .

. . . as the two creatures hidden within the tall grass now exploded outward . . .

They landed on either side of Thor, hulking four-legged creatures that looked almost bearlike save for their flattened heads and double row of twelve globular black eyes spaced in a semicircle around the front of their skulls. The "fur" covering their bodies was as red and as long and thin as the alien grass they had hidden in. A fin, more like a sail, ran laterally along the spine of each animal's back from the base of the neck to the end of the tail. As each thudded to the ground, they exhaled that same *tik-tik-tik* call, their heads shifting from dog, to human, to dog again, as if assessing which would be the easiest prey.

Rhiannon opened fire first, striking the creature on the left three times in the face, her hollow-point rounds exploding its head into bloody ribbons.

Emily brought her pistol up level with the second animal, expecting it to launch itself at them, then eased her finger from the trigger as, instead, it looked at its now-deceased brethren and wailed a long ululation as it scuttled to the dead creature's side in an unmistakable act of surprise. Completely ignoring the humans and dog, the creature sniffed around the remains of the other animal, prodded the body with its snout, and, when it did not move, lifted its head and wailed . . .

Rhillllll-tikk—

Crack! Crack!

Emily jumped in surprise as two shots rang out in quick succession, hitting the creature in the neck. It staggered once, then dropped to the ground, its head lying across the back of its partner, chest rising in deep, long pants, as it struggled feebly to regain its feet. A third shot from Rhiannon hit the creature in the temple and it too was no more.

■ ■ ■

Thor sniffed at the bodies of the two dead creatures.

"Get away from there," Emily scolded, her mind still caught up in the interaction she was almost certain she had seen between the dead animals. She was already beginning to doubt herself, but she was sure that in those final moments the second creature had shown clear indications of disbelief, maybe even grief, at the death of the first. Why she was surprised by that, she did not know. Perhaps it was simply because it was easier to label everything created within this world as monsters without emotion, without anything other than the base instinct to survive at all costs. There were plenty of examples of animals before the red rain that mated for life, or exhibited grief at the loss of a member of its family or friend; why then, should the new creatures of this planet be any different?

And Rhiannon . . . what about Rhiannon? Emily was beginning to worry about her. She seemed absolutely unperturbed after killing the two creatures, barely even looking at them once she was sure they were dead. That was disturbing to Emily. Neither creature had seemed intent on attacking them; as she reran the images of the past few minutes through her mind, they seemed more interested in driving them away from the field. And they had only moved outside the long grass after Thor had made the first aggressive move, and, even then, they seemed more interested in holding their ground rather than attacking. Emily had to wonder whether there was a connection between the spent pupae she had seen in the minivan and these two creatures. Could it be—

"Do you think we should go back and check out what's in those cases?" Rhiannon said, breaking Emily's train of thought.

There could be more of those creatures in there, but Emily's gut told her there wasn't, that these two were a couple. Mates, she was certain of it.

The drizzle still fell. The limp bodies of the two dead creatures only added to the depressing aura that seemed to have taken over their lives for the past couple of days. Maybe there was something useful in the two suitcases she had spotted in the back of the minivan. That would be nice.

"Sure," Emily said finally, "let's go take a look."

They followed the path they had created during their escape back to the minivan, a little more cautiously this time, but there was no sign that they were anything other than alone out here now.

Emily tried the back passenger door, but it was locked too. She headed to the rear of the minivan; it had a lift-up tailgate. Emily pulled halfheartedly on the door handle, knowing it, too, would be locked, but, to her surprise, she heard the click of the latch disengaging, and the door lifted up with barely more than a squeak. A musty smell, like old books, wafted out, and Emily turned her head away for a second.

In the storage compartment were the two leather suitcases she had seen earlier, a folded baby stroller, and an electric icebox. Red fungus grew around the edge of the icebox where the lid met the body. It was pretty much a forgone conclusion of what would be inside, but she felt the need to check anyway. Emily picked the box up and set it down. Opening the lid, she was surprised to see a six-pack of bottled water, pint size. Whatever food had been in there was long gone, but the water was a great find.

Rhiannon leaned in and pulled the smaller of the two cases out and popped the locks. She emptied the contents onto the ground and sifted through them; it was full of kids' clothing, diapers, and a bag of kids' toiletries.

The second case was locked. Emily pulled the knife from her ankle sheath and forced the cheap locks with that satisfying *thunk, thunk* sound only suitcases seemed capable of making. She flipped the lid open.

Winner!

It held a set of his-and-hers clothes—*Husband and wife? Boyfriend and girlfriend?* she wondered momentarily—enough for a couple of days away by the look of it. It wasn't hard to imagine the owners of the clothing on their way to visit family or maybe spend a couple of days with their children. Or maybe they had just decided to try and outrun the red rain and had died out here in the middle of nowhere. But at least they all died together, Emily thought, as she rummaged through the rest of the suitcase, which contained a couple of books: a romance and a well-thumbed copy of *The Stand*. She handed both books to Rhiannon, who glanced at them and put them into her backpack. "We can use them for a fire if we have to," she said. Emily nodded her approval, not sure reading Stephen King's book would be such a good idea, given their current predicament.

"This is more like it," she said, smiling at Rhiannon as she fished three pairs of women's jeans from the case. She held one against her waist. Too big, but then everything was these days; she had probably lost twenty pounds or more since this all began. But if she turned up the cuffs, they would work. She stripped off her soaked jeans and tossed them away, slipped into the new pair, and made a few adjustments until they fit her well enough that she could move freely. "Oh my God, these feel good," she said as she felt the cool, dry weave of the denim against her legs. There were socks too, and underwear—oh God, clean panties! Emily emptied out the kids' clothing from the first case and began packing everything useful into it.

Rhiannon fished a small roadside emergency bag from a side compartment, unzipped it, and pulled out a first-aid kit, which she promptly stowed in her backpack. "Are these dynamite?" she asked, holding up two red sticks that did bear a passing resemblance to the explosive.

Emily smiled. "Emergency flares," she said.

"Cool!" said Rhiannon, and stuffed them in her backpack too.

"Where's Thor?" Rhiannon asked, suddenly aware the malamute had vanished.

Emily looked around as if she expected him to be at her feet, but he was nowhere to be seen. A quick survey around the perimeter of the vehicle didn't turn him up either.

"Shit!" she said when she was sure the malamute wasn't just peeing on something, then, "Thor!"

There was silence for several long heartbeats, then Thor's bark came to them from off to their right; it was urgent, demanding.

"Thor," Emily yelled, "come here, now."

Again Thor barked that same almost playful but demanding bark.

"Leave the stuff here," Emily said. "Let's go see what he's gotten into now."

■ ■ ■

"Thor?" Emily called as she and Rhiannon pushed through the foliage in the direction of his excited barking.

Laced throughout the alien grass were what were obviously paths the two creatures they had encountered used on a regular basis, judging by how well-worn they were. Emily and Rhiannon followed one now toward the sound of Thor's insistent bark.

"There he is," said Rhiannon, then, "Whoa!"

The malamute was at the end of the path. He waited outside a—what? Emily couldn't call it a nest; it was too large, too intricately woven from the surrounding blades of grass. It was more like a work of art, big enough to have easily accommodated the two animals they had just killed with room to spare.

It was a den—yes, that was the right word. And Thor was sitting outside it, near a curved opening close to the ground that was probably the entrance.

"Thor, come over here," Emily said, suddenly aware that the den was easily big enough to accommodate more of the creatures. She drew her pistol in anticipation of another attack from within.

Thor ignored her command, instead dropping to his front paws, his butt in the air, and firing bark after bark at the opening.

Emily approached cautiously.

"Get over here, Thor," Emily insisted. This time the dog obeyed, meandering over to greet the two girls, no sign that he felt threatened. Emily took him by his collar to make sure he couldn't change his mind and run off again. It wasn't like him to disobey a command.

"Jesus, be careful," said Emily as Rhiannon stepped up close to the den and knelt down near the opening.

A faint but familiar *rhill-tik-tik-tik-tikkkkkk* rose out of the den.

"Emily, come look at this."

Emily ordered Thor to sit, then joined Rhiannon at the opening. "What am I . . . oh!"

Inside the den, toward the back wall, Emily saw three small bodies, slightly larger than her open hand, moving together, tangled almost into a ball.

"Babies," said Rhiannon. "Oh my God!" She turned and gave Emily a look of horror. "I killed their parents. Oh my God."

Emily was momentarily lost for words. "You had no other choice," she said eventually. Obviously the two creatures Rhiannon had killed were simply protecting their offspring and their territory. If Thor had not been so aggressive, they probably would have stayed in the long grass until the humans had left the area. But that would have meant they would have had to give up the clothes and other supplies they found.

"But what are they going to do now? How will they survive?"

"It's a hard, harsh world, kiddo," Emily said, reluctantly rising to her feet. "And you're doing about as well as anyone could be expected to."

She offered her hand to Rhiannon and pulled her to her feet too.

"Daylight's burning. We need to get moving."

CHAPTER 11

The travelers had passed only the occasional vehicle since touching down on the I-40. Most had been nothing more than wrecks, destroyed by either the passage of time or the great storm that had spread across the world. All save the minivan had been useless to them.

The freeway had seemed strangely deserted.

Over the last kilometer that had begun to change. The number of vehicles strewn across the highway gradually increased as what had been empty lanes began to fill with stalled vehicles. By the time they had travelled another two kilometers they were looking at three lanes of eastbound vehicles, mostly big rigs, nose to tail in every lane, as though they had all rolled to a stop together. The jam stretched ahead of them, before disappearing into the mist and drizzle.

The great storm had swept through and, seemingly at random, rocked some of the big rigs over onto their sides. As the companions cautiously made their way between the abandoned vehicles, they saw that the sheer density of the trucks had kept most of them right where their drivers had stopped them. But time and the weather had not been so kind to these relics, stripping the paint from the cabs and flaying the canvas and metal from the freight containers until they looked like row upon row of skeletons, strips of still-attached canvas flapping in the breeze like dead skin.

Still, some had managed to survive relatively intact.

"Do you think any of them still work?" Rhiannon asked as they walked up alongside a rig that still looked to be in good condition.

"Doubtful," said Emily as she climbed up onto the footplate of the cab and tried to look inside. A thin layer of red moss spun a frosty web across the window. Emily wiped it away with her sleeve. "And even if we found one we could get to start, there'd be no way to maneuver it out of this snarl-up. These things are packed tighter than sardines in a can." She tried the cab door, but it was locked.

Seeing nothing of use within, Emily climbed down and took a second to think. It was still raining, the sky was gray, and night was edging closer. With the heavy cloud cover, it was going to get dark much earlier. Emily estimated they had maybe an hour and a half of light left before it was too dark to travel safely. She stepped away from the convoy of dead trucks to the side of the road. The misty rain limited the distance she could see ahead, but there was no indication of the three-lane tailback of trucks ending anytime soon.

"We'll keep going until we get to the last truck or it gets so dark we can't carry on," Emily said. "Then we'll pick one to spend the night in so we can get out of this rain. That okay?"

Rhiannon nodded and walked on.

The trucks smelled. It was a new smell, made up of the scent of slowly decomposing wood, and metal, and gradually decaying plastic, sprinkled with a dash of whatever the trucks had been hauling, all bound together by the musky scent of the wet red vegetation.

As they continued on, Emily found unbidden memories, spontaneously activated by the web of scents popping back into her mind as they trudged onward through the vehicular graveyard. Here the plastic memory of splashing in a kiddy paddling pool in Mom and Dad's backyard when she was no more than four or five, a puppy, long since dead and gone—Rex, his name was Rex—running and yelping along the pool's perimeter, barking excitedly as she splashed and laughed. The vague recollection of her parents standing watchfully over her, shadows in her memory but always there for her. Here the unmistakable smell of wet pine, walks through the forest with her first serious boyfriend and secret meetings under the stars.

Her mind was tired, and she wished the memories would simply fade back into whatever part of her brain had been hiding them. The sense of melancholy these memories brought with them, of times she remembered so fondly, were now not only discolored by time but stained with the blood of an entire planet. It created a frisson of sadness and anger so intense it felt as though the emotions were alive within Emily, hollowing out a space for itself in her chest.

Emily looked at her companions. Rhiannon was such a dichotomy, surely as much a unique product of this world as her own son was. This tough young girl who should have been on the cusp of womanhood, excited by the prospect of dating, graduating high school, experiencing the heartbreak of first love, the joy of stepping out into a life that she could make and call her own. A husband. Kids. Grandkids. And a life well lived. What were the chances she would ever get to experience any of those things? Was she condemned to live under the boot heel of the Caretakers? Or, perhaps even worse, would she have to live in a world where people like Valentine still dictated how she would shape her life? Not if Emily had any say in the matter.

And Thor. Poor, bedraggled, loyal Thor, walking between the two women, eyes fixed ahead as always, ears up, his gray-and-white coat glistening with raindrops. The last of his kind, Emily was sure. Blissfully unaware of the fact, sure of only one thing, his love for his family. Emily knew she could not have asked for a more loyal companion. She had no idea what she had done to command the loyalty of such friends, and part of her also knew that she did not deserve it, but she was glad of it anyway. Because, even out here, in this barren alien world, she knew she was as rich as anyone left on this Earth.

The lines of vehicles creaked and moaned like condemned souls as the companions picked their way through them. For the first kilometer or so, the trucks and occasional car and even a Greyhound bus—a perfectly round hole drilled through almost every window—had all obviously been brought to a controlled stop by their now long-dead drivers. But that had changed over the past couple of minutes as the orderly procession of decaying vehicles had edged up the incline of the hill the travelers found themselves climbing. The farther up they walked, the more it became obvious that *these* vehicles had not stopped in time to avoid slamming into the truck ahead of them. It began as just minor fender benders, but a couple had obviously hit at some speed, despite the incline of the hill.

Visibility began to decrease the higher up they went, the low cloud covering the road with a mist of cold droplets, limiting their view to just a few meters. By the time they reached the summit, Rhiannon and Emily were holding hands to make sure they would not be separated.

The descent down was even more chaotic. The vehicles had become a tangled mess of crushed cabs and jackknifed trailers. They had to carefully pick their way through the carnage or risk a broken ankle or sliced foot.

"At least we can see where we're going now," said Rhiannon, about halfway down the opposite side of the hill, her face covered in a thin sheen of water left there by the thinning mist. Apparently, the heaviest cloud had been located on the western side of the hills, and their visibility was improving with every meter they took down now.

Ahead of them, a gas tanker had managed to skid to a stop, its shiny aluminum tanker-trailer jackknifed across all three lanes of traffic, blocking the road beyond, the cab twisted awkwardly like its neck had been broken. Emily and Rhiannon clambered under the trailer . . . and straight into a scene of utter carnage.

Directly ahead of the tanker were four partially destroyed vehicles, still recognizable for the trucks they once were, but after them the road was like a scene from a war movie. The freeway was littered with debris and the blackened scorch marks of what had obviously been an enormous inferno, a fire that had burned with such intensity it had boiled away the top layers of the freeway and even melted the guardrail along the central divide. What was left of the road was covered in the grime-encrusted remains of vehicles, none of them intact, all barely recognizable. The pieces were so scattered, and there were so many of them, it was impossible to tell how many vehicles they had originally belonged to. Even the open ground to the right of the eastbound lanes still bore the blackened shadow of the fire, the soil so devastated that the alien vegetation had not been able to take root there all these years later.

"Damn!" hissed Emily.

"Creepier than an uninvited clown at a kid's birthday party," Rhiannon said nervously, repeating one of Parsons' favorite idioms. She was right, though—the torn, smashed, burned vehicle parts were . . . well, scary looking. It didn't take much of a stretch of the imagination to picture some gigantic alien beast stampeding through the trucks, tearing them apart simply for the fun of it, leaving their chrome-and-fiberglass carcasses to rot in the New

Mexico desert. And, of course, in this strange new version of the world, that might just have been what had happened.

The truth, though, was probably much simpler, Emily was sure. As they reached the final quarter kilometer, the devastation was total; trailers and trucks had plowed into each other, merging together until it was almost impossible to tell one devastated vehicle from another. There had been a fire or an explosion or maybe both. It had consumed everything, reducing the big rigs down to little more than their chassis. Pools of rubber littered the ground, tires melted by the heat of the inferno that had ripped through here. Again Emily's imagination was more than eager to reconstruct the possible scenario that had led up to the devastation: an agitated driver wanting to get home had overestimated his luck and boom, catastrophe had rained down on him and everyone else for a half kilometer back who hadn't been able to stop in time. The tailback that had ensued, the one they had been following for the past five kilometers, had condemned everyone behind them to die in the cab of their vehicle or out in the desert if they had tried to make a run for it. Either way the end result would have been the same.

"Oh my God," said Rhiannon, stopping suddenly and pointing past the destruction. "Emily, look at that!"

Emily followed Rhiannon's excited pointing, following the line of the road as it dipped through the mess of burned-out vehicles, leveling off and then unerringly continuing east. But about a half kilometer after the road flattened off again, it curved through another set of smaller hills, the height of which Emily could not tell as their summit was hidden behind a misty veil of rain. And there, nestled in between the two hills Emily saw a squat, white building.

Emily felt a smile spread across her face. The first genuine smile she could remember since before Mac had left.

The building was boxlike with a flat roof and guttering running along the edges to drain pipes in each corner. Emily could see three windows along the freeway-facing wall. She could not be certain, but the windows looked to be intact.

"Thank God," said Rhiannon.

Emily's smile grew broader. The idea of having somewhere dry to spend the night was akin to offering a steak dinner to a starving man. The clouds above their heads had lost their silver-gray edge and were now becoming black; night was approaching fast. If the building was as undamaged as it looked from here, it would be a perfect place to spend the night.

"Come on," said Emily, almost laughing with exhilaration. "I'll race you."

They had taken only a few steps when Rhiannon let out another gasp of surprise and froze.

"Oh!" Emily said softly as she stopped too.

Behind the windows of the building, the unmistakable glow of man-made light now shined.

CHAPTER 12

"Do you think it's people?" Rhiannon said, her voice full of excitement.

Emily stared at the windows. There was no way the orange glow leaking from them could be mistaken for anything other than the illumination from a lightbulb. And that meant two things: there had to be power to the building *and* someone had to turn on the lights. Both of which were, well, stunning in their implications.

"It *is* people," Rhiannon insisted. "It has to be."

"Let's go and find out," said Emily, "but we have to be careful. This could be anything."

Rhiannon nodded and began to follow Emily across the road toward the safety barrier at the side of the freeway. The devastation of the crash, fire, and, by the looks of the debris pattern, subsequent explosion had flung parts of the vehicles everywhere, but the concentration of broken machines was still mainly on the freeway. If they wanted to avoid it they would need to get off the road for a while.

"Rhiannon, slow down," said Emily as the girl began to move at almost a jog. She stopped and turned around to look at Emily, her face brighter than Emily had seen in a very long time.

"But—"

"No buts," Emily interrupted. "We *have* to be careful."

Grudgingly, Rhiannon slowed.

Seventy meters away, Emily brought them to a stop.

"Get out your pistol," Emily ordered.

"But what if they're friendly?"

"If they are, then they'll understand why we had to be cautious, but if they're not, then I don't want any misunderstandings." Emily had already pulled her .45 from its holster and ratcheted a round into the chamber. She waited for Rhiannon to pull her own pistol and ready it.

Thoughts cascaded through Emily's mind, and a twinge of excitement, countered by an equal part of anxiety, set her heart racing. The possibility that others had survived the red rain and the megastorm that followed had vanished from her mind within the first week. Obviously there had been survivors, but they had been safely tucked away in submarines or at either end of the Earth's poles; she had given no thought to there still being life left on land since then. And out here, in the middle of the desert? How the hell had they managed to make it for so long? And where were they getting their power from? If they had lights, then they must have a power source. Maybe a generator? That was possible, she supposed, but where would they get the gas to power it for all these years? And generators were loud; this close to the building, she would have heard it running by now. Maybe there was still a power plant operational? If that were true, then it meant someone had to be keeping it running, and if someone was willing to maintain a power plant, then they had to be producing power for more than just a building in the middle of nowhere. Which meant that there might be more survivors, maybe even a town or a city. Her heart began to swell with the possibility. Maybe she had been wrong and Valentine had been right all along. Maybe.

"I can't see a surveillance camera or a lookout," Emily said, straining her eyes against the pale light of the dying day, "but that doesn't mean that whoever is in there isn't keeping an eye out. We'll get off the road and approach it from the blind side."

The west side of the building was just a large wall with no windows.

"Come on," Emily said, "let's move." They left the road and cut across the open plain in the direction of the building . . . and instantly regretted doing so. With so little red vegetation here to bind the dirt together, the constant rain had turned the ground to a thick, heavy mud. It sucked at their already-sodden feet and slowed them to a clumsy, lurching, slurping plod. Only Thor seemed to have little problem navigating the ground, but then he had four-wheel drive.

It took them twenty minutes of slowly picking their way through the mud to travel the remaining distance to the building. Emily's feet ached worse now than they had during the entire journey, thanks to the heavy coating of wet clay that clung to both of her boots. Her calves burned from the effort of pulling one foot after the other from the quagmire.

"Well this wasn't your best idea," said Rhiannon, a little too sarcastically for Emily's liking.

"Hush!" Emily hissed back. She scanned the building. From what she could see at this obtuse angle it looked remarkably intact. It was quite large, not a home, she thought, but maybe some kind of office building? Bisecting their position and the side of the building was a concrete driveway that led in from the freeway along the side of the building to a parking lot at the back. Two rusting cars still sat in the lot, but even from where they crouched Emily could see that the vehicles were weather worn, their tires flat as proverbial pancakes and the glass of their windshields scattered around the ground.

Nothing moved. There was no indication of life from within the building.

"Stay put," said Emily, turning to face Rhiannon.

"But . . ."

"No buts, I need you to wait here with Thor. If whoever is in there isn't friendly, I might need you to bust me out again, okay?"

Rhiannon did not look happy with the order. "Okay," she grumbled.

"Good girl. Keep your head down, alright, and only come in if I call you, understood?"

Rhiannon nodded.

"Thor, stay," Emily commanded and pulled her .45 from the holster, checked it again, and reholstered it. She looked left and right for any signs of movement, then slowly began to make her way to the concrete road leading to the parking lot just a few meters away.

Mud clung to her boots like concrete, slowing her movement to an exaggerated spacewalk as she hobbled across the road and leaned against the side of the building. She took a few moments to use the wall of the building to gently and as quietly as she could scrape the majority of the mud from her shoes. The damn stuff was like glue. When she was done, she followed the wall toward the back section of the building, bobbed her head around the corner, saw nothing, and cut left, edging toward the nearest window. When she reached it, Emily crouched down and slowly leaned in until she could see into the room within.

It was an office. An empty office, she noted after scanning it for a few seconds. It looked completely normal and untouched; papers were stacked on one side next to a mesh pen holder. Several metal filing cabinets lined one wall, and a couple of pictures, local landscapes, she thought, hung on the other walls. The ceiling light was on, glowing orange and spilling light out onto the concrete where Emily crouched. The door was ajar a few centimeters or so. Gradually, she adjusted her position until she could see through the crack of the door—just a gray wall of what looked like a corridor beyond. The corridor led to an external door about three meters farther on from where she stood.

When she was sure there was no sign of movement within, Emily ducked beneath the window frame and scooted past it. She reached the door and placed an ear against the cold wood, listening for any sound that would betray any occupants. Again there was nothing. Quiet as a tomb. *Probably not the most uplifting analogy,* she thought as she tried the door handle and eased it slowly toward her.

The door cracked open, allowing a thin sliver of light to bleed out.

Well, okay.

Emily took a deep breath and pulled the .45 from its holster. The weight felt good in her hand, reassuring, but she slipped it behind her back, out of sight of anyone she might surprise or who might be waiting for her. No need to present a threat to anyone she found within, she had already decided. Edging the door open another couple of centimeters, she stepped inside, pausing in the doorway, her body half inside, listening. After a minute of no sound she slipped through the doorway as quietly as possible and eased the door closed behind her.

The corridor ran from where Emily stood down to what looked like some kind of reception area at the front of the building; she could see a water cooler and the corner of a sofa. There were three more doors along this corridor, all closed.

It was significantly warmer inside. She wiped her sodden hair out of her eyes, then quickly covered the few meters to the doorway of the office she had peeked into from outside and ducked inside. A quick glance around the room confirmed it was still empty.

The room smelled . . . normal. There was no stench of decay. No signs of any infestation. No signs of life at all, in fact. Not yet, anyway, but there was still plenty of the building to explore where any number of people could be hiding.

The place seemed pristine. Frozen in time.

Emily moved back to the door and peeked into the corridor.

"Shit!" she hissed. A trail of muddy boot prints betrayed her entry into the building from the outside door. She silently berated herself as she quickly unlaced her boots and hid them next to one of the filing cabinets. Her socks were soaked through and felt like ice against her feet, so she pulled those off and tossed them with her boots, rubbing her feet against the carpet to dry them off. It would help her move more silently. This place *was* a lot warmer, and her naked toes had already begun to feel quite toasty against the tightly knitted weave of the carpet.

Emily edged out into the corridor, her eyes and ears open as she edged her way down toward the room with the water cooler. The second and third doors were both unlocked. She eased each door carefully open and looked inside, both empty save for almost duplicate editions of the furniture she had found in the first office. Emily closed each door again behind her, wincing as the third door creaked on dry hinges. The fourth room was locked, but there was no reason to suspect it was anything other than another office, so she moved on. The corridor ended in a larger room. It wasn't the reception area she had first suspected but some kind of waiting area with a large, comfortable-looking sofa and a couple of chairs scattered against the walls, a coffee table in the center with a lonely coffee mug waiting for its owner, and an industrial-size coffee maker next to a microwave on a waist-high cabinet.

On the opposite wall from where she stood was a glass-fronted snack machine. It still hummed quietly. Her heart sank at the same moment a feeling of relief washed over her when she saw the now-mummified rotted sandwiches behind the glass of the vending machine. If there were anyone living here those sandwiches would have either been eaten in the first few days after the red rain or at least cleaned out and the power turned off, she reasoned. That was an assumption, of course; it might just be that any survivors could not be bothered, or other survivors, immune to the red rain's effects as she was, had found this place after the fall. She didn't think so, though; the place looked so untouched, as though everyone had just stepped outside for a smoke break and would be back any second. No, the probability of humans still living here had dropped significantly in Emily's estimation. Of course, that did not rule out the possibility of something else setting up home in the building. So far, though, there was no sign of any kind of a resident, human or otherwise. Of course, empty or not, it did nothing to dispel the mystery of where the building was getting its power from.

There was another door on the other side of the waiting room. Emily opened it and found a second corridor leading deeper into the rest of the building. The corridor was dark, but there was enough illumination from the staff room that she quickly found the light switch. She flicked it on and the fluorescent overhead lights complained for a second, then flickered to life. At the farthest end of the corridor, she saw yet another door, but between her and it were two more offices. These contained filing cabinets and a table. The door at the end had the words "Service Area" stenciled across it.

The door opened inward, but whatever was beyond was completely hidden within the darkness, save for a few feet of light bleeding in from the corridor, revealing a stark gray concrete floor. Emily brought her pistol up, pointing it into the darkness while she felt around for a light switch on the wall. She found it and turned it on, flooding the room with light.

"Well, what do—" The words turned into a scream of fear as Emily felt a hand land heavily on her shoulder.

CHAPTER 13

Emily ducked and swung the .45 around like a club before she realized the hand on her shoulder belonged to Rhiannon.

"Jesus Christ, I just about peed my pants," she gasped, bent over at the waist, leaning both hands against her knees, sucking in a deep breath of air. She had to wait for her muscles to unclench and her heart to slow before she could manage to get out any more words between the thumping in her chest.

"I thought I told you to wait outside?" she managed eventually.

Thor stood at Rhiannon's side. He sat and stared at his mistress, his tail wagging slowly, unsure if it was him she was mad at. Rhiannon's face was a picture of barely suppressed mirth. "I know, but you were gone so long and it started to rain much harder, so I decided to come inside. I worried that you were in trouble. I didn't mean to scare you . . . sorry . . . ." The girl, bedraggled and sopping wet was trying to do her best to look penitent, but Emily could see the mischievous light in her eyes.

Finally, she smiled too. She took Rhiannon's hand in her own—it was cold, alabaster pale, and as wrinkled as if she had been sitting in a bath for an hour—pulled her close, and gave her a long hug. "It's okay," she said, "you did what you thought was right." She released Rhiannon, grinned conspiratorially, and said, "Here, look at this." Emily pushed the door open and ushered Rhiannon into the space beyond.

The room—*It's more of a bay,* Emily thought—was around forty meters deep and twenty wide. Strips of multiple fluorescent lights along the ceiling brightly illuminated the space. Six large roll-up doors, interspersed at two-meter intervals, ran along most of the long wall to their left. The opposite wall had narrow windows running along the top near the ceiling and workbenches at floor level. But it was what occupied the main floor of the bay that had Emily excited: four of the vehicle bays were still occupied.

"Do they work?" Rhiannon asked, a brightness entering her voice.

"I haven't had time to check them yet, thanks to someone trying to scare me to death." Emily gave Rhiannon a playful nudge with her elbow. "Only one way to find out, though. Come on." She beckoned for Thor to follow them. "But let's still be careful. This place looks deserted, but that doesn't mean it is."

Rhiannon nodded that she understood and slipped her pistol into her hand.

They approached the first vehicle, an imposing mechanical excavator. It was painted a bright orange. On the door to the cab, in black lettering, was "N. M. D. O. T." The hood of the excavator's engine compartment was propped open, and a toolbox still rested on the engine block.

"Of course, it makes sense," Emily said, walking around the lowered bucket of the excavator.

"What?" Rhiannon said.

"It's a storage depot or maybe a repair shop for the state department of transportation," Emily explained. She was already at the second vehicle, an even bigger dump truck, painted the same garish orange.

"It kind of looks like the snowcat," Rhiannon said as she joined her, ducking down to check underneath the vehicle.

She was right, Emily thought, it did remind her of the snow-cat, the tracked vehicle they had used to drive across the snowy wastes of Alaska to reach the Stockton Islands, oh, so very long ago now. It had the same sense of utility as the snowcat; when you looked at this machine, you knew exactly what it did. No need for speculation; its design yelled its function.

One of the ceiling lights flickered for a moment, splashing the bay with dancing shadows and freezing Emily midstep. They flickered again, then came back on. Emily held her breath, waiting to see if they would stay on.

"Can we use any of these?" Rhiannon asked, pointing at the big trucks as they walked toward the next bay, apparently unperturbed by the faulty light.

"Maybe." Emily wasn't sure what kind of a range the vehicles would have or if they even worked. They were extremely large, and she was sure they would usually be delivered to wherever they needed to be on a flatbed truck rather than driven directly. Still, any port in a storm, as Mac would say.

The third space was occupied by another dump truck.

"Does anything come in a color other than orange around here?" Rhiannon asked as they scouted around the front of it.

Sitting in the fourth bay, hidden behind the other oversized vehicles, was a pickup truck with a cluster of antennas fixed to the roof and side of the cab. It, too, was orange.

"That's more like it," said Emily, heading to the driver's side as Rhiannon gave the exterior of the truck a quick inspection.

"Crap!" said Rhiannon, pointing at the rear passenger-side tire. "We've got a flat."

"See if you can find a spare," Emily called back. In her mind she was crossing every possible part of her body as she reached for the driver's door of the truck. She pulled the door handle and it opened easily, but no cabin light came on.

"Damn," she whispered. The truck had been sitting here for over two years, so it wasn't really a surprise that the battery was dead, but still . . . it would have been nice to have caught a break. Well, another break if you counted finding it in the first place, she supposed.

"Found the spare," said Rhiannon, appearing at the door with Thor. "Will it start?"

Emily shook her head. "Battery's dead." She climbed down from the cabin. "We've got power to the building, though, and I'd bet there has to be a jumper cable here somewhere." She eyed the workbenches and cabinets at the opposite end of the bay.

The first couple of benches came up with nothing but neatly stored tools and parts.

"What are these?" said Rhiannon, pointing to a couple of brick-size boxes plugged into a power strip.

"I think that's what we're looking for," said Emily, smiling as she recognized the oversized crocodile clips of the battery charger, but she was confused as to why it would be plugged into a wall socket. A green light on the front of the units glowed brightly, which she decided to take as a good sign. She read the words on the side of the first unit: "Start-N-Go 900 Peak Amp Ultra-portable 12V Starter."

"I think," said Emily, reaching across and removing the first of the two units from the power supply, and smiling as the green light stayed on, "that it's a portable starter. Let's go give it a shot."

She carried the unit over to the truck and set it down on the passenger seat as she climbed inside. "Keys have to be here somewhere." She checked everywhere she could think of in the cabin for a set of keys but found nothing.

"Damn it!"

"Maybe they're in the office?" said Rhiannon. "There's a sign over there." She nodded toward the back wall and a spray-painted sign and arrow pointing into the far corner.

Emily climbed down from the cab and slammed the door closed. "Let's go take a look."

The depot's office was at the opposite end of the bay. It was locked.

There's always something else to break, Emily thought as she brought the butt of her pistol down hard against the glass of the office door. She reached through and unlatched the lock. "Hold on to Thor, there's too much glass on the floor." She quickly found a gray metal box fixed to the wall, opened it, and saw several rows of hooks and four sets of keys, each clearly labeled with a license plate number. She grabbed all of them.

"Let's see which one of these works," she said, jingling the keys at Rhiannon.

Emily quickly matched the correct set of keys with the truck's license plate and discarded the others. She inserted the key and twisted it, just on the off chance that the universe was paying them extra special attention, but there wasn't even the slightest response from the starter motor. "Deader than the proverbial dodo," she said to herself, while mentally adding, *Along with everything else on this planet.*

"Let's see if we can't get this big boy started?" She grabbed the portable starter unit, found the handle that popped the hood, and jumped down. Propping up the hood, she quickly found the truck's battery and removed the cover, attached the two crocodile clips to the terminals, and switched the charger to the "Engine Start" position. There was a crackle of energy across the terminals.

The two women smiled hopefully at each other.

A couple of seconds later Emily was back in the driver's seat, keys grasped between thumb and forefinger. "Here goes nothing," she said, turning the keys to the start position and pressing the brake.

The starter motor whirred, then whirred again. The dash lights flickered briefly to life, then glowed brightly as the powerful V-8 engine coughed once and fired up, filling the bay with a deep rumble. A large plume of gray-black smoke escaped from the exhaust, and Emily felt the truck vibrate violently for a second, then settle down into a low tremble. She revved the engine a few times, and the truck responded, eager to be moving again.

Rhiannon gave a whoop of joy and jumped in excitement. Emily smiled back.

She checked the lights, windshield wipers, and heater.

"Looks like we'll be travelling in style," Emily said, smiling as she rolled down her window.

"What's that for?" Rhiannon pointed at a box with dials, displays, and buttons.

Emily picked up a microphone from the side of the box. "It's a radio transmitter. I think this might have been used as some kind of communications relay for the work crew when they were out of range of cell towers." She turned a knob to the on position and the cab was filled with the static hiss of empty airwaves. "I guess it works," she said before switching it off again.

Emily checked the truck battery's charge indicator: it was flickering at about the quarter point, which she knew should be higher, but it was going to take some time for the battery to actually gather a charge. There was no way that she was going to leave the engine running for as long as it would need to fully charge. Even though the gas tank registered as full, she still had no idea how far they were going to have to travel, and every single drop of gasoline was going to make a difference on this journey. They were just going to have to rely on the portable starter for at least one more start. The important thing was that the engine seemed to run fine, a testament to the grease monkeys and mechanics who had worked on it before the collapse. Reluctantly, she turned the engine off.

"We need to conserve the gas," she told Rhiannon, "besides, we're not going anywhere until we change that flat tire. Wanna show me where the spare is?"

Rhiannon led Emily to the back of the truck and pointed to the underside where the spare was stored. Emily opened the rear door and quickly found the jack kit in a compartment. The rear of the truck was enclosed, with plenty of space to stow their gear, perfect for Thor too.

"Here, give me a hand with—"

The ceiling lights flickered again, crackling as they pulsed on and off, dimmed to a low orange glow, pulsed on again for a half second, then went dark; and this time they did not come back on.

■ ■ ■

"Emily!" Rhiannon's voice, sharp with panic, cut through the darkness.

"It's okay, just hold on a second." The last time Emily had been in darkness this profound she had been alone in the stairwell of her apartment, still blissfully unaware of how far-reaching and terrible the transformation beyond her building would be. "Just wait here."

She used the flat of her hands against the body of the truck to guide herself around to the front of the cab, fumbled blindly for the door handle of the truck, found it, and pulled the door open. The faint orange glow of the cabin light illuminated just enough for Emily to see Rhiannon crouched next to Thor, her arms wrapped around the dog's neck.

"Hold on a second." Emily searched for the headlight switch, found it, and turned it on. Without the engine running only the parking lights came on, but it was enough light for Emily to see where they had left Rhiannon's backpack resting against the garage door.

"Rhiannon, it's okay. Go grab the flashlight from your pack." Rhiannon reluctantly let go of Thor, ran to the pack, and rummaged through it until she found her flashlight. She turned it on and made her way back to the truck.

Emily released the breath she had been holding. The second the lights had failed her fear of the dark had immediately pounced. It was amazing, she thought, how light fed humans' bravery. Without it, we were all just cavemen cowering in the blackness.

"You okay?" Emily asked.

Rhiannon nodded, the momentary panic already gone as she quickly collected herself. "Why did the lights go out?"

Emily had been pondering why there was power since they had first discovered the building to be empty of any human life. The light's sudden demise so close to sunset more or less confirmed the conclusion she had come to. "I think this place has some kind of solar-panel system, or maybe even a wind turbine that powers it. I think if we scout around we will probably find a battery bank in here somewhere."

"So why did the lights go out?" Rhiannon asked again.

"How should I know?" Then, regretting the edge of sharpness in her voice, added, "Maybe there's a problem with the batteries or with the solar panels. Maybe there just wasn't enough sun for the past couple of days. Who knows? It looks like whoever worked here left in a hurry and didn't bother turning off the lights, and this place has been empty for two years or so now. And we've turned on a lot of lights, which probably drained the power even faster. It's a miracle it's still functioning at all. Come on, that tire isn't going to change itself."

Half an hour, several scraped knuckles, and more than a few harsh words later Emily released the jack and allowed the truck to sink down onto its newly changed tire. The lights had still not come back on, and Emily figured they had seen the last of them, at least for tonight.

"Not bad if I do say so myself," she said, moving Rhiannon's hand until the flashlight illuminated the wheel well so she could tighten the wheel nuts.

"Can we go now?" said Rhiannon, eager to be on her way.

Emily was tempted to leave right then and there too. Now that her mind was free of distraction, the constant pull Adam exerted on her was almost irresistible, but it would not be fair or safe to travel the freeway after dark. She was just going to have to deal with it for tonight.

"It's almost dark out there now. Too dangerous. We'll plan on an early start tomorrow, so it's best we get an early night too," Emily told Rhiannon. She contemplated spending the night in the cab of the truck, but it was pointless sleeping in such cramped quarters when there was a perfectly good sofa in the waiting area. They grabbed Rhiannon's backpack and headed back there.

"I'm going to check the doors," she told Rhiannon and retraced her steps back to the rear entrance of the building. She turned the thumb lock to the closed position, then recovered her boots and socks from the office. The mud had dried to a solid cake on her boots. She banged them against the side of the desk until the majority fell off, picked off the few stubborn pieces that remained, then walked back to their makeshift bedroom.

Rhiannon had already unpacked her sleeping bag.

"You take the sofa, and I'll take the chair," Emily offered.

"Thanks," said Rhiannon. She smiled, handed Emily the blanket from her backpack, yawned, then picked up her sleeping bag and moved over to the sofa.

Emily checked the two doors to the room. Neither of them had any kind of lock, so she took two of the high-backed chairs from under the table and jammed one under each of the door handles. That left them only exposed via the two windows that looked out toward the freeway, but there was little that could be done about that.

The setting sun was at the opposite end of the building, pushing long shadows across the ground as she looked out across the open space toward the freeway. It wouldn't be long before night edged out the gray evening, but there was just enough light left for Emily to be able to see that the clouds that had dogged them for the past few days had begun to thin, and the faintest hint of light-blue sky was now visible. Maybe tomorrow would be a better day, although the weather didn't really matter anymore, now that they had a vehicle. It was going to make the trip so much easier. To the north Emily saw a distant gleaming on the horizon, a scintillating glimmer like light reflecting on glass. Maybe another building catching the final dying rays of the sun.

She was suddenly aware of just how tired she was. And how cold her feet were too. The previous residents of this place had apparently left the heating on, but as soon as the power died the air had gradually begun to chill. She took off her jacket and then stripped out of her clothes, laying them over the table to dry. She changed into a clean pair of jeans and a sweater. By the time she slipped under the blanket, the windows were almost black with night, and the only sound was of Rhiannon's and Thor's sleep-soothed breathing.

"Good night, Adam," she whispered as her eyes closed. "Your mommy is coming for you."

CHAPTER 14

She was a million different souls rushing through the night. And yet, even as she was all, she was still one. The I/They flowed together, a mathematical wave of such purity that, if the I had still possessed its individual personality, it would have been reduced to an emotional pool in the presence of such coordinated perfection and beauty. The constant ebb and surge moved over the ground like a living tsunami, a luminescent tide swelling inland looking for a shore to break over.

Through tens of millions of eyes, I/They observed the landscape moving before them, disappearing beneath the rolling wave of life as it moved through the darkness, driven by an insatiable hunger shared equally by each member of the great swarm.

I/They felt the need glowing within her, the hunger that roared within each of them. The Need was a song, and each of them contributed their voice, urging the others onward, drawing power from the others' emptiness.

A pinprick of light appeared to the west, distant and tiny to any human eye, but to the I/They's multitude of senses it was a flash so bright and so intense it could mean only one thing . . .

Sustenance!

As one, the wave swelled toward the light, still distant, but irresistibly drawing them in. Even if the mass of tiny collective minds had wanted to ignore the call, it would have been impossible, the Need was so very, very strong.

EXTINCTION POINT: GENESIS

I/They felt a vibration akin to excitement shudder through the swarm, and with it came a sudden acceleration, both a push and a tug at the same time, toward the light source, urging each other onward, faster, and faster, and . . .

The world turned a blinding orange for a split second, disorienting the human portion of the I/They mind, but the They swept onward, unaffected by the confusion of the I.

A noise that the I recognized as being a word but was unable to process brushed against her, then the orange light was back once more, flooding her vision. More words, loudly spoken, pattered against her psyche like stones thrown against a window.

And like that pane of glass the connection suddenly shattered into . . .

■ ■ ■

"Emily! Emily, wake up." The sting of a slap across her cheek and a dazzling explosion of light dragged Emily panting and heaving back to consciousness. Her vision swam, her eyes blinded by light that filled her entire head. It took Emily several heartbeats before she realized that the light was coming from Rhiannon's flashlight.

"Get that out of my face," she gasped, the words stumbling from between her dry lips.

Rhiannon complied, dropping the beam of the flashlight to the floor and giving Emily a glimpse of the girl's pale and frightened face in its glow. Rhiannon knelt on the floor. Thor sat next to her. He gave a low whine, raised a paw toward Emily, and then dropped to the carpet, his nose inches from Emily's.

Carpet? Hadn't she been asleep in the armchair?

Emily closed her eyes. Projected onto the black screen of her eyelids she saw the image of the darkened plain from her dream, felt the wavelike surge of bodies heading toward *something* . . . a distant light. The food?

What the hell is going on here? As her senses returned Emily realized she was lying on the floor next to the coffee table. Her blanket, looking uncomfortably like the shed pupae of one of the spider aliens, lay on the floor at the foot of the chair. She sat up and immediately regretted the decision. Her head throbbed and her vision blurred again. Raising a hand to her forehead, she felt a stickiness there just above her hairline, and the tips of her fingers came back coated with drying blood. What the hell had she done now?

"You were yelling and thrashing in your sleep," Rhiannon said. "Then you tried to get up and you tripped over your blanket and hit your head and started to bleed, and I didn't know what to do, because I tried to wake you, but you just kept yelling and thrashing and then . . . and then . . ." Her words gushed out without a pause.

"Breathe!" Emily demanded, reaching out a hand to calm the frantic girl and also to steady herself, her senses still woozy. Emily put her hand to her head again; the cut was just above her hairline. It stung as she probed it with her fingers. Not that bad, though; the gash was about an inch long, the blood congealing already. "Just tell me what else happened."

Rhiannon paused and took in a deep lungful of air. "You kept mumbling and swaying, like you were drunk. You wouldn't wake up. I turned on the flashlight, and you were lying there bleeding and you wouldn't shut up. I tried to wake you, Emily. I didn't mean to hit you but that was the only thing I could think of."

"You hit me?"

"You were mumbling something over and over again. I'm sorry, I had to slap you." Rhiannon was distraught.

"What was I saying?" Emily asked, wetting her chapped lips with the tip of her tongue.

Rhiannon paused, as if she was afraid to let the words out.

"It's okay," Emily said, trying to not let her agitation make it to her voice. "I'm not angry. You did the right thing. Just tell me what I said."

"Hungry!" Rhiannon blurted out. "You kept yelling 'Hungry' over and over."

Well, that made no sense. Hungry? Why would she be yelling that?

Her mind flashed back to the dream, and the deep insatiable hunger of all those minds. And the light, the distant light on a darkened plain.

"Oh no! Rhiannon, get your gear together, we need to leave now." Emily scrambled to her feet, felt the world sway for a second, ignored it, and virtually leaped to where she had dropped her blanket.

Rhiannon looked confused. "What? Why? What do you mean?"

"We don't have time for me to explain anything, just grab your stuff. We need to get to the truck and get out of here. *Right now!*" Emily pushed the blanket unceremoniously into her suitcase and dropped it at the door.

The keys to the truck, where had she left them? Her head was still woozy as she fought to focus. On the table, right there. She pocketed the keys and turned to check on Rhiannon, who was slowly packing her sleeping bag into the backpack.

"Why do we have to leave?" she asked, confused.

"Because . . ." Emily thought about it for a second. Why did they have to run? Because she knew that these dreams were not really dreams. Because each one was becoming more and more intense, more real, almost prescient. Because lately she felt more real when she was dreaming than she did when she was awake. Because she knew that, somehow, some kind of connection had been established between her and the life-forms that now dominated this planet. Because she recognized the building she had seen in the dream. *This* building. Because . . .

". . . something is coming," she said.

■ ■ ■

"What do you mean something's coming?" Rhiannon said as they hustled down the corridor to the vehicle bay. Her voice was a high-pitched squeak at this point. "What's coming? Emily, please."

"I don't know how to explain it," Emily said, exasperation, fear, and pain making her own voice shriller than she intended. She tried to ignore the sharp throbbing spasm in her head that came with every footfall as she jogged alongside the girl and the dog. "My dreams, they . . . I think they show me things. Like how I knew Adam was still alive. And if I'm right, then that last dream means we're in terrible danger."

"Danger from what?" Rhiannon insisted, pushing open the door to the vehicle bay, her flashlight illuminating the way.

"I don't know that either. Whatever it is, there are a lot of them, and I think they're heading this way." Emily realized she didn't even know what time it was. She glanced at the windows that ran along the top of the vehicle bay doors. She had gone to sleep just after nightfall, but now she could see a growing radiance through the dirt-stained windows, so it must be close to dawn at least. God, she felt like she had only just fallen asleep.

They negotiated their way around the other vehicles and headed to the truck. Pulling open the rear door, Emily threw in the suitcase and Rhiannon's backpack. "Thor. Up," she commanded, slapping the floor of the truck with her hand. The malamute leaped joyfully into the back of the truck, his tail wagging furiously, tongue lolling. Despite everything, Emily had to smile. *The damn dog always was a sucker for a road trip*, she thought as she slammed the door behind him and made her way to the front of the truck. Rhiannon was already inside. Emily grabbed the battery starter from the driver's seat, ran quickly to the front, and attached it to the battery on her second attempt, cursing her shaking hands. She wedged the starter down between the battery casing and the side panel, then slammed the hood shut again. There wasn't going to be time for her to get back out again and retrieve the starter once the engine was running.

Rhiannon was already inside as Emily climbed back into the driver's seat.

"Fasten your seat belt," Emily ordered and was immediately overcome with a sense of déjà vu. Sitting in a similar vehicle, in a garage, two kids in the car that time, though. Their father outside, trying to lure them to him and the thing that had taken control of him.

Emily forced the memory from her mind. Pushing the key into the ignition, she held her breath a moment, then turned it. The engine instantly roared to life. She gave it a second, then turned on the main beams and looked up at the bay door windows. Morning was fast approaching; she could see its illumination now through the glass, pushing back the shadows on the ceiling. Thank God.

"Shit! The door. I need to open the door." The door could be manually operated by a chain-and-pulley system that was clearly visible on the wall between their bay and the next one over. Emily began to unbuckle her seat belt.

"No, I'll get it," said Rhiannon, eager to help. She was out of the door and running to the pulley before Emily could even say no.

Sprinting to the door, Rhiannon took the chain in both hands and started to pull it hand over hand. The door rose with each smooth tug from Rhiannon. Light filtered in through the growing gap between the concrete floor and the bottom of the door.

Emily's fingers thrummed impatiently against the steering wheel. *Come on! Come on!*

As the gap between door and floor grew, more light began to flood inside and, unless by some miracle every cloud had disappeared from the sky, the amount of light that was now spilling across the service bay floor was just too bright.

"What the . . . ?" Emily muttered. The bay door was halfway up, and if she tilted her head she could get a good view of . . . *Oh! Shit!*

A wave of white light, shimmering like liquid metal, filled the entire width of the gap left by the roll-up door. It dipped and rose again, flowing silently toward them.

Emily recognized it instantly from her dream. In the dream she had been one of them, linked somehow via this weird and growing interconnection that had been established when Adam was kidnapped. A residue of that connection must still have existed, because as the wave of light moved inexorably toward their position, growing larger with each passing second, she felt a thrill pass through her, and she was the hunter again for just a moment. She knew what they wanted, and in that instant, she was almost willing to give it to them.

Thor started to bark frantically from behind her, shocking Emily from her trance and severing the connection. She shook her head as though that would dispel the filaments of disorientation she still felt floating within her mind.

Focus, Goddamn it.

Rhiannon's back was to the truck, and the pulley system was set back against the interior wall; Rhiannon would not be able to see the approaching danger until it was too late. Emily flashed the truck's headlights and hit the horn hard.

As soon as she had done it, she knew it had been the wrong thing to do. A ripple, slightly brighter than the main white light, passed through the onrushing wave, and Emily thought she saw the wave accelerate, shifting ever so slightly toward the bay where she, Rhiannon, and Thor waited like trapped rabbits.

It was a split-second decision, but in her mind the thought process seemed to stretch on for an eternity: Should she just chance it, bundle Rhiannon into the truck, and make a run for it and hope that she could outrun the wave? She calculated the risks and probabilities—beyond the beautiful shimmering light was nothing but the darkness; the wave was moving with lightning speed; her ability to avoid any obstacles in the road—and came to the conclusion that there was no way they would make it. The light wave was moving far too fast for her to be able to guarantee she could safely navigate them out from this place.

So that left only one option.

Rhiannon had stopped pulling the chain, the door raised to her chest height, and was now looking back at the truck, the quizzical look on her face silently asking Emily, *What?*

Emily threw open the truck door and rushed to Rhiannon's side.

A hum, like a high-tension power line throbbing with energy, was beginning to fill the air ahead of the wave, barely audible over the deep rumble of the truck's engine but growing louder with every second.

"What are you doing?" said Rhiannon. Emily ignored her, snatched the chain from her hands, and shouldered the girl aside. As quickly as she could she pulled on the chain and the door began to gradually drop back toward the floor. As the crack between door and floor became smaller so the intensity of both the sizzling sound and the luminosity increased, until the inside of the vehicle bay sounded like fat sizzling on a red-hot skillet, and the shadows had all been forced to the room's corners.

Rhiannon noticed it now too. "What is that? What's going on?"

Something white and glowing brightly zipped through the shrinking gap between the floor and flew up toward the ceiling, then another and another followed it.

"Emily, what are those?" Rhiannon screamed, but Emily ignored her and continued to drop the door the final few inches, her hands slick with sweat, slipping on the chains. Another blur of white incandescence zipped under the space—*Come on, come on*—until, finally, with a metallic clunk, the door met the concrete.

The crack of a pistol being fired deafened Emily for a second. Instinctively she ducked and turned to see Rhiannon, her pistol drawn and aimed into the air over Emily's shoulder. The girl's face was a mask of concentration, her eyes slits, both arms extended the way Emily had taught her, as she tracked something through the air. Emily turned in the direction the girl was aiming in time to see a white and glowing flash of light diving toward her. She scuttled back, rattling the roll-up door as she collided with it, then gasped as Rhiannon's pistol barked twice in quick succession, and the glow exploded into tiny splotches of liquid light that cascaded through the air like miniature fireworks, fading to nothing before they even hit the ground.

A ragged shape hit the concrete near Rhiannon's feet with a wet *splat!*

It was about as big as Emily's hand, a corpse-gray body that was almost translucent. What might have been an abdomen until Rhiannon's nine-millimeter slug ripped through it was now nothing but a ragged, torn bag leaking a still-glowing viscous liquid onto the concrete. A pair of red wings—feathered, Emily thought at first, but on closer inspection, she saw that the wings were covered in what looked more like long, fine scales—sprouted from the joint that connected the torso to the abdomen. A hundred or more limp black tendrils that might have been legs hung from the body. They still twitched spasmodically, but any chance of further examination disappeared as Rhiannon brought her boot down hard on the creature's body, turning it into a pool of goo.

"Ugh! I think I'm going to be sick," Rhiannon said as she lifted her heel and regarded the mess on her sole.

Thor had somehow hopped from the storage area of the truck, across the backseat, and into the front cab. He now sat in the front passenger seat, his paws on the dashboard, barking furiously, spittle streaking the windshield. Emily looked up in time to see five more of the glowing creatures zipping around the roof space between the support beams and girders. Their abdomens seemed dim by comparison to the brightness she had seen approaching, and they appeared disoriented, uncoordinated even, nothing like the elegantly organized mass of creatures she had experienced in her dream. Perhaps being separated from the main group broke the intense connection she had experienced when she dreamed among them?

A loud metallic clang made both women jump. Something had just hit the sheet metal siding of the building. Hard.

As Emily searched for where the sound had come from, she heard another and then another bang as more of the creatures hit the outside of the building. Dimples were beginning to form in the walls where the light bugs were barreling into it.

"Come on," Emily yelled. She grabbed Rhiannon's hand and dragged her toward the car, threw open the passenger side, and let Thor down. She was about to head to the back to retrieve their packs when one of the panes of glass above the farthest bay door exploded inward, raining glass down onto the concrete. A stream of light flowed in through the broken window space and twirled around the ceiling, absorbing the five stragglers who had made it inside first, their abdomens now glowing as brightly as those of their kin. A second and third pane shattered almost simultaneously, the sound of breaking glass smothered beneath the hissing of the wings of thousands of the creatures flooding into the vehicle bay and the constant barrage of bodies hitting the sides of the building with a sound like hard-bounced tennis balls.

Emily did not wait to see how many more creatures would make it inside. She stretched across the center console and switched off the engine, pocketing the keys. If her dream was accurate—and there was no reason to doubt it wasn't, not now—then she knew there were millions, maybe even tens of millions of these creatures out there, like a swarm of starving locusts, and all that kept them separated from the swarm were the walls of the building.

Rhiannon stood silently mesmerized by the light show swirling through the metal rafters above her head. Thor barked crazily, scooting back on his hind legs with every yelp. They had to get out of here now, before these things gathered themselves and realized that lunch was just a few meters below them.

Leaping from the truck, Emily grabbed Rhiannon by the shoulder and pushed her toward the door leading back to the staff room. She tried to yell "run," but her voice was drowned beneath the cacophony of thrumming and buzzing. Thor seemed to bark silently at the creatures, and she had to grab him by the collar and force him toward the door too.

They sprinted through the semidarkness, ghost-lit by the creatures' bioluminescence that turned the two humans and Thor into a weird stop-motion shadow.

A ball of light streaked past Emily's face like a bullet, its wings thrumming.

"Faster!" Emily yelled, not sure if Rhiannon could even hear her over the cacophony of sound.

Rhiannon reached the door first and flung it open, stopped, and held it ajar as Thor ran past her into the corridor. Emily's eyes met Rhiannon's and in that weird strobing flash between darkness and light she saw her face transformed into a mask of horror, her eyes glowing white with the reflected light of the swarm Emily knew was behind her. She felt the air change as the pressure wave of so many creatures moving as one washed over her. A part of Emily wanted to turn around and look—it was so tempting to just stop and see this astonishing thing that no human had ever witnessed before. Instead, she dove into the corridor headfirst. Thor yelped and leaped over his mistress as she slid across the polished floor, colliding with a wall. She managed to look up just in time to see Rhiannon pull the door into place, her muscles tensing as she grasped the door handle and leaned her body weight backward.

■ ■ ■

The thud of hundreds of the light bugs hitting the walls and door sounded like a mob of angry men smashing at them with baseball bats. Thank God the door closed inward, or they would have been overwhelmed in seconds, but there was no way to tell how long it was going to stand up to this kind of violence. A faint glow emanated from around the edges of the door, seeping in through the cracks.

"Emily!" Rhiannon cried. "What are we going to do?"

Emily's mind raced. The memory of the dream and the knowledge of just how massive the swarm actually was—it was petrifying. No way they could make a run for it; they would be overwhelmed before they even made it a few hundred feet from the building. And where would they go? Apart from the ghostly glow of the swarm, it was pitch black beyond the building. They would stumble around in the darkness, and the second they flipped on a flashlight the creatures would zero in on them, Emily thought, remembering how the swarm had converged on the light of Rhiannon's flashlight in her dream, and that had been from many kilometers away. The vehicle bay was already overrun with the creatures, making it impossible for them to make it to the truck. They needed some way to distract these little horrors away from the building, something that would hold the swarm's attention for long enough that the three travelers could get to the truck and make their escape.

Light, that was the key, but from where?

"Emily?" Rhiannon yelled, her knuckles white against the doorknob as she tried to maintain her grip. "What do we do?"

"Hold on," she snapped. The light bugs had stopped throwing themselves at the door—which, Emily thought, disconcertingly suggested a coordinated intelligence or, at least, a sense of self-preservation—but her voice was still only barely audible above the cacophony of thrumming wings that filled the vehicle bay.

"I need to think." What they needed was a lighthouse. But where would you find a lighthouse in the desert?

Perhaps if they managed to put themselves far away from this section of the building, out of range of whatever senses these little bastards possessed, it might buy enough time that the creatures would give up and move on, or at least give her time to formulate an escape plan.

"On the count of three, I want you to let go and run as fast as you can back to the middle office in the corridor, okay?"

Rhiannon nodded. Emily could see beads of sweat glinting on the girl's forehead.

"One . . . two . . . three!"

Emily waited for Rhiannon to pass her, stole a glance at the door to make sure it wasn't going to explode and let the creatures through, then took off after the teenager, Thor at their heels. They burst through into the waiting area where they had intended to spend the night, and, as soon as they were all through, Emily again set the chair against the doorknob. Through the windows, the light from the swarm lit up the entire perimeter of the building, almost as far back as the freeway. The swarm seemed to have focused its attention on the bay door, the glow of the mass throbbing like a heartbeat, elongating and shortening the shadows within the room. A lightning bolt zipped past the window, describing a perfect parabolic arc across the night and leaving a residual afterglow on Emily's eyes.

"Get to the office," Emily hissed when she saw Rhiannon had stopped. Three seconds later and Emily was following behind her.

They sprinted down the corridor toward the back exit, then cut right into the first office. Beyond the window there was only darkness. The creatures had not made it to the rear of the building—not yet anyway.

"What *are* those things?" Rhiannon demanded.

"How the hell should I know?"

"You're the one who said that they were coming, remember?"

"I . . . I don't know what they are, some kind of alien locust, but I know they're connected. Goddamn it, everything is fucking connected in this world. It's like everything talks to everything else. But these things, they communicate and they hunt together. They're like a giant shoal of land piranha."

"So, how do we stop them?"

"They're attracted to light, I think. When you turned on your flashlight to wake me, they saw that and headed right for it. So we need to create a distraction to draw them away from here to buy enough time for us to get to the truck and get the hell out of here."

"How are we going to do that?" Rhiannon asked, her voice despondent.

"Do you still have the flares you found in the minivan?"

Rhiannon rooted through her backpack and pulled out the two emergency flare sticks.

"Give them to me," Emily said, taking the two red cardboard tubes. She ran her fingers over them, inspecting each as best she could in the dim light. Hopefully they had not gotten wet to the point they would be useless. There was no way to be 100 percent sure; she was just going to have to hope they would work when the time came. She didn't think the flares alone would be big enough or bright enough to distract the swarm. It was going to take something much bigger than that.

Goddamn it, she was missing something. She searched her memory . . . something she had seen back on the road, just before they had spotted the building.

"That's it," she said, suddenly remembering.

"What are you going to do?" Rhiannon asked, her voice nervous now.

"I want you to stay here with Thor—"

"Why? What are you going to do?"

"—and close the door behind me when I leave. When the swarm leaves, I want you to run to the truck"—Emily pressed the truck keys into Rhiannon's hands and closed the girl's fingers around them—"then I want you to take it, and, if it's safe to do so, I want you to wait five minutes for me. Don't turn on the lights until you have to go, okay? If I'm not back in five minutes, I want you to drive away from here. Wait until it's light, and then I want you to head back to Point Loma, okay?"

"But what are you going to do?"

"When you get back to Point Loma," Emily continued, she didn't want to say "if you get back," but she knew the chances of the girl making it all the way back to California were slim at best, "then I want you to tell Valentine that I killed the guard when you were visiting me and that I kidnapped you, okay? You tell them anything you have to to stay alive. Keep your head down and stay out of trouble, but when Mac comes back, I want you to tell him everything, do you understand?"

Even in the dim light of the office, Emily could see the fear in the girl's eyes.

"Emily! What are you going to do?" Rhiannon said.

"Do you understand?" Emily insisted, and, when Rhiannon nodded, Emily continued, "Five minutes. You wait five minutes, that's all."

And with that, Emily headed for the back exit.

CHAPTER 15

"Jesus! What the fuck am I thinking?" Emily whispered to herself as she eased the rear exit of the building open just enough to be able to squeeze out into the night.

A halo of white light danced like the aurora borealis above the roof of the building. Pressing herself against the door, Emily prayed to whatever god might still be willing to listen to her that the swarm would not spot her; although, thankfully, they seemed preoccupied with assaulting the front of the building. She edged herself as tightly against the outer wall as possible and slinked as quietly as she could toward the western corner of the building.

The otherworldly glow of the swarm made shadows jump and leap across the parking lot, a constant distraction in Emily's peripheral vision. For what she had planned, she was going to have to reverse her route back up toward the hill and the jam of trucks they had passed on the way here. In her mind, she tried to replay the terrain they had crossed when they had first arrived—not that it really mattered, because first she was going to have to cut back diagonally away from the building and head deeper into the desert if she wanted to guarantee that she would not be spotted. She needed the darkness, but no matter which route she took there was going to be a stretch of ground where she would be vulnerable to being sensed by the swarm.

The air was filled with the thrum of wings, like tiny chainsaws. The sound of the swarm resonated and echoed across the desert, fading and growing like a sea of sound. It was actually quite beautiful, Emily thought, terrifying but entrancing.

She sucked in three quick breaths, aimed for the nearest, darkest shadow she could see, and on the third breath, began sprinting away from the building.

"Don't fall. Don't fall," she repeated under her breath as she ran, her eyes fixed on the darkness, but her brain fascinated by the length of her shadow as it extended in and out with each swell of the swarm.

And then she was flying. Her mind registered the impact of her toes on the raised concrete curb surrounding the parking lot a split second before she hit the ground, the wind knocked from her lungs as effectively as if she had received a boot to the stomach. She lay facedown, feeling the silky softness of the alien grass against her hands, the wet splatter of mud across her face as she panted for each painful lungful of breath.

A second passed. Then another second and a third, delineated only by the thumping of her heart and the thrumming of the light bugs. She opened her eyes and could see nothing; she had fallen into the arms of darkness, and it embraced her willingly. Emily allowed herself a few more seconds to regain her breath, then sluggishly rolled over until she was facing back toward the depot.

The swarm looked gaseous, like a living white cloud of light pulsating around the silhouette of the building. It was breathtakingly beautiful, like the northern lights rendered into flesh and given wings. If she had been a God-fearing woman, it would have been easy to believe these were angels . . . but she had seen what they really were, had ridden with them across the darkened plain, sensed their desire, felt their hunger. She knew their intentions. These were no angels.

She *had* to get moving.

"Shit!" Emily hissed as her hand flew to the pocket where she had stashed the two flares. "Shit! Shit! Shit!" She could only feel the outline of one of them. She pushed her hand into the pocket and confirmed the worst: one of the flares must have fallen out when she took her spill. She rolled onto her side and began blindly feeling around for the missing flare. Could she could risk turning on her flashlight briefly? Absolutely not, she decided instantly. That brief flash of light would be like a sonar ping to the swarm, and they would be on her in a moment. She would just have to keep trying to find it with the light they cast.

Minutes later, she resigned herself to the futility of wasting any more time looking. The flare was lost, but she still had the one. It was just going to have to suffice. She pushed herself to her feet, reoriented herself to where she thought her destination would be, and took a step.

She felt something beneath her foot give.

"You've got to be fucking kidding me?" She knelt down and moved her hand to beneath her foot and felt the outline of the missing flare. Her boot had pushed it deep into a pool of muddy water, and, even as she wrapped her fingers around the cylinder, she already knew it was pointless; the hard cardboard wrapper was soaked through already, and her fingers pushed through into the interior of its rotten guts. She flung the remains away into the night, trying to resist the urge to scream her frustration. There was nothing to be done about it now. She was just going to have to make do with what she had. Besides, the chances of success were small, she knew that already. But if her plan did not succeed, she was going to try and make a big enough distraction that at least

Rhiannon and Thor would be able to escape. It would give them a chance at survival, even if it was only a minimal one at best.

Emily headed deeper into the darkness, walking as quickly as she felt safe to. She began counting off in her head—one one thousand, two one thousand—a trick Mac had taught her to gauge her distance. When she thought she had reached a half-kilometer distance from the depot, she stopped and reoriented herself, using the light of the swarm to judge her position.

"My God!" she said, looking back the way she had come. The ground had risen a hundred meters or so, and now she was looking down on the depot and the swarm. It was like looking at a lake of silver light collected around the front of the building. The pool embraced the depot's front and sides and was gradually creeping over the roof, slowly swallowing it whole, like some amorphous snake.

Time was running out. At some point, the swarm was going to find a way into the building, and then it was only a matter of minutes before it discovered Rhiannon and Thor holed up inside.

She had to beat feet right now.

Reorienting herself toward the freeway, Emily started off at a brisk jog. Moving this quickly was a calculated risk that had to be taken. The sky was as black as the ground around her. The memory of the moon, distilled to nothing more than a smudge, glowed dimly overhead, the thick layer of cloud denying even its measly assistance to her. She kept going, putting one foot in front of the other. She was almost to the point of thinking that somehow she had managed to miss the freeway—*How the fuck do you miss a* freeway? her inner voice chided—when she felt the hard surface of the I-40 beneath her boots.

Exhaling a sigh of relief, she turned to the west and started up the freeway. She had no idea where she was in relation to where she wanted to be, but, as if the gods in all their capriciousness were finally willing to cut her some slack, even if it were only to prolong her agony, the clouds thinned sufficiently to allow a sliver of moonlight to bathe the ground. And in that light she saw the shadowed outline of twisted wreckage that had once been a tractor-trailer about five meters ahead of where she stood. The moonlight lasted a few seconds longer before being swallowed up by the cloud again, but it was long enough for Emily to see that she was almost on top of the crush of vehicles at the head of the line of rusting trucks that had led her to this place.

In the daylight it had been relatively simple to pick her way through the field of debris strewn across the freeway, but under the cover of night she was soon kicking and stumbling over pieces of metal and broken truck parts, slowing her search down considerably. By the time she had almost tripped and fallen headlong for the third time, her mind was made up: there was no way she was going to be able to find the truck she needed in such complete darkness. She was just going to have to risk turning on her flashlight.

Emily took a deep breath, pointed the flashlight uphill, and flicked it on. She played the beam of light over the nearest truck carcass; it rang no bells in her memory whatsoever, so she moved the light to her left and saw that she was about three trucks up from the jumble of twisted metal that had brought this convoy to a stop . . . and her heart seized.

A tributary of white light had broken away from the main body of the swarm and was now snaking its way diagonally toward her. It would be here in minutes.

It took all her willpower to turn her back on the approaching threat, but if she had any hope of surviving this situation, she was going to have to move her ass right now. It was pointless turning off the flashlight; the damage was already done. She played the beam off the side of the ruined trucks, searching for the wreck she was looking for as she jogged up the line.

No . . . No . . . No . . .

Then, there it was, the beam of her flashlight glinting off the side of its brushed aluminum tanker, the name "Bryant Gasoline" barely visible along its side. She ran to the tanker, glancing briefly back over her shoulder. Through the space between the trucks in front of her she could see the glow of the approaching swarm marching toward her like ghosts through the night. She had to hurry.

Of course there was more than enough of a chance that her plan was already doomed; the tanker could be empty, or the gasoline she hoped was inside could have long turned to sludge, or the flare might be useless.

But there was only one way to find out.

"Come on, come on. Where is it?"

Emily searched along the side of the truck and finally found the bank of three valves the driver would have connected the hose to when making deliveries to gas stations. Each valve had a metal handle pointing upward, the plastic grips brown and crumbling from exposure to the elements.

Looking back toward the depot, it was plain to see she had a couple of minutes at best before the swarm reached her.

I have to move fast.

Emily stepped to the side of the valves, away from where she guessed the gasoline, if there were any, would flow. She slipped the flashlight under her right armpit, clenching it tightly, then with both her hands free took hold of the middle handle and pulled downward. The handle was stiff, but she repositioned herself slightly in front of it and allowed her body weight to help in the effort. She felt the handle give, stepped back to the side, and pulled the handle toward the ground. Before the handle was horizontal, a thick stream of liquid gushed out of the valve and began to pool on the road, flowing down the incline of the road back toward the depot and the oncoming lights of the swarm. The unmistakable smell of gasoline reached Emily's nostrils almost immediately. If she had had more time she would have done a little jig; instead, she reached over the spurting stream of gasoline and pulled the second lever, but this one would not budge at all, so she quickly shifted her hands to the third, and, with a couple of short tugs, had that valve wide open too. Now a veritable lake of gasoline had begun to form on the ground around the tanker.

Emily felt her mind fuzz over for a second as she breathed too deeply from the vapors. Staggering, she fell lightly against the side of the truck.

She felt wetness against her leg. Pointing the flashlight down at her feet she saw both her boots and her jeans were now soaked in gasoline. *Shit!* She was going to have to be extra careful when she lit the flare.

The lake of gas flowed across both lanes and quickly spread beneath the tanker.

A flash of light zipping past her head made Emily realize she was out of time; the first of the swarm had arrived. It was now or never.

She reached into her pocket and pulled out the flare. Looking behind her, she spotted a mass of swirling lights only a couple of trucks away. Several of the swarm had broken away from the mass, flying out in front like scouts. One dived directly at her, barely missing her head, startling her enough that she dropped the flashlight to the ground. Before she could stoop and grab it again another of the light bugs made a beeline for her, forcing her to duck under the truck, putting the body of the tanker between her and the advancing creatures. She splashed her way through the pool of gasoline to the other side of the truck.

Another of the creatures flew under—the others seemed more interested in her flashlight—and headed straight for her, but its wing must have clipped one of the rig's metal struts, because it made an odd whirring noise and spiraled away to her right, bouncing off the ground until it was nothing but a rapidly dimming light in the darkness.

She scrambled out from under the tanker and began to run for the edge of the freeway, her hand grasping the flare as if it was all that stood between her and the devil himself. There was no way she was going to be able to perform the next part while she was moving. She forced herself to stop, the instinct to run overwhelming, and risked a look back at the tanker, which was about ten meters or so away from her now. The glowing creatures swirled around her flashlight, but some must have spotted her in the eerie glow of their light and were rising over the top of the tanker. Emily popped the plastic endcap off the flare, exposing the striker surface, and held her breath as she struck the flare across the igniter.

A bright-red bloom of light appeared at the end of the flare, turning the ground around her blood red, before vanishing behind a blossom of acrid smoke for a moment, then sinking back to a steady hissing red flame.

Jesus! It freaking worked. She had fully expected the flare to simply fail and was actually struck motionless for a second.

Now throw the damn thing!

She lobbed the flare overhand like a hand grenade, watched it arc through the air, spinning end over end until it hit the side of the tanker and dropped toward the pool of gas. Before the flare even hit the ground she saw the first flicker of blue flame as the gas vapors ignited. She allowed herself a second to watch as the flame quickly spread out across the pool, frying some of the creatures midflight. The flames spread quickly under the tanker toward the valves. The last image she saw before she turned and started sprinting back across the desert toward the depot building was a gushing waterfall of flame as the fire reached the trailer's valves.

Emily allowed herself a smile as she chased her shadow across the ground back toward the depot.

Couldn't have asked for a better re—

She did not hear the gas tanker explode; the shock wave had already hit her, and, for the brief couple of seconds before she hit the ground again, she was too concerned with figuring out how she had suddenly learned to fly.

■ ■ ■

Emily opened her eyes to a world of flame. All around her fire raged, and the acrid smoke of burnt fuel filled her nostrils.

She looked down her body. Someone's boots and jeans were on fire.

It took a few seconds for Emily's muddled mind to make the connection that it was *her* feet and *her* legs that were burning.

"Oh! Oh! Oh!" she hissed, flailing at the flames. The heat from the burning gasoline was already beginning to singe the hair of her legs through the thick denim. She began batting at her jeans, but all that did was scorch the soft flesh of her hands. She pushed her hands into the pool of cold, wet mud she had splashed down in, and began scooping up huge handfuls of it, slathering it over her burning clothes. Her flames died quickly. Not so for the hundreds of tiny fires that still burned around her.

Thirty meters from where she lay, where the tanker had been, a huge pool of fire now burned in the shattered remains of the tanker, a heavy plume of smoke rising up into the night sky, spreading southward. A mist of light flowed all around the inferno, dancing through the smoke and circling the fire like a sentient fog: the swarm. The ground was littered with charred and burning debris, more remains of the gas tanker, and probably several of the wrecks that had surrounded it. A stream of burning fuel still leaked from what was left of the rear portion of the tanker, running down the slope toward the depot.

The plan worked! Holy crap, it actually worked.

She had no recollection of what had happened after she'd thrown the flare and started to run; her plan had obviously worked a little *too* well. She looked down toward the depot and could only identify it by the reflection of the fire dancing in its windows. The swarm had left the building completely, the final stragglers zipping toward the burning wreck of the gas truck like earthbound shooting stars. The main body of the swarm seemed fascinated by the fire; they danced and weaved around it, the occasional unlucky one getting too close and falling into the flames. She could hear the pop of their bodies boiling and exploding in the heat as they fell to the ground, sizzled lumps of goo.

Emily eased herself to her feet, her legs still unsure they were willing to hold her up. She patted down the last smoldering spot on her jeans. She was *so* going to have to get a new wardrobe when all of this was finally over, she told herself.

The fire cast long shadows over the landscape, its light pushing deep into the surrounding darkness. Emily began to stumble her way back toward the depot, picking through the scattered fires that burned like tiny funeral pyres. By the time she reached the rear entrance of the building, her legs felt leaden and a dull pain, like she'd been punched hard, pulsed in the muscles of her right shoulder.

She was pretty sure she had lost consciousness, but there was no way for her to gauge exactly how long she'd been out. Long enough for the swarm to have made its way to the fire, at least. But that could have been minutes or half an hour. Either way, it would mean that Rhiannon would have followed her instructions and left in the truck with Thor. Emily had instructed her to head east and put some space between the swarm until daylight, then double back and try and make her way back to Point Loma. Rhiannon would have to come back along the I-40 eventually, so all Emily would need to do was stay on the road. They would inevitably run into each other at some point. She pushed through the rear door and headed straight to the office and was instantly blinded by the beam of a flashlight in her eyes.

"Emily!" Rhiannon yelled and ran to her friend, throwing her arms around her and hugging her hard.

"Are you kidding me? Do you *ever* follow my instructions?" Emily said, too exasperated and bone weary to do anything but speak.

"I couldn't," Rhiannon said. "I couldn't leave you here. I love you, Emily."

"I love you too," Emily said eventually and hugged her right back. "Now let's get the hell out of here."

CHAPTER 16

Emily led Rhiannon and Thor back through the depot.

"Let me take your flashlight," she asked Rhiannon at the door to the vehicle bay. "I lost mine out there." Pausing, she pressed her ear to the door, listening for any sign the swarm still waited beyond it. Hearing nothing, she eased the door open and swept the beam of the flashlight through the room.

The opposite side of the door, its wooden frame, and the wall it sat in were a cratered mess. Crushed bodies of the swarm were piled around the doorway like dead autumn leaves, and many more were scattered over the concrete floor.

"Stay away from that, Thor," Emily whispered as the malamute sniffed inquisitively at the bloodied pulp of a dead bug, prodding it with his nose. Emily stepped out into the bay. "Come on, stick close to me." They walked in single file toward the truck.

The windshield of the first dump truck looked as though someone had taken a baseball bat to it; squashed bugs were splattered across the windshield, bodily fluids streaked across the glass. More bodies lay around the tires of the truck, and Rhiannon gasped in horror when one of the creature's legs twitched convulsively as they passed it. Emily stopped any future movement with the swift application of the heel of her boot.

The other vehicles had suffered less damage, and their own truck just had a few dents and bangs; aside from a spiderweb impact crater that dripped a glowing blue ichor on the passenger side of the windshield, the damage looked minimal.

"Get in," Emily ordered Rhiannon, opening the passenger door while she scanned the shadows for any movement. When Rhiannon was safely strapped into the passenger seat, Emily made her way to the back of the truck and ushered Thor up and inside. Their gear was still where they had stowed it. She slammed the rear door closed and flinched as the echo reverberated around the silent room.

At the roller door, Emily began pulling the chain as quickly as she could, not caring how much noise she made at this point; they would be gone and on their way before the swarm could react to the sound anyway.

At the halfway point, she ducked her head under the opening and looked outside.

The gas truck still burned brightly back along the freeway, the swarm still apparently entranced by the flames. Good. When the door was fully retracted, she kicked as much of the broken glass out of the way of the tires as possible and jogged back to the truck. She was about to climb up into the driver's seat when a blur of motion snapped her attention to the roof space.

It had probably been resting on one of the metal girders, she thought in the split second she had to register what was happening. The light bug swooped down from the ceiling like some kind of dive-bomber, its abdomen igniting suddenly within the darkness.

Emily instinctively batted at it with the hand holding the flashlight but missed, and it swept through the open door and into the truck.

Rhiannon screamed as the creature zigged and zagged inside, bouncing off the interior walls.

Thor snarled, flecks of foam flying from his mouth.

EXTINCTION POINT: GENESIS

Rhiannon screamed again, throwing up a hand to protect her face from the creature. It whirred around her head for a second, then dived at Rhiannon again, fastening itself to her wrist with its tentacles, its wings wrapping around her arm in an unwanted embrace.

Rhiannon screamed again, this time in shock and pain.

Emily lunged into the cabin, but, as her hand reached for the bug, the creature released Rhiannon's wrist and headed toward Emily's face . . . only to disappear in an explosion of glowing blood as Thor plucked it from midair and shook it to pieces between his jaws.

"Shit! Holy shit! Rhiannon, are you okay? Let me look," Emily said, leaning in to inspect the girl's arm.

"It bit me," Rhiannon said, hot tears spilling down her face, her voice full of anger and disgust rather than fear.

"Give me your arm." Emily unfastened the buttons of Rhiannon's shirt cuff and rolled the sleeve up to her elbow. There was a single puncture wound just above the inside of her wrist. A spot of blood had welled up and now trickled down the girl's arm.

"Ow, ow, ow," said Rhiannon, her fingers rubbing at the spot.

"Quit rubbing it and let me take a look." Emily shined the flashlight on the wound and saw that in the seconds since the bug had bitten Rhiannon the wound had swelled and reddened deeply, but the bleeding looked like it had stopped, at least.

"It's okay," Emily said. "How do you feel?"

"It stings a lot," Rhiannon said, "but I don't think it—"

Rhiannon's body curved like a bow, her arms snapping to her side, her head arcing backward as the seat belt engaged, the only thing, Emily realized, that stopped her body from flying from the seat as a convulsion exploded through Rhiannon's muscles. The girl's jaws clamped shut, and Emily saw a thin splatter of blood—*Oh God! Oh God, please, please, no*—fly from her mouth. Her eyes rolled back into her head, and a low hiss, like escaping gas, whistled from between her clenched teeth.

"Rhiannon?" Emily yelled, taking the girl's shoulders with both her hands. Rhiannon was completely unresponsive, her back arching, then relaxing slightly before snapping back against the seat belt again. "Rhiannon!" Emily yelled again, but there was not a damn thing she could do to help her.

Outside, Emily saw a sudden shift in the light of the swarm as it broke away and began to head back in their direction, the truck's headlights finally too much for them to resist.

What do I do? she wanted to yell, but there was no one and nothing that could help her right now.

Rhiannon's body convulsed once . . . twice . . . then sank back into the chair like a deflated balloon, all her muscles limp, her head lolling toward her chest.

"No, no, not again, Goddamn it, not again," Emily repeated as her fingers checked for a pulse against the girl's throat. She exhaled a sigh of relief when she felt the slow but steady pulse of Rhiannon's heart and saw the shallow rise of her chest.

Rhiannon was alive, but if Emily wanted them all to remain that way, then she had to get them out of there right now.

Sliding back into her seat, Emily pulled her door shut and slipped the truck into drive, edging out of the bay. Her attention was split between the unconscious body of Rhiannon slumped in the seat next to her, navigating a route to the freeway, and the glowing cloud of the swarm advancing rapidly across the half kilometer or so of open terrain still separating them. Multiple strands of the swarm extended into the air in front of the main body like antennae, probing ahead for something they knew was there but seemed unable to pinpoint.

"Hold on," Emily said, stealing a glance at Rhiannon's motionless body. Flipping on the high beams lit up the landscape ahead of them like it was day. She might just as well have painted a target on the truck, because the swarm instantly began to accelerate toward the vehicle. The road leading from the depot to the freeway was broken and uneven, and Emily had to resist the urge to just floor the accelerator and pop another tire.

"Come on. Come on," she mumbled to herself as she navigated the truck over a slab of road forced up almost a quarter meter by a tangle of plants. The swarm was picking up speed now, and Emily could sense its collective excitement as it closed the gap with its prey.

The headlights illuminated the freeway ahead of her, the road in front of them clear. She pressed the accelerator pedal hard and felt the supercharged engine kick in. The truck's front tires found the freeway, its rear tires momentarily losing traction, fishtailing the rear end of the vehicle until the tires caught again and the truck lurched forward onto the I-40. Emily swung the truck in a wide semicircle until the nose pointed toward the east.

The first few scouts of the swarm rocketed alongside her window, dodging in front of the truck, the rest of the swarm only seconds behind them now.

Emily pressed the accelerator all the way to the floor, and the truck roared. In the rearview mirror the light of the swarm began to recede into the distance. Emily checked her speed; she was going a smidgen under eighty. Her eyes flicked to the rearview mirror again; she had already put a half kilometer between them and the swarm, but the tenacious little fuckers were still following. She forced herself to breathe deeply; her concentration *had* to remain on the road. At this speed, if there was anything in the road she was going to have a matter of seconds to react.

Ten minutes later, Emily began to ease her foot off the gas pedal, allowing the needle to gradually drop to thirty. In the mirror, there was nothing but night. The glow of the swarm had disappeared completely.

• • •

With the threat of the swarm far enough behind them, at least for now, Emily pulled the truck over to the side of the road, left the engine running, and leaped out. She sprinted around to the passenger side and pulled the door open.

Rhiannon was deathly pale, slumped forward, her arms hanging loosely at her sides. Emily checked for a pulse; it was there but slow and weak. Gently lifting the girl's injured arm to the light, Emily examined the bite or sting or whatever the fuck it was the bug had done to her. Memories of another time, with another child, tried to crowd into her mind. The bite mark on Rhiannon's wrist looked angry and inflamed, the dot at the center a dried scab of blood. Emily lifted first Rhiannon's left eyelid then her right with her thumb; they were both dilated, but at least they were no longer rolled back into her head. A good sign? Emily had no idea whether it was or not, because, if she were being perfectly honest, she had no clue what she was supposed to do. The light bug must have injected some kind of venom into Rhiannon when it bit her, because the reaction had been so damn fast. It had been almost a half hour since the attack, and she was still breathing, so that had to be a good thing, right? Maybe the swarm relied on multiple bites to kill its victims; maybe a single bite would simply render the victim immobile. She was still alive, so that meant there was hope.

The voice in her head tried to get her attention again: *Just like Ben was still alive, remember?*

Emily cursed under her breath and ran to the rear of the truck. She lifted up the cargo door, ushered Thor out, pulled the blanket and a sweater from Rhiannon's backpack, and pushed their gear farther back until it was up against the backseats. She ran back to the front. Unbuckling the safety belt from around Rhiannon, Emily slipped one arm under her knees and the other around her back and carefully lifted her limp body out of the seat. The kid felt like she weighed as much as a sparrow, if there had been any sparrows left, and her skin was cold, clammy with sweat. She carried Rhiannon's unconscious body to the rear of the truck and gently slipped her into the cargo compartment, resting her head against the rolled-up sweater, then pulled the blanket over her.

Emily took a step back from the truck and allowed herself to breathe. *Now what?* she wondered. She answered herself: *Now we wait.* That was all she could do: keep the kid warm and watch her as closely as she could . . . and if the worst-case scenario became a reality? Would she, *could* she, really do that again? Emily already knew the answer to that question: she would do whatever it took.

"Jesus!" Emily exhaled the word as though it had been caught in her throat for the last day. She leaned forward—sank, really— until her forehead rested against the window of the truck and allowed its coolness to sink into her skin. Maybe she could just stay like this, silent in this eye of the unseen storm she knew was whirling around her.

Thor's soft but insistent whine brought her back to the moment. He sat at her feet, looking up expectantly at his mistress.

"She's going to be okay," Emily said, not sure if she was reassuring the malamute or herself.

Thor watched her, his tongue lolling from his mouth until she reached down and scratched behind his ear. The thought of losing Rhiannon was just too painful to think about, but she knew that the kid's future was out of her hands now. Her only recourse was to watch over her and wait. And hope—she could still hope; there was still some of that precious liquid left in that shallow well.

Emily leaned her back against the side of the truck. She looked back in the direction they had come from; the very faintest glow of the fire still flickered there, but the western horizon was still clear of any sign of the swarm following them. To the east was another glow; the first rays of the morning sun, illuminating a sky peppered only with buckshot cloud and the promise of a day finally free of rain. There was nothing else visible around them other than the slightly swaying red weed.

The ache to keep moving toward her son tugged at her, but she had already decided that she was going to spend the next few hours here, watching over Rhiannon. She wasn't going to risk moving the girl, and, if she had learned anything since the red rain, it was that the resolution would come quickly, and this was as good a place as any to wait out whatever form that resolution might take.

Emily had to pee too. She found a spot a few meters away from the side of the road. When she was done, she checked in on Rhiannon. The kid looked the same, which Emily supposed was a good thing; at least she hadn't deteriorated. She let Thor back in the truck, then climbed into the passenger seat, locked the doors, and waited for the future to arrive.

■ ■ ■

"Em-uh-lee." The voice floated into Emily's sleeping mind as though blown there by a breeze. She opened her eyes, jerking awake, momentarily confounded as to why she was sitting in a vehicle in the middle of nowhere, unsure of whether she had heard or dreamed her name.

Outside the truck, full-fledged morning now surrounded them.

"Em-uhhhh-leeee." Rhiannon's voice, barely a whisper, drifted from the back of the truck. Emily whipped around in her seat and looked toward the back cabin. She couldn't see Rhiannon's prone body from where she sat, but she *could* see a pale arm waving back and forth beyond the rear seats like a wind-bent reed.

"Rhiannon! I'm coming," she called out, already out the door, then standing at the rear bumper in what felt like a second. She levered the hatchback up and climbed in beside a now-conscious Rhiannon, her eyes open, her pupils still dilated, though, Emily noted.

"Hi, how you feeling?" she cooed, her hand instinctively going to the girl's forehead. She was warm again and definitely had more color than before.

"Thur-stee," the girl replied weakly through cracked, dry lips.

Emily reached across Rhiannon to the backpack and grabbed a can of soda. She pulled the tab, slipping her free hand behind Rhiannon's neck. "Here," she said, lifting her head to the can.

Rhiannon drank deeply from the soda can.

While she drank, Emily snuck a look at the bite mark. The inflammation had all but vanished, and it was no longer quite as angry looking; now it was just slightly raised with the red dot at its center, like a bad mosquito bite.

"Oh my God, that tastes *so* good," she said after she had emptied almost half of it.

Emily could not contain her happiness and broke into a wide grin. "Any pain?" she asked, lowering Rhiannon's head back to the makeshift pillow, smoothing the girl's cheek with the backs of her fingers.

Rhiannon nodded slowly. "Head hurts and all my muscles feel really, really tired. Fingers have needles and pins."

"Do you think you're gonna be sick?"

Rhiannon shook her head. "Where are we?" she asked after she took a few more sips from the can.

"About twenty kilometers from the depot," Emily said. "You hungry?"

"Yes," said Rhiannon. "What time is it?"

Emily checked her watch. "About ten."

"At night? I slept a whole day?" Rhiannon said, her voice disbelieving.

"No, silly. Ten in the morning."

Emily saw the color drain from Rhiannon's face again. She pulled an arm from under the blanket and waved the hand in front of her eyes, blinking her lids exaggeratedly.

"I can't see," Rhiannon said matter-of-factly, as if she were simply delivering a line from a script. "Emily, I'm blind."

■ ■ ■

It took Emily a few moments to react. "What?" she said, not sure she had heard Rhiannon correctly.

"I can't see anything. It's all black." Panic had begun to creep into Rhiannon's voice.

Emily reached out and took Rhiannon's hand in hers. "It's alright. It's okay. I'm right here." Perhaps it was the simple accretion of problem laid upon problem, but Emily found herself surprised at how easy it was for her to accept this latest development in a long line of "hindrances and bothers," as her grandmother would label any kind of setback in her own life. In this world, things did not ever seem to get better—they only stayed the same or got worse.

Slowly Emily waved the flat of her left hand in front of Rhiannon's face. "You can't see my hand?"

"No," Rhiannon said, biting her lower lip to stop it from trembling.

"It's okay, it's all going to be alright." Emily's reassurances were just a distraction while her mind tried to process the situation. Perhaps Rhiannon's blindness was just a temporary affliction, a side effect of whatever poison that single minion of the swarm had injected into her. Or perhaps not. Perhaps it was permanent and Rhiannon would never see again.

And if permanent blindness was the worst-case scenario for Rhiannon, then by God Emily would take that, because the darkness in the back of her mind was already coming up with other ways—much, much worse ways—that this could have ended. Again Emily surprised herself with her level of fatalism. But, really, what could she do about any of this? Nothing. Not a Goddamn thing. The only option she had was to try to ensure that Rhiannon remained safe, and the only way to do that was to keep moving.

Emily reached across and squeezed Rhiannon's cheek with her hand. "It's okay, don't worry. It's probably just a temporary thing. Do you feel strong enough to stand?"

Rhiannon said, "Maybe."

"We're going to get you to the front seat, okay?" Emily backed her way out of the rear compartment and stood. She picked up the blanket, threw it over her shoulder, then reached back inside and took both of Rhiannon's hands. "Okay, scoot your butt forward. That's it, now you're on the edge of the tailgate, so just put your feet down and let me guide you."

Rhiannon did as she was told, and Emily led her unsteadily around the truck to the front passenger door and opened it. "Okay, left leg first," she said, guiding Rhiannon's foot up onto the footplate. "And up." She maneuvered the girl into the seat, placed the blanket over her body, and then fastened the safety belt. "Comfortable?"

"Yes."

Emily placed the can of soda in Rhiannon's hand. "Let me know if you need more."

■ ■ ■

The clouds that had dogged their journey since they left California were finally in full-on retreat, leaving only a few stragglers behind in an otherwise lonely blue sky.

Emily drove and Rhiannon slept for most of the next two hours. Emily couldn't tell if she was fitfully dreaming or in any discomfort, but every few minutes Rhiannon would groan and struggle against the restraint of the seat belt. A hand against her forehead or a stroke of her hand seemed to calm the girl until the next time.

The freeway was mostly clear of debris, and Emily found her mind beginning to drift as the thrum of the truck's tires against the hardtop lulled her into a meditative state; she was confident she would find her son, of that there was no doubt in her mind, but after that . . . ? What then? The future was opaque. They could go back to Point Loma, as long as she had Adam. The original charges against her would have to be dropped, but she knew that Valentine would be quick to level more accusations against her for the deaths of the two guards. She might be able to fight them too, with Rhiannon's help, but any semblance of a trial would be colored by Valentine's influence. And who knew if the woman had any more assassins willing to carry out her dirty work. Besides, all of that was a moot point anyway; she had no way of getting *back* to Point Loma. The red jungle lay between them and what had become home. Hundreds of kilometers deep, Emily had already learned her lesson of how deadly even a small sortie into it could be. The chances of them making it all the way back to California were all but nonexistent.

Of course, there was always Mac and the crew of the *Vengeance*. If there was just some way that she could contact him . . .

Rhiannon moaned and twisted in her seat. Emily's eyes flicked to her, her fingers mechanically reaching to take the girl's hand. Rhiannon settled again, her head resting against the leather back of the seat. Her arm was exposed, and Emily got a good look at the wound on her wrist, half expecting to see the same striations that had marked the transformation of her little brother. But there was nothing. The inflammation had all but subsided, leaving only the small red puncture wound marking her pale skin to show that anything had happened at all. And the blindness, of course.

It must have been some kind of nerve toxin, Emily thought. Like a spider bite, it was designed to paralyze, immobilizing the victim long enough that the swarm could overwhelm rather than outright kill. Still, Emily's mind kept returning to Rhiannon's brother, Ben, and how swiftly he had changed. But that did not mean the same was going to happen to Rhiannon.

Rhiannon stirred, yawning as she woke. She stretched both arms above her head, pressing the flats of her hands against the truck's roof, yawned again, and pulled the blanket back around her.

"Hi. How'd you sleep?"

"Okay. My neck's a bit stiff."

"Well, you were sitting kind of awkwardly," said Emily. She glanced over at her passenger . . . and stared, her heart suddenly grasped by an icy fist that threatened to squeeze it until it burst.

"Christ!" The truck had drifted almost into the center divider in the few seconds that Emily had been looking at Rhiannon. She yanked the wheel to the right, buffeting everyone inside, and slowed the truck to a stop.

"What is it?" Rhiannon said, panicked. "What's happening?"

Emily continued to stare at the kid. "Nothing . . . just something in the road," she lied.

Rhiannon relaxed and turned her unseeing eyes back toward Emily, eyes that were now nothing but red orbs staring out from Rhiannon's pale, freckled face. "I'm the one who's supposed to be blind," she said, mustering a convincing laugh to accompany the statement.

Emily took a shallow breath. "How are you feeling?" she said, attempting to sound as nonchalant as possible.

Rhiannon must have caught something in the tone of Emily's question. "Why?" she asked, suspicious.

"No reason. You feeling okay? No fever? Any pain at all?" She reached out a hand and laid it against Rhiannon's head. It felt normal.

Rhiannon pulled back. "Like I said, apart from a stiff neck, I feel okay. What's wrong, Emily?" The last three words were spoken with a tone that said she suspected Emily wasn't telling her everything. "Tell me."

"Nothing's wrong. Just checking you're okay, is all." Emily's feigned lack of concern was about as far away as possible from what she actually felt. It was unsettling to see those two blood-red orbs blindly looking back at her, but, apart from the physical change to her eyes, Rhiannon seemed perfectly fine. When Ben had been stung by the thing back in Stuyvesant, he had become sick soon after, quickly deteriorating as the venom swept through his body, changing him into . . . *something* that Emily did not want to remember. She leaned in closer to Rhiannon, looking over every inch of visible skin. There was no indication of change. In Emily's experience, nothing of the old world *ever* survived contact with this new world without changing in *some* way, even if it were only in some minor manner. So maybe *this* would be the extent of it, for Rhiannon. So many damn "maybes."

"What *are* you doing? I can feel you breathing on me," Rhiannon said, looking directly at Emily as if she could see her.

Emily pulled away. "Sorry, I was just reaching for your soda. Here." She grabbed the almost empty can and placed it in Rhiannon's hand.

"Thanks. Can we go now?" The kid obviously wasn't convinced, Emily thought. She sensed something was wrong. Emily almost told her then, but why worry her when there was nothing that could be done about it? And Emily knew Rhiannon well enough that if she had *really* wanted to know, then she would not have given up so easily. When the time was right, she would tell her.

"Sure," said Emily, sounding as upbeat as she could. She moved the gear stick into drive and pulled away.

She checked Rhiannon one final time and again was struck by the feeling of utter helplessness. There was *nothing* she could do for the girl, other than watch her and hope that there were no other changes.

But that at least was something she *could* do.

■ ■ ■

Emily did not realize she'd grown a lead foot until she swung the truck so sharply to avoid a tree sprouting from the right lane that she startled Rhiannon awake and sent Thor rolling into the side of the rear cabin.

"Emily? It feels like we're going really fast," Rhiannon said, both hands searching for her seat's armrests and grasping them tightly when she found them.

"What?" Emily checked the speedometer; it hovered just below fifty-five, much too fast for this uneven road. "Shit!" Her foot found the brake, and she slowed the truck down to a much safer thirty. "Sorry. You okay?" She placed the palm of her right hand against the girl's forehead. Her temperature seemed normal, perfectly normal if she were being honest.

"Mhmm," said Rhiannon, then, "What's wrong? Why were you driving so fast?" The girl might be blind, but she certainly couldn't be accused of being unobservant.

"Nothing," said Emily, then sighed. "It's Adam. That pull I told you about, for the last hour or so, it's gotten stronger. It's all I can do not to floor the accelerator."

"Do you think that means we're getting closer?" Rhiannon said, sitting up straighter.

"Yes." Emily's answer was as definitive as if Rhiannon had asked her to say the first word that came to her mind. She didn't even have to think about it. "It's almost physical," she continued, "like someone's grabbing hold of my clothes and pulling me, guiding me. I think we're really close now."

"Where are we?" Rhiannon asked.

Emily had no idea. She had seen no road signs during almost the entire journey, all victims of the great storm that had followed behind the red rain, she assumed. Beyond the cabin the scenery remained more or less the same as it had for the last however-many-hundred kilometers or so, but in the distance, near the northeastern horizon, Emily could see the black silhouette of a Titan tree forest curving away. There seemed to be more plant life around this area too. For the majority of the journey the vegetation had sprouted from between cracks in the road put there by lack of maintenance and weather. But here—wherever "here" was—the red tendrils had made their own holes, forcing their way through the blacktop. The tree she had swerved to avoid a few minutes earlier was a prime example. The level, almost turf-like fields of red weed on either side of the road they had started their journey with had now become more irregular and much, much taller, the occasional larger plant or red bush also putting in an appearance. It all meant one thing: somewhere close by, there had been an abundance of extra biological material, maybe a city or large town, probably near the forest of Titan trees she had spotted.

"I don't know where we are," Emily admitted. "If I had to guess, I'd say we're probably still in New Mexico, but we could be in Texas for all I know."

"Do you see anything at all?"

The rainstorm had moved on, leaving behind just a few large gray clouds to guard the sky and obscure the midafternoon sun. The land on all sides of the truck was pretty much laid out for the next twenty kilometers or so, and, apart from the cluster of Titans in the distance, the only thing that stood out was the absolute nothingness of this flat, empty land.

"Nothing," Emily said. "There are some trees, but that's about it." Her eyes kept creeping over to the silhouette of the copse of Titans, pulled there as though her peripheral vision sensed movement, but when she looked directly at it there was nothing but the solid shadowy outline of the densely packed forest.

She slowed the truck down to a crawl so she could get a good look at it without risking colliding with something in the road. The sun finally freed itself from the grasp of the clouds, lighting up the landscape.

"What's going on? Why are we stopping?" Rhiannon said, sitting upright in her seat like a gopher sensing danger as Emily leaned hard on the truck's brakes.

"There's something . . . hold on . . ." Emily exhaled the next word in a long breath, "Wow!"

"What?" Rhiannon insisted.

Emily had been mistaken; freed from shadow she could see the distant silhouette was not a forest after all. It was a Caretaker ship.

And it was huge.

CHAPTER 17

The truck sprayed a wave of gravel as it slid to a halt on the side of the freeway.

"I'll just be outside for a second," Emily assured Rhiannon, laying a hand on the girl's knee, never taking her eyes from the Caretaker ship. She was outside before Rhiannon could reply. The clean, warm air should have been refreshing after so many hours cooped up inside the cramped cab of the truck, but Emily did not notice it. What she did notice was how bright the sun was, straining her eyes until a deep furrow appeared between her eyebrows. Sunglasses had been the last thing on her mind when fleeing Point Loma, but right now she kind of wished they had made the list. Her hand made a decent enough shade, but a pair of Ray-Bans would have done the trick a lot better right about now.

The Caretaker ship was maybe three kilometers away, Emily estimated. She had thought the structure was shadowed, but as her eyes slowly became accustomed to the brightness she could see it was actually ebony black and convex. It was difficult to judge the exact size of the ship from this distance, the space between here and there filled with tall vegetation, but it was big, really, *really* big . . . and obviously not man-made. There were what looked like tubes or roots sprouting off its sides, but it was almost impossible to pick out any real detail at this distance.

This was where they were keeping Adam. She knew it, could feel it with an intensity that felt like electricity in her gut. And if she had needed more proof that this was the destination she had been drawn to, each time she turned to face the ship she felt the constant pull increase like short, sharp tugs against every molecule she was made of.

Shhhhssshuck! The sound of the truck window dropping brought Emily's attention back to Rhiannon.

"What can you see?" Rhiannon said. Thor's head poked out from between the front seats, his eyes bright with the possibility of an excursion. "Is it there?"

Emily looked back at the ship and described what she saw.

"You're going to have to leave me here," Rhiannon said when Emily was finished.

"Yes," said Emily. She stepped in close to Rhiannon's open window and placed her hand on the girl's arm. "But I *will* be back. I promise." Emily checked her watch; it was just after midday. She had a good six or so hours of daylight if she left soon. She couldn't make out any sign of a road leading out to the ship ahead of them; it was basically in the middle of nowhere. She could try and drive the truck to it, but if it had been raining even half as hard here as it had during their trip, then the ground would be waterlogged and muddy. It wasn't worth the risk of getting their only means of transportation stranded. But that would mean leaving the truck, and Rhiannon, here alone. Not an option she was happy with, but she saw no other way around it.

"I can't take you with me. But I'm going to leave Thor here with you, so you don't have to worry, okay?"

Rhiannon nodded. There was no mention of the fact that if Emily did not come back, then Rhiannon was as good as dead. Locked in her permanent darkness, the probability was that she would not survive the night if Emily did not make it back to the truck. Emily pushed the thought aside. She *was* coming back, and she *was* going to get them all home.

"Bring him back," Rhiannon said. Emily felt her love for this kid, this young woman, grow.

"I will. I promise." Emily leaned in through the door window, took Rhiannon's right hand in her own, and guided it to the water bottle and a couple of protein bars she had pulled from her bag. "And your pistol is here," she said, moving her hand to the butt of the PPQ she had placed on the seat between Rhiannon's knees.

Emily moved over to the driver's side. "Thor! Here," she said, tapping the driver's seat. The dog hopped over and sat quite happily in the seat.

"And Thor is right here," Emily said. Thor licked the girl's hand as Emily guided it to his head. "He'll be here to keep you safe, okay?"

Again, Rhiannon nodded, biting her bottom lip.

"I'll be right back."

Emily had already taken two steps toward the ship, but she still heard Rhiannon whisper, "Don't be long."

■ ■ ■

Emily stepped off the road and into the field of red weeds. She hadn't walked more than twenty paces before she knew she had made the right decision not to bring the truck; the ground was muddy—not as bad as they had encountered back at the depot, but the mud still sucked at her boots, slurping wetly with each step she took.

The day was beautiful now. The few clouds had moved almost to the horizon, the sun warm against her back as she trudged across the open plain toward the Caretaker ship. It could have been a nice leisurely walk on a Sunday afternoon if weren't for the incongruous slash of silver arcing from the horizon, the Caretakers' ring, tattooed across her world's sky. She barely had to move her head to spot the glowing arc of this anomaly that now circled the Earth, shining almost as brightly as it did against the backdrop of the sky at night.

Ahead of Emily, the silent black outline of the Caretaker ship waited. And somewhere inside it was her son. She knew that for a fact now; it was an unflinching certainty, confirmed by the magnetic tingle that grew with each new step she made toward it.

Answers! She needed answers to all of . . . *this*. And that ship was where she was going to find them.

The red vegetation came up to her waist. She pushed through it as though it were corn, her hands trailing at her side. There was no sound other than the dry rasp of the plants moving against her clothing.

A kilometer closer and the truly monumental size of the ship or structure—she was unsure which of them this thing actually was—had become apparent. It sat in a circular crater, the walls of which were maybe fifteen meters high and rose sharply. From where Emily stood, it looked as though the crater surrounded the craft quite snugly. The part of the ship visible above the crater was also circular, with a domed top similar to an inverted saucer. Whatever material made up the outer skin of this machine, it was abyss-black and nonreflective. It seemed to absorb the light of the sun, sucking it into itself so that even the air around it seemed dimmer, darker somehow. The closer Emily got to it, the more she felt as though she were staring into the deepest, emptiest region of space, as though the Caretakers had taken whatever material made up a black hole and then forged it into this craft.

The tubes she had seen from the road resolved themselves into huge black tendrils that looped over the lip of the crater, pushing deep into the soil out to about twenty meters around the circumference of the crater. They looked like giant worms intertwined around each other, similar to the roots of the Titan trees but extending much farther out and far less biological in their appearance.

A light sweat had begun to form on Emily's brow. She stopped and wiped it away with a dirt-stained hand. The urge, the constant pull toward Adam, was now a drumbeat that resonated through every cell; it was not a bad thing, pleasant even, and the closer she got to the craft the more the sensation became satisfying like a scratched itch. Standing here, with the sun shining warmly over her body and the odd, yet not unpleasant, smell of the plants and wet soil filling her senses, was . . . comforting. Almost hypnotic in how it lulled her senses.

Almost a full kilometer separated her from the craft. The Caretakers undoubtedly knew exactly where she was, had likely tracked her journey this entire time. She already knew they could simply pluck her from the air when they wanted to. They probably expected her to sit and wait for them to bring her to them, but fuck that. She highly doubted that they would simply allow her to walk up to their craft, knock on their front door, and demand her son back. So, she decided, that was *exactly* what she was going to do.

The Caretakers had summoned her here for a reason. *They* had kidnapped Adam. *They* had somehow hijacked the psychic connection between her and her son, compelling her to come here. *They* had a plan. *They* wanted something from her.

Well, she wanted something from them too, and fuck them if they thought she was going to simply stand here and wait for them to come and pluck her up.

She strode toward the crater surrounding the ship.

• • •

The sides of the crater turned out to be steeper than Emily had thought—almost sheer, in fact. She circled around the base, looking for the easiest route up through the tangles of tendrils that roamed over its embankment. When she finally found what looked like a good spot for entry, Emily took hold of one of the smaller tendrils and, using it like a rope, began to climb hand over hand, her feet slipping in the loose dirt of the crater's side. It took her five minutes to reach the top. Sweaty and dirt-stained, she swung herself up onto the lip of the crater.

"Ho-lee shit!" she exclaimed, looking out at the craft. It was mind-bendingly huge. You could probably fit six football fields on top of it and still have space to spare.

It sat at the center of the crater. This crater was far more compact than the long, scarlike rut caused by the crashed ship in Las Vegas. It was as though this machine had burrowed straight down into the ground.

The visible part of the ship was at least five, maybe even seven, stories high. It was hard to tell exactly because of the chaotic mesh of tendrils that crisscrossed each other like the roots of some giant plant. They varied in size, some as thin as her pinky finger, the largest over a meter and a half in diameter.

The roof—truth was, it could have been the base for all she could tell—of the craft was convex, curving slightly from the highest point at the center down to the edge. The edges were sharply defined lines, about ten of them. Whatever the material was that made up the outer skin, it certainly was not any kind of metal she was familiar with.

There was a gap all around between the farthest edges of the ship and the crater. From what she could see, it extended down the side of the ship before the sunlight could not penetrate any further, leaving a space of about a half meter. More tendrils extended out through that space before disappearing into the wall of the crater. The roof area seemed clear of sprouting tendrils, other than around the edge where she now stood. The exposed surface was pitted with dimples every few meters. Emily saw pools of liquid reflecting in the afternoon sunlight within them. She leaned out across the gap and scooped a handful from the nearest pool in the ship's flesh, brought it to her nose, and sniffed it, then touched it to her lips. It was water. Nice and clean too. She drank what was in her hand, then scooped another into her mouth before using the water from the next dimple to clean away the grime and dirt from her hands and face.

The shape of the ship struck a chord in Emily's memory: it looked like a nerve cell, the myriad tendrils thrusting deep into the ground like the dendrites that transmitted impulses to the cell.

Emily began walking along the edge of the crater. The ridge was quite loose and the dirt tumbled away down both sides as she walked, so she leaned one hand against the roof of the ship for balance. She skirted around the edge of the pit, looking for some kind of an entrance but found nothing obvious. At this rate it was going to take her forever to get all the way around.

"Okay then," she said to no one in particular, then leaped across the gap and onto the roof of the ship. At least this way she wouldn't have to worry about falling off the edge of the crater.

Emily began to search for an entrance, looking for any kind of anomaly on the surface. The gradient of the roof was so gradual that she could see quite a bit of the ship, but it was still going to take more time than she was willing to spend to search its great expanse. She worked her way carefully up to the apex of the ship's roof. From there she looked down, turning in place until she had prescribed a full circle. Still no sign of an entrance. She had wasted the good part of an hour before she was certain there was no way she was getting inside through the roof.

She was just going to have to go down into the gap between the ship and the crater and find a way in from there.

Emily jogged back across the roof to the crater. The gap between the edge of the craft and the rim of the crater was too tight for her to squeeze through. She knelt down near the edge of the roof and began scooping dirt away with her hands, tossing it back down the slope. The dirt was not that hard, and it had been a *long* time since she had received anything even vaguely resembling a manicure, so she wasn't particularly upset when she broke two nails within the first couple of minutes.

When she finally scooped out a big enough space for her to safely slip through, she pulled out her flashlight and shined the light down into the darkness below. The space seemed to widen as it got deeper, as though the sides of the crater went straight down, while the body of the Caretaker ship tapered away, so the farther down she went, the more room there was to maneuver. Tendrils extended out from the body of the ship, crisscrossing each other in a wild tangle within the gap, but there looked to be enough room for her to squeeze through. She would use them like rungs on a ladder, she decided.

About four feet down, Emily spotted a tendril that looked like it would bear her weight; she swung her legs over the lip of the ship, flipped around, and used her arms to lower herself down until her feet touched its thick body. Still holding onto the lip of the craft with both hands, she crouched and examined the surrounding area, plotting a route down into the pit. There was enough light for her to see about ten meters or so down before the rest of the ship was swallowed by darkness.

Okay, deep breath, and let's do this.

She reached out, took hold of a nearby vinelike tendril . . .

. . . rustling through tall red grass. Fear gripping her heart as something huge exploded out of nowhere, teeth dripping with saliva, jaws closing around her neck . . .

. . . and promptly released it as if she had grabbed a live electrical line.

Emily screamed, instinctively ducking away, her hand grabbing for the lip of the ship again as her foot shifted and she almost slipped.

What . . . the . . . fuck . . . was . . . that?

Her heart hammered in her chest, her system flooded with adrenaline.

Jesus!

It felt as though she had woken from the worst, most vivid nightmare of her life. It took a while to convince herself that she was actually alone; the experience had been so terrifyingly real.

Okay, so, obviously that was fucking freaky, she thought as she steadied herself against the ship. But the similarities between her dreams and this—whatever you wanted to call it—were unmistakable. Touching that tendril had connected her somehow with that creature—*lunch, that creature had been lunch,* the darker side of her mind filled in. The question now was: Would she go through the same experience every time she touched one of these tendrils?

Emily reached out and tentatively placed the tips of her fingers against the same tendril, ready this time for . . .

. . . water all around her. Waves rippling across the surface far, far above her head as she slid through the sea toward a darkened mouth of a cave . . .

. . . anything. This time the experience had been distant, as though she were observing it, watching rather than participating.

Maybe being prepared for it gave her some control over whatever process she was connecting with?

She reached out a third time, steeling herself for what would come, and . . . found only the warm, uncomfortably fleshlike texture of the tendril beneath her fingers. It was as though touching it had established some kind of tie to whatever creature she had found herself linked to, just like in her dreams; but, this time, she'd been awake, and the sudden switch between her reality and that of whatever was on the other end of the connection had been far more jarring. Either the effect had worn off each time she touched the tendril or being aware and ready for it had reduced its influence. Whatever it was, she didn't have time to think about it right now; she had to find a way inside.

Emily lowered herself down the embankment, dropping a few feet into the concavity of the pit, her feet resting on a thicker tendril, then she tentatively reached out her hand for another. Thank God, there was no sensation other than the disconcerting fleshy warmth of whatever material it was constructed from. She had dropped another five meters or so deeper into the pit before realizing that the sense of constant pulling she had felt almost from the second Adam had vanished, that had only grown more amplified the closer she got to this machine, had disappeared.

She stopped for a second and caught her breath. It was getting warmer the farther down she climbed. She wiped sweat from her eyes as she rummaged back through her memory of the last ten minutes, searching for the last time she had felt Adam's pull. It had been the moment she had felt the shock of that first connection, she was sure. Her heart skipped a beat at the thought of what that could mean. Had something happened to Adam, or did it have something to do with the link that she had established? Had she somehow shorted out the connection between her son and her?

Absurdly, now that the constant pull had left her, her need to find Adam had only grown stronger, more urgent. While it was there it meant she was still connected, could still feel her boy, but its passing left a hole that was quickly filling up with panic and fear.

Keep moving. You must keep moving, she told herself. If she stayed still, the panic she felt swelling up like a high tide would drown her, and that would be it for all of them.

Emily pulled her flashlight out again, directing its beam down and around her. The outer skin of the craft was just about a meter away from her. It stretched down another fifty meters before disappearing beyond the limits of her flashlight. She eased herself across a section toward the body of the ship. The outer skin was a sheer surface, no sign of those pockmarks she had seen on the exposed top—or bottom, she still wasn't sure which—of the craft. She reached out and lightly placed the flat of her hand against its skin, half expecting that same shock of displacement from her body into another.

Nope, still here. But she did feel a slight electrical tingle run up through her fingertips. She braced herself for another vision, throwing the crook of her arm around the nearest tendril, so she wouldn't slip and fall if her consciousness was suddenly relocated to some new creature. A second more passed and she was still exactly where she should be. She pulled her hand away, confused.

Keep moving, she told herself.

Emily began to use the tendrils to move laterally around the circumference of the craft, looking for any clue of an opening. Her arms and legs were already beginning to ache from the exertion of climbing down through this tangled jungle of tubes, and the warm air was not making it any easier.

By the time another hour had passed, Emily's spirits were almost as exhausted as her muscles. She dropped down another level and began the same route around the ship again. The body of the craft began to taper inward, but the farther down she climbed the thicker the jumble of tendrils grew, and by the time she had carefully maneuvered herself down another two meters, she could see that there was no chance she would be able to progress any lower than this. The tendrils were thick enough that she could use them as a bridge if she were careful not to catch a foot and twist an ankle.

Emily began to follow the body of the craft again, looking for the elusive doorway or even a way to drop down farther beyond this barrier growing out of the ship, her frustration increasing with every step she took. By the time she had prescribed another full circle around the perimeter, her anxiety had brought her close to tears.

It was simply unfair. There was nowhere left to go. No sign of any way inside the ship.

Emily pummeled her fist against the skin of the Caretakers' craft. Despite its fleshlike surface, it was as solid as metal and just as impermeable. Not even an echo from it, just the dull thud of solidity.

"Goddamn you! Open up. Open up!" she yelled, her voice echoing in the darkness.

She sat down heavily on a tendril. Uncomfortably warm. Exhausted. Out of ideas.

That was it, then. Not that she had ever actually had a plan, but she had at least been able to anticipate getting here. But how was she supposed to have known the Caretakers would not let her in? She'd made the assumption that she would either be able to walk right in to the craft or that the Caretakers would be waiting for her. Having the bastards simply ignore her had never even crossed her mind.

"Fuck!" she yelled, venting her frustration to the slit of sky high above her head, past the mesh of tendrils, and into the heavens.

And that was when the knowledge of exactly what she was going to do overtook her.

Her child was inside that thing, and if the Caretakers were trying to keep her away from him, well, fuck them! They had taken almost everything that she had ever loved from her, so she would be damned if she let them keep her son from her.

Emily directed the beam of her flashlight upward, scanning the levels of thicker tendrils above her. She quickly spotted one about halfway to the surface that would suit her needs just fine.

Pulling the knife Mac had given her from its sheath on her ankle, she placed it between her teeth and began to climb toward the light.

CHAPTER 18

It was the perfect candidate for what Emily had in mind. The tendril jutted out from the side of the ship, and disappeared into the ground with a barely perceptible curvature. Its circumference was as thick as an oil drum. The only problem was that there was no way she was going to be able to climb to it directly.

She had chosen this particular tendril because it was one of the only ones with an exposed area surrounding it. She was going to need that space to work. It looked strong enough to support her if she could reach it, but there was only one way to be absolutely sure. Emily climbed up another tendril two meters above her target, took hold of one of the smaller ropelike tendrils hanging loosely between the ship and the wall, tested it would hold her weight, and then jumped.

She swung out once and almost made it across the distance separating her from the big tendril, the tips of her boots touching it, but she had underestimated the distance and had not given herself enough of a boost; she swung back to her perch. The second time she pushed harder and overshot . . .

"Ooomph!" she exhaled hard as she collided sideways with the ship, the knife still between her teeth. She began to swing back, but her body had twisted so her back was toward the target. She was going to have to guess . . .

Oh shit! Oh shit!

She let go . . .

Emily dropped through the air, praying she had judged her timing correctly. Her feet hit the curved skin of the tendril and immediately slipped out from beneath her. She teetered for a second, her arms flailing wildly, her feet trying to get some kind of purchase on the slippery skin of the tendril but finding none.

She fell . . . Her hands brushed against a thin vine. She grabbed on and allowed herself to hang there, her legs dangling over the hundred-meter drop to the bottom of the pit. Her teeth hurt from biting down so hard on the metal blade of her knife. No way was she going to lose that.

Emily grunted as, hand over hand, she began to pull herself up the tendril. It was only a matter of a meter or so, but by the time she threw a foot up onto its thick, slick body and shimmied herself to safety, her shoulders ached and her forearms burned like nobody's business. She lay on her back against the flesh of the stalk, panting hard from the exertion, regaining what strength she could.

Emily carefully maneuvered herself to a sitting position, then swung her right leg over the tendril's body, straddling the tube as if it were a horse, facing toward the body of the ship. She plucked the knife from between her teeth, careful to keep a strong grip on it, and then dropped her torso to the tendril until her cheek was flat against its warm skin. From the interior she could feel a deep, thrumming pulse, like a distant heartbeat thumping against her inner thighs.

Slowly she reached her right arm around the tendril. Its circumference was too wide for her to get all the way around, but she figured it should work anyway. She pointed her blade back up toward the bottom of the stalk, took a deep breath, and plunged the blade deep into the flesh of the tendril. She plunged her knife in, pulling toward herself as hard as she could.

There was a hissing sound like gas escaping from a balloon as the knife sliced through the fleshy bottom of the stalk. Something wet, warm, and slimy dripped over her fingers.

Oh sweet Jesus, that reeked.

Emily fought her gag reflex. Whatever gas was escaping from the core of the tube stank like decaying vegetables. She prayed silently to any god that might still have an interest in the world that, whatever this stinking gas was, it wasn't toxic. A minute passed and the hissing finally began to slow. Thirty seconds later and it stopped completely.

Emily allowed herself to breathe again. Now for the difficult part.

She began sawing with the blade, cutting a slit in the flesh. More liquid began to spill out, pleasantly warm against her hand.

Emily's shoulders, biceps, and forearms were soon burning with an intensity she had not felt in years, but she was making headway. She allowed herself a moment's rest, then began that sawing action again. When she estimated she had sliced a good meter along the length of the tendril, Emily began to draw the knife in a gradual arc up toward her on the top of the tendril.

Another twenty minutes passed and her arms now felt numb. She had to stop frequently or risk losing her knife from her aching fingers and wrist. When sensation finally returned, Emily began cutting a line parallel to the first back along the length of the trunk. When she was sure she was done, she sat upright and placed the knife between her thighs, massaging her aching right arm with her left hand until she got some kind of feeling back into it.

Emily checked her wristwatch. Three hours had passed since she had left Rhiannon and Thor. Darkness was drawing steadily closer, and if she did not get her ass into high gear, then she was condemning both of them to defending themselves against a hostile world that would have the upper hand. Emily sheathed the knife at her ankle. She slipped her right thumb into the cut and pulled, but the muscles on that side of her body refused to cooperate; she was just too tired.

Ignoring the pins and needles in her lower half, Emily moved to a kneeling position, wobbling slightly, her jeans offering little grip on the sheer surface of the tendril's skin. She tightened her grip and pulled as hard as she could.

She felt the skin give a little.

She tried again with the same minimal result.

What she needed was more leverage. Emily edged her body backward along the trunk until her feet touched the body of the craft, pushed her thumb deeper until the rough edges of the incision cut into the web of skin between her thumb and forefinger, and yanked *hard*.

A chunk of the tendril's skin came away in her hand and went spinning down into the darkness, the suddenness of it almost sending her right along with it.

Finally! She smiled at the minor victory, and thrust her fingers into the larger hole she had created and began tearing away chunks of the skin, tossing them into the pit below.

With an almighty *crack* the outer skin broke along the incisions she had made, and she pulled the large, curved piece of the tendril's skin away.

Fluid cascaded from the opening, spilling into the darkness like the intestines of some slaughtered animal. When the gush finally subsided, Emily looked over the ledge and into the hole she had created. The inside of the tendril was hollow as she had hoped. Rivulets of the goo she had felt flowing over her hand hung from the opening, dripping obscenely off the ragged edges. *God, does it stink*. She pulled back in spite of herself and took a couple of breaths of clean air.

There's no time left for nerves. Don't think about this, just do it.

Emily swung her head back over again and checked that her estimation had been correct: it looked good. She was going to have to be careful at the beginning for sure, and all that lay ahead was uncertainty, but, hey, these days, that was the best any of them could expect.

Emily took one final look up at the sky, took another long deep breath as though she were about to dive to the bottom of the ocean, swung her torso over the side until she was facing the doorway she had created, and slithered herself into the red darkness of the tendril.

CHAPTER 19

Emily managed to hold her breath for a little over a minute.

If the smell outside had been bad, inside the belly of the tendril was much, much worse.

When she finally sucked in a breath of the fetid air within the tube it instantly burned the back of her throat and mouth, turning them to sandpaper as the saliva dried up. She gagged, trying to resist the urge to vomit. Her eyes had teared up again almost the instant she crawled inside the gutted tendril, giving her sight a hazy distortion, as she elbow-crawled her way along the slime-covered floor.

Her eyes throbbed as she tried to blink back the constant stream of tears. The urge to wipe them was almost too much to resist, but her hands were coated in the same burning excretion, and getting that shit in her eyes directly would probably end up blinding her too. So she did her best to ignore the discomfort as she slid onward through the alien muck.

Her entrance into the shaft of the tendril had been close to the outer wall of the Caretaker craft. She estimated she had been crawling now for a good five minutes through this stinking mess—her watch was covered in the crap too, obscuring the dial—so she knew she must be well past the outer wall. She had no idea where this conduit would lead her, but she knew it must have some importance to the Caretakers, so it must go *somewhere*.

She just had to keep crawling.

There was no sign of anything even vaguely resembling an outlet or a valve or, preferably, some kind of a hatch. Just meter after meter of this shiny-sided tube leading farther into the guts of the craft.

Her flashlight illuminated the way ahead, but all she could see was more of the same red-tinged wall. It was like being on the inside of an artery.

Well, if she had her way, she would follow this thing all the way to whatever dark heart it was connected to and split the bastard wide open.

Elbow knee elbow. Elbow knee elbow. That was all that mattered. Move forward. The sides of the tendril were just a few centimeters from her face. A mucouslike substance covered every surface, oozing out of small pocks, scattered like pores along its surface. It was sticky and pretty fucking disgusting. The discharge slid down the walls and formed a pool of goop at the base of the tube.

A gradual warmth spread through Emily's hands and the knees of her jeans. The liquid she was sloshing through was getting warmer. She looked down at the puddle of red goo beneath her fingers, except it wasn't just a puddle anymore, and, where a few minutes earlier she had been able to clearly see her fingers, now the goo had risen to just above her wrists. And now that she was paying attention, the amount of the goo oozing out of the walls was increasing, quite quickly in fact. In the few seconds since she had noticed it, the level had risen another centimeter.

"Oh, that's just wonderful." Her voice sounded raspy, squelched within the narrow, wet confines of the tendril's insides, and she instantly regretted speaking as she inhaled more of the crappy air into her lungs.

Emily began moving faster, shuffling as quickly as she could, acutely aware of the rising level of the fluid. By the time she had travelled another ten meters, the goo was almost at her elbow. The tube was filling up again . . . fast. It made sense that the damage she had done to gain access to this tendril would not simply be ignored; it would be repaired, of course. Apparently, those repairs had now been made, and the tube was replacing the goo and gas she had let out when she had cut her way inside. There was no way to know how full the tube would become. It could be just a couple of inches or it could fill completely; either way, it was going to force her to do something about her predicament.

Emily shined the flashlight back down the way she had come; it was too far for her to go back, and, besides, if her entrance had already been sealed and repaired, retreating would be pointless. The light illuminated nothing but the red walls of the tube ahead of her. Looked like she was screwed whichever way she chose to go.

That left only one other way out, then. She unsheathed her knife again. Blade facing down, she plunged it into the flesh of the tendril in front of her and began slicing. She wasn't interested in making it neat this time; she just needed a way out, something she could squeeze her ass through.

It was a much easier job to cut this incision without having to work at such an odd angle. She simply grasped the handle of the knife with both hands and pulled backward, sawing as she went, tearing a slit in the floor of the tube that was beginning to feel more and more like a sarcophagus with every passing second. As if it were aware of her butchery, the tube began to fill with the goo even faster. Emily stopped for a second as she noticed the first few centimeters of the slit she was cutting begin to seal over.

"Oh, come onnnnn." Emily pushed hard onto the hilt of the knife and pulled with all of her rapidly waning strength, tearing the blade through the floor.

It was probably her weight that did it, she decided, in that last split second as a sound like a T-shirt being torn apart filled the tube. The next instant she was falling, hands flailing for purchase but finding none on the wet lips of the split as she slipped through the tear, carried out in a waterfall of stinking liquid. She landed ass first with a teeth-crunching *"Ugh!"* of expelled air, swallowed a mouthful of the goo that clogged her throat, bounced, slid, and rolled to a stop against what could only be another wall.

Coughing and spluttering, Emily rolled onto all fours, and promptly puked up the crap she had swallowed during her fall. She knelt there, panting for twenty long seconds.

Open your eyes, she commanded herself.

She couldn't see a damn thing. Both eyes were thick with the gunk from the tube and still watering from the noxious air she had had to breathe. There was still more of the crap in her mouth; she spat it out in a long dribble, wiping her lips with her equally disgusting goo-encrusted jacket.

Damn, her eyes burned. She used her fingers to try to scoop the ooze from them, but all that did was smear it across her eyelids. Blindly, she pulled her undershirt from beneath her jacket and used that to clean the remainder away.

When her eyes finally began to stop burning she opened them again and looked around her new surroundings.

She was in a corridor with fleshy-looking gray walls, ribbed like a corrugated pipe, the ribs set at three-meter intervals, which only added to the illusion of being inside a living, breathing body. The majority of the corridor was curved like a tube too, but a flat walkway ran along the base.

The tendril she had used to get inside the ship ran along the ceiling. The cut she had fallen through still dripped the occasional teardrop of goo, but the wound was already knitting itself back together.

The flashlight had spun from her fingers when she fell the meter and a half to the corridor floor. It lay nearby, its light shining up the wall.

God, her butt hurt, and the wound on her head had started to throb again.

But she was finally inside. She had made it.

■ ■ ■

Emily picked up her flashlight from where it had fallen and realized she did not actually need it. The corridor was filled with a dim light, although she could not say from where exactly the light emanated. As the black external skin of the Caretaker ship had seemed to suck in the sunlight, so the very air within this corridor seemed to emit it.

This place smelled . . . *off*. Sweet, sickly, biological. She was surprised she could actually still smell anything at all after the stench she had endured in the tendril; this might just as well have been honey. Of course, the smell could actually be her. She hadn't had a change of clothes in how many days? And after crawling through that disgusting crap . . . She shuddered at the thought.

There was no sign of the Caretakers, not yet, anyway, but the same distant thrum of power she had heard outside the ship now reverberated up through the soles of her boots. If there was power then where were the Caretakers? *Someone* had to be taking care of her son, after all. Still, there wasn't much about any of this that made sense to her. She had just cut her way into this ship. Effectively, she was an invader, so whatever systems ran the ship must have notified whomever was in control about the damage she had caused getting in. That meant there was no way the Caretakers would be unaware of her presence. Where was her welcoming committee?

"Hello, you bastards. I'm here," she yelled. "Now take me to my Goddamn son."

She looked around in anticipation of one of the gangly Caretakers appearing, but she remained alone in the corridor. What kind of a game were they playing with her? Did they expect her to find them herself?

The fall had deposited her just before the elbow of a gently curving corridor. On this side of the corner Emily could see that the passageway ran back toward the exterior wall of the ship. It was pointless going that way. She dipped her head around the corner; the corridor continued inward toward the center of the ship. That seemed like the logical direction to take; the chances of her son being near the outer skin seemed unlikely. She started walking, following the corridor for a few minutes until it terminated at a ramp that curled up into an opening in the ceiling and down to what was, presumably, another level. Obviously a staircase of some kind. She wondered why the Caretakers would need something as simple as stairs to move about their ship when they could teleport at will. Maybe it just used a lot of energy to do something like that? Maybe their teleportation was not accurate enough to move confidently between levels? Who knew? Either way, she had to make a decision on which direction she should take.

Up or down?

Jesus! How was she supposed to figure this out? Guess? The ship was massive, and she was somewhere on the middle level along the outer edge. It could take days, weeks even, wandering around the inside of this place, and she still might not find Adam. It seemed so ridiculously illogical that she could be guided all this distance so accurately, only to spend her time blindly searching for him once she got inside. There *had* to be another way.

Emily thought back over everything that had happened since Adam had disappeared: the dreams that had not been dreams and that connection to *something* much, much larger had always seemed to be there, in the back of her mind. There had been the constant, inexorable, magnetic pull of her child's energy. And then, when she had first started to climb down into the pit she had touched that tendril and her mind had instantly transferred to those other creatures. All of these events added up to something that she had not seen, had not had the time to consider deeply enough—something that involved her child, the firstborn on this alien Earth. In her mind, she saw his red speckled eyes reflecting the red flecks of her own.

And she understood.

Tentatively, Emily reached out and laid the flat of her hand against the corridor wall . . . and gasped.

She was everywhere. Swirling through a red galaxy of connections, instinctively knowing that each dot—some infinitesimally tiny, some massive, the rest every shade in between—represented a life somewhere on her planet. Every dot was connected to the next, an incredible biological weave, the complexity of which should have been overwhelmingly complex, yet it made perfect sense within this context. And with a flat realization devoid of any emotion, Emily understood that she was as much a part of this tapestry as every other life force that glowed within the lines of its warp and weft.

And there was clarity for her, the falling away of boundaries. From the moment she had been abducted and awakened on the alien ship outside Las Vegas all those years ago, she had ceased to be Emily Baxter. The woman who had awoken within that ship was different, irreversibly altered, inextricably connected to this bioweave, and she hadn't even realized it until this very moment.

The red motes in her eyes were a tattoo of her assimilation. Her key to belonging.

Emily slipped from soul to soul, body to body, instantaneously, frictionless, tumbling helplessly from one to the next, her conscious mind removed from each slip, but her soul caught in a dizzying uncontrolled plummet from body to body.

Control, she had to regain control.

Slow, slow down.

Emily willed herself to slow her momentum, and, gradually, she did. The headlong tumble through Earth's life began to ease. Back, she thought, edging her consciousness away from the perspective of an individual soul until she was once again looking out at the vast collection of life arrayed around her. Back further . . . and there he was, the brightest light, at the center of all of this life, burning so strongly that even in this metaphysical embodiment the heat from her son was overwhelming. Emily tried to follow the red pathways to reach him, but the connections, ever changing, proved too complex for her nascent awareness. There was so much connected to him, he kept receding each time she got close.

But that was okay, because now she knew exactly where he was.

Emily tried to pull her hand away from the wall of the ship, but it felt stuck, as though it were glued. She pulled harder, and this time her hand moved back, dragging with it long black fibers off the wall like melted plastic. In horror she yanked her hand to her chest. The fibers released her with tiny audible pops, snapping away as they melted back into the wall. An imprint of her hand remained on the surface, gradually filling in as she watched, until the wall was again perfectly flat.

Emily's legs felt weak. She sank to the floor, her hand rising to cover her mouth as the full realization flooded through her. She was not Emily Baxter. At least, not the same Emily Baxter who had been plucked from that clearing in Las Vegas. She understood now that she had been changed, augmented, adapted by the Caretakers. She was an experiment. *Jesus Christ!* She might not even be the same woman . . . they could have created this body and implanted the *real* Emily Baxter's memories in her head like a scene from some bad fifties science-fiction B movie.

No way. No way. No way. Her mind repeated over and over, refusing to accept the possibility.

But does any of it really matter? her inner voice asked. *If I feel like Emily, if I love like her, look like her, then surely that means I am her.*

The only way she would ever know for certain would be to question one of the Caretakers. If she had to, she would beat the truth from the ones that had done this . . . this *abominable* thing to her. But they didn't exactly seem interested in her, judging by their lack of contact since her arrival. And this ship—if that was what it actually was—she wondered if it were connected to everything they had created, acting like some kind of conduit to gather data? Or monitoring the progress of the alien takeover? Maybe the Caretakers weren't even on board. Emily had had no sense of their presence within that fantastic web of connections she had just been connected to. Maybe this was all just automated.

But all that really mattered to her, right now, was to get to her son. Now more so than ever.

Emily pushed herself to her feet and made a conscious effort to breathe slowly and deeply as she tried to make sense of the jumble of thoughts bouncing around inside her head. The most important thing was to find Adam; that was why she was here. He was an innocent in all of this, and, Goddamn it, she was going to make the Caretakers pay for taking him from her. She was no longer worried about finding him. From the second the wall had released its grip on her, Emily had felt his presence again, and this time the sensation wasn't a subtle tug. Instead she felt as though someone had grabbed her by the lapels of her jacket and yanked her hard. His position within the jumbled bioconnection had been ever shifting, almost impossible for her to follow within the context of an entire multidimensional metasphere, but back here in the physical reality of this ship, he was fixed in place. And she knew exactly where he was.

Emily began to climb upward.

CHAPTER 20

Emily stepped off the staircase three levels up and straight into a corridor almost identical in appearance to the one she had just left. This one was shorter, though, terminating about twenty meters ahead of where she stood. On the left wall, halfway along, there was some kind of a recess, the rounded edges of a frame defining its clearly visible outline. By the time she reached it Emily saw it was an opening into a room: no door, just a gap in the wall leading into a sharply curving alcove several meters long, filled with shadow. She had stepped into the darkness and had taken a few paces before she stopped dead in her tracks.

Ahead of her, the alcove opened up into a dome-shaped room. At the center of the room, a thick column rose up from the floor and disappeared into the ceiling ten meters above. The column pulsed with vibrant colors, shot through with silent lightning-bolt flashes of energy.

Arranged in a circle around the base of the column was a row of Caretakers. Each of the aliens' oddly humanoid bodies leaned against a slanted board that protruded from the floor. Tubes extended from the center column, each one radiating a different lambent color, each fleshy tube terminating, no, *melding*, with the body of an individual Caretaker.

The memory of her first encounter with these aliens in Las Vegas had faded, apparently, because Emily's breath caught in the back of her throat, frozen there by the sheer strangeness of these creatures. The distilled light from the central column played over their metallic-gray skin, creating the illusion of movement where she knew there was none. Their featureless oval heads faced straight ahead, as if their attention was drawn to some distant point.

From the shadows of the alcove, Emily counted ten of the humanoids, but she knew there must be more on the opposite side of the room, obscured by the central column of light.

Emily slowly backed up into the shadows of the alcove. The ring of Caretakers hadn't sensed her yet; none of them had so much as lifted a skinny digit in her direction. Carefully she edged a few centimeters closer, scanning the room. On the opposite side to where she stood was an alcove mirroring the one in which she now hid. Each time she looked at it, she felt that same molecular tug toward it, like Ariadne's thread guiding her through the Minotaur's maze.

Other than the column at its center and the motionless Caretakers surrounding it, there was nothing else in the room, no furniture or architecture she could use as cover to reach the other side. Emily ducked back the way she had come, double-checking the corridor to make sure she hadn't missed another door or junction that might give her another way past the room. Apart from the stairs, the alcove was the sole way out of this corridor. If she wanted to get to her son, she was going to have to cross the twenty meters in plain view of the Caretakers.

Emily slid the knife from its scabbard on her ankle, grasping it tightly in her right hand she walked back through the alcove. If any of these alien *fucks* so much as twitched, she was prepared to cut its Goddamn head from its shoulders. She took a step into the room, then another and another, her back against the wall while keeping her eyes fixed on the still-motionless aliens. She had to pass within a meter of them.

She held the knife at arm's length. If they tried to come after her, she assumed they were first going to have to jettison the filaments that stretched between them and the central column. That should give enough warning of their intentions, but their eerily still forms had set her nerves jangling. Each step felt like a moment in a horror movie when the music stops. The watcher knew that at any second *something* was going to spring out of the shadows with heart-shattering surprise. The unsuspecting never saw it coming. She wasn't going to end up like one of those fictional victims.

The Caretakers remained motionless, their bodies as still as a frozen pond. Their overly elongated arms rested against the curve of their thighs, each of their three slender fingers raised slightly in an arc.

There was the vague memory of a smell captured within the air of the room . . . a scent of sulfur, like someone had dropped a lit match into a box of matches, or maybe spent gunpowder? Emily had the distinct impression of something having been burned, energy expelled.

She reached the opposite alcove unmolested and was about to step out into the mirror image of the first alcove when the peal of curiosity bells ringing in her head got the better of her. *Oh, for God's sake, this is* exactly *what the idiots in the movie would do.* Her inner voice berated her to just keep on going; she'd gotten by them for whatever reason, so why ruin a good thing? *Keep on going, for fuck's sake.*

But it had just been too easy. Something was out of place here. Emily twisted around in one sharp movement, her mind made up, and strode to the Caretaker nearest the alcove.

It gave no indication that it even knew she was there.

Switching the knife to her left hand as she approached, Emily waved her empty hand in front of the alien's featureless face. "Wake up, dummy!" she said, loud enough that she knew the Caretaker would hear her. She was just waiting for one of those skinny arms to flash up and grab her wrist in its equally skinny digits. That would be all the excuse she would need to plunge the blade into the dome of the fucker's head. She shifted anxiously from foot to foot, her muscles clenched, ready to explode.

The Caretaker did not move, did not even flinch at the bark of her voice.

Emily moved the knife back to her dominant hand, extending her arm out until the tip of the knife pressed against the creature's throat. Maybe the threat of death would motivate it into action? The Caretaker remained perfectly still.

She pushed gently . . .

. . . and screamed in surprise. It was like pushing the knife into a deeply burned log; the blade sank all the way up to the hilt and then the knuckles of her fist. The Caretaker's body cracked and a moment later collapsed like a condemned building, crumbling into a gray mound on the floor at Emily's feet. It was nothing more than ash.

"You have got to be shitting me," Emily said, trying hard to maintain a semblance of composure. The knife and the hand that held it were covered in a gray dusty residue that she wiped away on her jacket. "You have got to be fucking shitting me," she repeated in utter disbelief.

Were they all like this? All of them equally as desiccated? She moved from alien body to alien body, carefully pushing the knife into each of the remaining Caretakers' chests. By the time she was done with the last of them, there were thirty piles of ash lying on the floor.

Emily stood back and surveyed the room, unsure. Something incredible had happened. Something . . . inexplicable. But what, exactly? The Caretakers, these seemingly unstoppable creatures that had destroyed her world in a day had in turn now been destroyed. These ones, at least.

Emily stared down at the last pile of dust at her feet. That smell of expelled energy she had picked up when she first entered the room made sense now. The Caretakers' bodies had somehow been incinerated where they stood. She leaned in and checked the weird board each body had been propped against. No scorch marks, no signs to indicate a fire or instantaneous combustion. But the question of who, and why, and, most importantly, *what* could be capable of accomplishing something like this escaped her. What could overpower these omnipotent creatures so swiftly and absolutely that they had not even had the time to react before they were reduced to dust?

Perhaps she had been wrong all along. Perhaps there was a God watching over the sad remnants of humanity after all, because that was the only entity she could think of that could have moved so swiftly and completely to defeat these aliens.

And that idea scared her more than the Caretakers.

■ ■ ■

Emily's thoughts were in free fall as she exited the room of dead Caretakers. The implications of this were, well, just overwhelming, and confusing, and, quite frankly, terrifying.

She supposed it was possible that what she had just experienced was some kind of medical bay, or maybe even a mausoleum, but that seemed unlikely. From what she understood from the conversation she had had with the Caretaker she'd encountered in Las Vegas, these aliens were tools of a much higher, much older race—sentient, yes, but still effectively machines programmed to carry out a very specific job. And they were just as capable of transforming themselves as they were of transforming an entire planet. They were cold, calculating biological machines, with almost no understanding of human emotion. Emily did not think they were any more capable of caring for their brethren than they were for the billions of human lives they had destroyed, and she was certain they would not honor their dead . . . if they even died in the sense that humans did. Emily shuddered. Humans had been pretty good at screwing themselves over, but the Caretakers . . . they were a whole new level of cold-bloodedness.

She had to find Adam and get both of them out of this place. Throughout the entire journey, right up until the first Caretaker had crumbled to dust, Emily had never really doubted that it was her son who was guiding her, calling her. But after what she had just seen back there in that room, she was not so sure. She felt a sharp splinter of doubt lodge in her chest.

Was it too much of a stretch of her imagination to think that whatever had managed to stop the Caretakers in this ship so completely could, under the disguise of her son, just as easily manipulate her to come here? But what would that achieve? And why her? Surely whatever was capable of doing this could just as easily have abducted her when it took Adam. Hell, judging by what had happened to the Caretakers, whatever "it" was could have killed every last living human being left in Point Loma without breaking a sweat. There were just too many threads at this point, and none of them seemed in any way connected. It made no logical sense, which meant that there was some other force at play here that she was not able to see . . . not yet, anyway.

The new alcove led into another corridor that looked exactly the same as the others.

She could still feel that constant ping from Adam. It grew stronger with every step she took, in fact, but Emily moved with caution now. It was all very well following her instinct, but if she were being manipulated . . . she let the thought go unanswered because the answers she felt swirling around in the shadows were just unacceptable to her.

A little farther along, the corridor ended at a T-junction.

Ping! She felt a tug to her left as she approached it.

Rounding the left corner, Emily almost stumbled over the prone body of another Caretaker. It was on its knees, slumped forward as if it had simply collapsed on the spot, one spindly arm reaching out and propping the body against the wall. Its pose reminded Emily of an exhausted marathon runner. She reached out and tapped the thing's chest with the tip of her toe and watched the torso crumble away, leaving only the midsection and legs intact, like a biological exhibit at some weird intergalactic sideshow. She could see the remains of organs she did not recognize within the exposed torso, all turned to cinders.

Emily stepped gingerly over the Caretaker and carried on down the corridor.

The ping had become a beat, thrumming through her limbs. A sense of anticipation, not the good kind, had begun to take hold of Emily as she grew nearer to the source. A half hour ago she would have expected herself to be running at this point, but now, with what she had just witnessed, she was actively resisting the urge to sprint, and it hurt. She faced the very real possibility that her son was not even alive, and with that possibility came the probability she was not going to make it out of here alive either.

And hanging over everything was the unnerving sensation that she had been manipulated, played all along.

So no way was she going to run into any trap that might be waiting to spring shut on her.

The pulsing throb running through Emily was now almost tangible. She was surrounded by a sea of energy, and every two seconds a wave of it would crash over her, urging her forward, staggering her with its intensity. Despite her conviction that she was not going to run, she found herself walking faster, unable to resist, her mouth hanging open as her breathing increased, her heart pounding in anticipation and fear. The contradictory energies at play like tidal forces eroded her will, forcing her to do their bidding.

But still she resisted.

"Too much," Emily breathed, "too much." She staggered forward. Ahead of her, in what had only a second ago been nothing but a blank wall, an opening appeared, the material of the wall peeling back like skin to reveal a room full of shadows.

There! In there.

From within the room, Emily sensed the source of whatever energy compelled her forward, dragging her toward the opening. This close, its pull was irresistible. She was no longer in control of her limbs. She was a marionette, whoever held her strings forcing her forward. She was Dorothy, standing before Oz the Great and Powerful.

Emily almost fell through the doorway, her eyes blinded by sweat from her forehead as she staggered inside . . . and then her body was hers again. The pull that had been a compulsion since Adam had been taken was suddenly gone. She slipped to her knees, what little energy she had left sucked out of her. Her lips were dry, her throat parched. She lay still, limp now that those marionette strings had been severed, allowing her muscles a few moments to recover.

A minute slipped by.

Emily's breathing slowed, the cogs within her mind began to turn again, pushing back the fog of confusion and exhaustion that had filled her. Gradually, she rose to her feet and looked around.

She stood in a large room. The same odd there-but-not-there lighting filled it, but in here it appeared dimmer. Some unlit spots allowed shadows to take up residence, as though whatever energy the light drew its power from was running low or was overloaded.

Along the nearby wall Emily saw black extrusions, irregularly shaped bumps, each about the size of her fist pushing out, the random shape of the bumps at painful opposition to the smooth, flawless design of the rest of the craft. The light was too sporadic for her to be able to see much farther than a couple of meters around her, so she took a few steps deeper inside.

As though waiting for her, a trio of blindingly bright lights snapped silently on from somewhere high above, the three beams directed down like spotlights, illuminating a refrigerator-size cylinder suspended upright in the center of the room. It was made of some kind of clear material and filled with a liquid that looked disconcertingly like blood. Emily could see no wires attached to it; it just hung there, the red liquid churning slowly within.

Emily took a step toward the object, her head moving left and right, scanning the room for any suggestion that she was not alone. She tilted her head sideways and looked under the container's base; there were no apparent connections that she could see. It just floated in midair like a levitating magician's assistant. The red-hued liquid within swirled and roiled, folding in and out within itself.

She stepped closer, her heart surprisingly still.

There was something else in the container, a darker shape, but the liquid was too thick and the light too strained for her to be able to make it out clearly.

Another step, then another, until she stood less than a meter from it.

The shadow within the glass resolved into a silhouette, cruciform in shape, suspended at the center of the liquid-filled cylinder. Perhaps the material that made up the cylinder was responsible or the liquid within it; either way, the shape and detail of whatever was at its center was grossly distorted.

After a final step, Emily stood at the cylinder, a gap of about half a meter between the floor and its base. She leaned in closer, her hands lying flat against the curiously warm transparency of the container. The liquid thinned for a moment, and, to her horror, Emily realized she was looking at the body of a child, a human child, its legs fully extended, ankle touching ankle, the arms pointing straight out from its sides. The face was blurred but recognizable . . . *her* child.

Adam! Her son was suspended in that container like some prized specimen.

Emily screeched and staggered backward, her hand flying to her face to stifle the scream of horror before it could escape.

"Adam!" she said through the mesh of her fingers, her son's name shattering in her mouth. "Adam!" she yelled, starting forward again, slapping the flats of her hands against the container's wall. Her eyes were fixed on the shadow of her son slowly rotating within the glass cylinder, but her peripheral vision caught movement from within the deeper shadows of the room.

Emily turned her head in time to see the slender arm of a Caretaker reaching from the darkness for her.

CHAPTER 21

Emily screamed, leaping out of range of the alien's grasping hand. In one fluid motion she drew her .45 from its holster, the anger within her raging like she had never felt before. She was suddenly and completely on fire.

The Caretaker took several juddering steps out of the shadows toward the center of the room. It was unsteady on its feet, shaky, as though it were unsure of its movements.

Emily took two steps toward the Caretaker until she was less than a meter from it, brought her arm up, and pointed the .45 straight at its head. "What the fuck have you done to my son?" she demanded, her voice barely able to make it past the rage that had seized control of her throat.

The Caretaker stopped. It teetered for a moment as though it were a drunk, then threw one long, spindly gray arm out and landed a multifingered hand on Emily's shoulder.

Emily gasped. Too slow and tired to react in time, she flinched but stood her ground. In her mind, she played out what it would feel like to kill this *fuck*, and the pleasure she felt shudder through her at the thought of it was . . . well, it was close to orgasmic. She was *so* near to pulling the trigger, the possibility of seeing this thing's head explode was almost too much to resist . . .

. . . almost . . .

But she needed it to help her release her son from whatever fucked-up experiment they were conducting on him. And she needed answers. Lots of answers.

The alien's hand was incredibly light against her shoulder, and she heard it crunch dryly like autumn leaves as the Caretaker leaned its weight against her. Even though its head hung down as though it were exhausted, it was still at least thirty centimeters taller than Emily. And its skin was *hot*, not warm, but uncomfortably hot, like standing a little too close to a campfire.

Instead of blowing the Caretaker away, she shrugged the hand from her shoulder.

The alien staggered, its legs no longer able to support its weight. The alien's legs snapped midpoint with an audible crack, dropping it to the equivalent of where its knees should be. Now the Caretaker was face to face with Emily, the blank orb of its head centimeters from her own. Emily leaped backward as features—a pair of black eyes and a lipless slit of a mouth—emerged from the gray flesh in a weird reverse melting. She could see her own face reflected back in the shiny surface of those orbs, her anger written like words across her features.

Fuck it! She would figure this out by herself. This thing was dead. She brought the pistol back up and placed the muzzle against the Caretaker's forehead.

And it was in those newly formed eyes that she registered her own shock when the creature croaked a single word . . .

"Mom-me."

■ ■ ■

Emily staggered back.

Stunned, she let the pistol drop to her thigh.

"What did you say?" she demanded. When the creature kneeling before her did not respond, she took another step forward and yelled the question into its face, spittle flying from her mouth. "What the fuck did you just say to me?"

"Mom-meee," the Caretaker mouthed, the slit that passed for a mouth barely moving. That single word, so small and yet so powerful.

Emily felt her heart twist behind her ribs. Memories of Rhiannon's father, Simon Keller, came flooding back to her. She remembered the creature that had manipulated him like a puppet and had tried to use the children's love for him to lure them to it—and how it had succeeded, costing the life of Simon's son, Ben. The Caretaker she had encountered in their Las Vegas ship had attempted to pass that thing off as having some kind of place within the new ecosystem they had created here on Earth, and now this Caretaker was trying to do the same thing to save its own worthless skin, apparently.

Emily's anger flared again at the idea. "You son of a bitch!" She raised the pistol above her head, poised to bring it down across the creature's skull.

A glimmer, like evening heat on a road, moved across the Caretaker's body, and Emily's hand froze midstrike. The alien was gone, and in its place stood Nathan—beautiful, long-dead Nathan, the man she had loved until he had died so horribly in her apartment the day the red rain had fallen. The man she had thought she would spend the rest of her life with. Or, at least, Emily's overclocked mind quickly decided, a perfect facsimile of what had once been the man she had loved so deeply. Her pistol hand dropped limply to her side. She took a step backward and sat down hard, her hands wrapped around her knees. The first tears began to roll down her face.

"What are you trying to do to me?" she sobbed. "Are you trying to drive me insane? Is that it? Is that what you want? Tell me, God-damn it."

Nathan sat up and regarded her for a moment with those same blue eyes that had once looked at her with such warmth but now seemed cold, as lifeless as a photograph.

"Mommy," the facsimile said, in a voice that certainly did not belong with Nathan's body. "I have missed you." The hint of a smile creased his mouth. "You must listen to me. I have so much that I need to tell you, and there is little time left with this body."

Emily looked up, hot tears washing over her cheeks now. "Don't you dare call me that. I'm not your mother. Tell me what you've done with my boy," she spat.

The thing that was Nathan watched her for a few seconds, his chest rising and falling as rapidly as if he had just jogged up a flight of stairs, adding to the illusion that he was actually alive. When he spoke again, the voice was Nathan's, and it was with the same calmness he would reserve for telling her something he knew was going to upset her.

"Emily, I know that what I am about to tell you will seem strange and hard to believe, but it is the truth. I've chosen this visage, as we know that you had feelings for this man. Our name is Tellus and we are . . . *I* am your son."

Emily giggled. Oh, good God, the utter ridiculousness of it all. She laughed loudly. This was just, well, it was just . . .

Nathan raised his hand, not in a demand but a request for silence. "I know that it seems impossible, even repulsive, to you, but, please, let me tell you our story, then you will understand." He did not wait for her permission. "When I . . . when your son, Adam, was born, we, the ones you call the Caretakers, became aware of his presence within the connections and nodes of the life we created on this planet. All life is a part of that network, and together, those combined intelligences made up the I . . . the We. As your son grew, so we became aware of his connections to us. And with each connection he made, so we became more intrigued by him. In all the time since our creation by the First Ones, all the planets and races we have reconstituted to create new life, never have we encountered an entity such as Adam." Nathan pushed himself up until he was resting on his knees; the effort seemed to exhaust him, and he took a few moments to catch his breath. "When he began to share his connections with you while you slept, we became too intrigued not to act, and we decided to bring him here, to this ship, for further examination."

Despite her misgivings, Emily found herself fascinated to hear what this thing that resembled Nathan so closely—what had it called itself? *Tellus?*—had to say, even if she did not believe a word of it. But at the mention of her dreams she found herself blurting out a question. "How did you know about my dreams?"

"Adam, the I, the *We*, sensed the connection to us and to you. We felt his inquisitiveness, his willingness to allow his fledgling self to merge with the self of the subject he connected with, and become a part of the Whole. His lack of fear and his innocent desire to share his experience with you was . . . intriguing to the Whole. But it was only once we had brought him here that we realized just how unique he was." Nathan looked around the room, as though seeing it for the first time. "This biomachine is the node." His hands rose weakly to indicate the room. "It serves as the central connection to the entire ecosystem we have created here on your planet. We wanted to see how he would adapt to being interfaced directly with it. The consensus among the Whole was that he would perish, that the power of the information that flows through this node point would destroy him in an instant. The majority were confident we were correct. The majority were wrong."

Nathan dropped his hands back to his side, pressing them to the floor to support himself more easily.

"Once we had obtained Adam, we brought him here and placed him in the access point." He nodded toward the container. "The expectation was of instantaneous destruction. We expected him to be overwhelmed within seconds of the connection being established; instead, he thrived. The Whole, of course, was fascinated by him. We observed him make connections at an exponential rate. Within minutes we realized his consciousness had spread across the planet, processing information from every life-form. It was exhilarating for the Whole to observe. We believed we were in control of him, but within the first hour he had obtained access to our ship's biological systems. We were unaware that he was in fact in control of us."

Nathan's skin had taken on a sheen of what at first Emily thought to be sweat, but as she looked closer, she could see it was the faintest of heat shimmers, like a halo surrounding his skin.

Nathan had noticed it too. His forehead creased, and his eyes closed in concentration. The shimmer faded until it was barely noticeable. "There is not much time. Even as we observed Adam's progress we were unaware of what he was accomplishing. The ecosystems we have created on each new world have always existed independently of us; we have always been the observers within the network, ensuring that the life we created progressed along the course of the plan. But the cumulative connections Adam had made created something new, an intelligence that had never existed before."

"Tellus," Emily said, surprising herself. "My son created you?"

Nathan smiled. "Yes. Your son gave this world its consciousness. Before him we, Tellus, could not have existed. And without you, there would be no Adam, and hence no us. You are the mother of this world, Emily."

"But . . ." The hand holding the gun had fallen to Emily's side, and she placed the pistol back in its holster. "I . . . I . . ." The words faltered on her lips. "This is all . . . it's *crazy*."

Nathan held up a hand to stop her, then continued. "Within another hour Adam had delved deeper into our archives, finding memories and records stored on a molecular level that we had not accessed for millennia. And he found something, a truth obfuscated from the Caretakers, hidden from them by an enemy that we did not even know existed." A new tone entered Nathan's voice. Was that anger she was hearing? In both of Emily's encounters with the Caretakers, first in Las Vegas with the creature that had taken on the form of Jacob, and now with Nathan, the creatures had exhibited a distinct lack of empathy and emotion. This, as Mac would say, was a turn up for the books.

"What!" Emily said. "What enemy?"

Nathan ignored the question, continuing his elaboration. "When Adam broke through the barriers erected to block access, his young, eager mind was set loose on all our memories. He was free to roam around histories so ancient, so buried, that we had not accessed them since before the first original life on this planet even began. And it was there, buried deep under eons of history, that your son found our greatest shame and exposed it to us. And when he showed that truth to us, a trigger was thrown. And we began to die."

"What do you mean 'a trigger'?"

Nathan raised an unsteady hand as though lead ran through his veins and inhaled a shuddering breath. His cheeks seemed to sag for a moment, melting into his lower jaw, before springing back to where they should be as he started talking again. "Please, just listen to me. I am being kept alive now only by the sheer force of will of Tellus, and I have little time left. Adam showed us a history that we did not, could not, remember. Ten thousand worlds

PAUL ANTONY JONES

ago, our scouts encountered a planet. It was fertile, full of life, and with a sentient species who, while technologically backward, were true custodians of the world and all life on it. It was a prime candidate for our assistance. But when we arrived, the planet had been devastated, the cities lay in ruins, with no trace of life left anywhere. Our scouts were waiting for us, but they had been changed, reprogrammed on a genetic level. We could not have known that they had been ambushed, and, once they reestablished their connection with the Whole, the infection they carried spread to all of us. We did not even notice the switch between our true purpose and what we have now become. From that moment onward, we were bent to our Hosts' will, our true goals forgotten as though they had never existed, replaced with a new program to fulfill."

A tingle of apprehension had been rapidly building within Emily, growing with each new piece of information Nathan added to his story. Now it thrummed in her like power surging through a conduit.

"What . . . ? What were you supposed to do?" she asked, leaning forward, all thoughts for her own safety now gone. She did not want to know the answer, but she knew that she had to hear what this dying creature had to say.

"Augment," Nathan said, his words heavy. "Our original program was to augment any life we found, not reconstitute it. We were capable of enhancing, educating . . . *helping* the life-forms we discovered, greatly increasing their chances of survival in a universe where life was as delicate as a flower growing within a furnace. And that was what we had done for hundreds of worlds before that, nurtured and grown life throughout this universe. But from the time of the change, we became something else; we became puppets for the unseen intellects that manipulated us to their own desires, eliminating every new ecosystem we found and

replacing it with the one that they desired. Your son, in his innocence and his youth, revealed this truth to us, exposed us to what
had been done to us, showed us our corruption."

Emily felt as though she had been hit square in the chest with
a sledgehammer. "But if you know all of this, then why don't you
do something about it? Why don't you just stop? You could just go
back to your original programming. You could help us."

Nathan looked at her with what amounted to pity; the muscles in his face had begun to twitch, spasming uncontrollably.
A thin trickle of green spittle dribbled from the right side of his
mouth, and that side of his face seemed to now be paralyzed,
as though he had suffered a stroke. The heat-haze halo had also
returned. Emily felt the heat pulsing from his body in waves now.

Nathan's words came out in gasped, slurred fragments: "Self-
destruction . . . built into us by . . . the entities who did this to us. To
ensure . . . we could not trace the originators back . . . cellular petrifi-
cation cannot be stopped or reversed. Too late for us but *not* for you."

Instinctively, Emily reached out and took one of Nathan's
hands in her own. It was almost too hot to touch. The energy was
draining fast from him now, his body seizing up like some complex engine deprived of oil. Her inner reporter kicked in, sensing
there was little time left. *Keep the questions short, get the most
information you can.*

"The other Caretakers on the ship in Vegas and the ones
Commander Mulligan saw from space? What happened to them?"

"The ships are intact. But my brothers are gone, all gone. I
am the last."

"What did this?" Emily hissed.

"We have . . . very little information. The original constructs who
brought this plague to us had only shards of memories remaining.
But Tellus believes that the entities that committed this crime against

life did so to benefit themselves, to provide a ready-made energy source for them. The only logical conclusion that we could reach for the repurposing of life to such a very specific design is that the entities would be more able to assimilate the planet's resources."

"Holy shit! You mean, they're going to take everything that's left?"

Ever so slowly, as if it was the hardest thing to do, Nathan's head turned to look up at her. "No, Emily . . . I mean they intend . . . to use this planet as food."

Emily dropped his hand like it was a red-hot stone. "Wha-what?" she stuttered and scooted backward. "Food?" She seemed incapable of anything other than single-word questions, but, in her mind, she was asking herself a more pertinent one: *When was this fucking nightmare ever going to end?*

"You must know *something*?" she pleaded.

"We have analyzed the process . . . we undertook on each new planet we located. On all worlds since we . . . first encountered them . . . we have simply processed the planet . . . in the same manner. Reconstituting the living matter in . . . a very particular way. We believe the entities . . . move from each planet we have reconstituted to the next . . . stripping it of its resources like locusts. They meet no resistance as we have already prepared the world ahead of them. Millions of worlds over the ages, Emily. All that life, gone to feed the greed of these faceless creatures."

"But . . . but how would they find you? I mean, do you send them messages or leave them some kind of"—her words trailed off, and she knew the answer before she even said the next words—"some kind of sign?" Her head involuntarily looked skyward to where the ring whose perplexing appearance over the past several weeks would be glowing in the sky.

"Yes . . . the . . . ring." Nathan's lips seemed almost incapable of moving now, like they were made of quickly setting cement. "When the ring is placed around a candidate world, it tells them that the process is complete, that the world is ready for them."

"Jesus, you have got to be joking. No, don't bother, I know you're not. So, that's it? How are we supposed to defend ourselves against something that you couldn't even stop? There's only a handful of us left, and I'm pretty sure that the majority of them want me dead."

Nathan shook his head.

No? "No, what?"

"There are more survivors. Groups scattered around the planet that we were unable to reach."

Emily had not believed she could be any more surprised than she had over the past hour, but this floored her. "Where are they? How many?"

"Adam knows. He will show you when he is ready."

"But he's just a *baby*. How are we supposed to defend ourselves against an enemy we know nothing about?"

Nathan's breathing had become more labored with each passing moment. "He . . . he . . . is the center. Tellus. He is Tellus. He must remain."

Emily leaped to her feet, the implication of what she had just been told sinking in. "No! No fucking way. He's my son, and he's coming home with me."

"No," said Nathan. "Emily, he is so much more than that. You can take him from the node, I will not be able to stop you, but understand something: he does not want to leave. He is a part of this world. But if you release him, you will doom this planet, and all life on it, to destruction. Do you understand?"

Emily felt her hand ball into a fist. She had never wanted to smash something so badly in her life. She wanted to pound that Goddamn face into powder.

"My son!" she moaned, as if that would make him understand. Emily stared at the shape suspended in the red liquid. She knew it was a cliché, but, oh dear God, it felt as though her heart would explode.

"Soon he will begin to grow, quickly," Nathan continued, oblivious of her suffering. "But he is just a child now, and you *must* protect him until he is able to protect himself. He must remain within the ship."

"I never got a chance to tell him how much I love him," she said, her focus entirely fixed on her boy.

A familiar smell had begun to waft from Nathan: burned matches. It reeked, and Emily coughed involuntarily.

"Emily," Nathan said in a voice that demanded her attention. "He sees you. He hears everything that you say. You are as connected to him as I am. He knows." Then, with what seemed like a gargantuan effort, he reached for her hand and unfurled his fingers, dropping an object into her open palm. "Take . . .this. They . . . are . . . coming. You must . . . be . . . ready."

Emily caught the object. It was a square box, glowing slightly.

Nathan's arm froze in place, his hand outstretched toward her. His skin gray. He looked like a statue perfectly hewn from granite, she thought.

Emily sat there—for how long, she did not know—staring into the lifeless eyes of a man she had once loved but who had been dead for years and now had died all over again. She ran the tips of her fingers across Nathan's petrified cheek . . . and pressed. His head crumbled first, breaking apart into three separate pieces, followed by his torso, until nothing was left but a pile of dust at her feet.

The last of the Caretakers was dead, and humanity was once again the master of its planet.

For now.

EPILOGUE

MacAlister stood on the ice-crusted deck of the HMS *Vengeance*, two hundred meters off the shore of Svalbard Island. The submarine had dropped anchor in an estuary off the western side of the island an hour earlier. Even with his cold-weather parka fastened up to his neck and several layers of clothing below that, the biting-cold wind blowing in from the Greenland Sea had already managed to find its way to his skin.

He raised a pair of binoculars to his eyes and glassed the shoreline.

A line of craggy mountains blocked the horizon, their snow- and ice-covered flanks barely discernible against the light-gray clouds that swallowed the entire hemisphere in every direction he looked. White everywhere. Nothing else to see but more snow and ice no matter where he looked. And that was just fine by Mac, because, for the first time in over two years, there was also not a single sign of the alien life that had squashed the rest of this planet under its boot heel. He felt a surge of hope replace the uncertainty that had dogged him since he first set foot on the sub for this mission. There was *still* a chance for them, for all of them. Now all that was needed was for his team to make it happen.

The Svalbard Global Seed Vault waited just a few kilometers northeast from this spot, on the opposite side of the line of craggy mountains, hidden within the rock and permafrost that made up this inhospitable land. Humanity's last, best hope for returning this world to a semblance of what it had once been, it contained hundreds of thousands of seed samples, stored there as a failsafe against disaster, a final chance to restart humanity's food supply in the event of a global apocalypse. Well, that apocalypse was now. All he had to do was get in there and get the seeds back to Point Loma.

His mind drifted for a moment back to Emily and his family. He wondered what they might be doing right then. In the weeks since he'd set sail, leaving everything that was precious to him back in California, he had had little else to do other than train and think about his life, his family. It seemed so odd to him that in the midst of the shit-storm that had swallowed this world, while almost everyone on the planet had died horribly, he had lucked out. By some amazing, screwed-up twist of fate, his life had actually become better. God, he missed them, but he also knew that Emily was more than capable of looking after herself *and* their family. *I just hope she's keeping herself out of trouble,* he thought, then smiled when he realized that that would be so unlike his wife. *Let me rephrase that*: *keeping herself out of* too *much trouble.*

The world was silent. No sound but that of the waves lapping against the hull.

Mac spoke into a throat mike, "Alpha Team, we all set?" Behind him seven men, similarly clad in all-white snow camouflage, responded one after the other that they were ready. "Let's move our arses then; we don't have all day."

The men climbed into the Zodiac boat moored to the side of the submarine's hull, stowing their gear and equipment at the bow before sitting. Mac gave a nod, and the boat's engine coughed into life. Two seconds later, they were bouncing over the waves, heading toward the island. Three minutes after that, and the nose of the boat was buried in the shale of the rocky beach.

Six men leaped to the shore and fanned outward, their weapons drawn to cover the area ahead of them while their remaining comrades pulled the boat higher up onto the shingle and secured it. The shore was just as deserted as it had appeared from the deck of the *Vengeance*. As Mac began to help unload their equipment, he caught a final glimpse of the submarine as it slipped below the waves again, a precaution they had decided on in case the Caretakers decided they wanted to put in an appearance.

They were now well and truly on their own.

"Single file," Mac said, turning to face his men. "I'm on point. Keep your eyes and ears open."

The snow crunched loudly beneath their feet as the soldiers followed the base of the hill north. The vault was cut into the mountain on the opposite side from their position. It took them twenty minutes to cover the distance.

"I'm guessing that's what we came here for," Mac said as the team rounded the bluff and pushed inland along the southern edge of a cove. Ahead of them, halfway up the slope, was the unmistakable outline of a man-made structure, a huge monolith of concrete that jutted out from the face of the mountainside, about a kilometer or so in the distance.

Mac stopped and pulled out his binoculars again, scanning them over the terrain leading up to the vault.

"There's a road about fifty meters up there," he said, pointing toward the rocky incline. He led his group up the side of the mountain until they intersected with the road, following it until they stood outside the entrance to the vault.

The entrance would not have looked out of place in a sci-fi movie or as the entrance to some ancient tomb. The concrete slab stood eight meters tall and two and a half wide, cantilevered out of the natural chaos of the land around it, its sharp lines and flat sides an obvious attempt to ensure it would be seen. Near the apex, at the front, a mosaic of mirrors, prisms, and glass glowed with a scintillating blue-and-white light, turning the entrance into the equivalent of a lighthouse, visible for kilometers. It was the absolute opposite of camouflage, Mac thought, which he supposed stood to reason when you thought about the actual purpose of the building.

A short metal gantry led up to the doorway. Richardson, the team's demolitions expert, stood on it now and examined the locking mechanism. "It looks almost like a regular household lock to me," he said, the surprise evident in his voice, stepping back so Mac could get a better look.

"It's not like they want to make it hard for people to get in, after all," said Mac.

"Want me to blow it?" asked Richardson casually, his hand already reaching into the satchel of C-4 he carried.

"Not if we can help it. If we expose the interior to the elements, we don't know how long anything we leave behind will last," said Mac. They had brought a portable oxyacetylene torch with them, which would be preferable to blowing the door. Mac was prepared to use it if he had to, but it would still leave them with the same problem of leaving the entrance open to the elements.

Mac thought for a moment or two then called out, "Ryan! Get your backside over here."

"Sir?" Ryan crunched his way to Mac's side. He was a gangly twenty-something, a good lad in Mac's opinion, and a fast learner. He'd joined the navy when he was nineteen. A misspent youth had culminated in him being caught and prosecuted for burglary. Offered the choice of either a prolonged stay at Her Majesty's pleasure or a tour with the Royal Navy, the kid had wisely chosen the latter.

"If I remember right, you've had a bit of experience with locks in your time," said Mac, thumping his gloved fist against the ice-encrusted steel door. "Think you can get that open?"

Ryan knelt to scrutinize the lock. "Not a problem, boss, but I'm going to need something that can—"

They seemed to appear from nowhere, materializing from the snow like ghosts, but Mac knew they had probably been there long before he and his men had arrived. Even as Mac registered their presence, he could tell his men were easily outnumbered three to one, and he knew that there would probably be several more that remained hidden, their weapons covering their comrades on the off chance Mac had backup hidden away somewhere. He also knew that if these soldiers had wanted them dead, they would have been dead already.

"Hendene opp! Hendene opp!" the newcomers yelled.

"Hold your fire," Mac snapped as his men instantly took up a defensive posture.

One of the newcomers stepped closer, a pistol in his hand but held at his side, Mac noted. Not like he needs it, anyway, he thought, not with all the firepower trained on them by the rest of his men. Mac quickly counted twenty figures that he could see, all armed with fully automatic weapons, and, by the accent, he thought, maybe Swedish or, more probably, Norwegian.

"Hvem av dere er kommandoen i?" the man said, his voice muffled by the hood of his parka.

"We don't understand you," said Mac, noting the white-clad soldier's head turn to him instantly.

"You are British?" the man with the pistol said, switching to heavily accented English.

Mac nodded.

"You are in charge?"

PAUL ANTONY JONES

Mac nodded again.

"If you would please order your men to drop their weapons. We would prefer for there to be no bloodshed."

Mac sighed, but it was obvious these guys had them well and truly over the proverbial barrel. "You heard the man. Drop your weapons, lads."

One by one, Mac's unit placed their weapons at their feet.

"Thank you. Now, your name please."

"MacAlister, James. Sergeant."

"And what are you and your men doing on my island, Sergeant MacAlister?"

"Take me to whoever is in charge, and I'll explain to them," he said. The prescribed reply after being captured by an enemy force was name, rank, and serial number, but if the truth be told, Mac thought, he didn't even know if these blokes were the enemy. Still, he was taking a chance here. They could just kill him and his men and leave their bodies here, and no one would ever be the wiser. But Mac prided himself on his ability to suss people out, and the man standing across from him did not strike him as the coldhearted-killer type . . . he hoped.

The officer—and Mac was certain that was what he was—regarded him with steel-gray eyes for a couple of very long seconds. Mac wasn't sure, but he thought he saw a smile crease his face, all but hidden within the hood of the parka. He said something in his native tongue and the other soldiers advanced on Mac and his men.

"Very well," the officer said eventually. "We will take you to meet the *kommunestyret*. Please inform your men it would be in everyone's best interest not to resist."

Their captors led Mac and his team along a path and into a small valley where four large military snowcats had been hidden. His men were split up into twos and bundled inside the vehicles. Mac and Ryan found themselves sitting across from the officer and two of his men, their backs to the driver, their weapons trained unwaveringly on the two of them.

"Where are they taking us?" said Ryan, his voice barely betraying the nervousness Mac knew he must be feeling.

"Just sit back and enjoy the ride, please, gentlemen," the officer interjected, then ordered the soldier at the controls to get under-way. The snowcat's engine kicked in. Mac felt the tracks slip, then gain traction, and they pulled out of the valley and headed inland.

To the north, through the frost-webbed window, Mac saw the unmistakable profile of an airport, a hangar, and several smaller buildings. And an airplane. A plane that looked to be in perfect working order. He leaned in closer to the window. It looked like a passenger plane, maybe an old DC-10? It was hard to tell, really; the snowcat was bumping and jostling him as it made its way over the rough terrain.

The airport ran parallel to the opening of a bay, a kilometer-and-a-half-wide U-shaped concavity, like someone had taken a bite out of the mainland.

"Where *are* you taking us?" Mac said, turning his eyes back to the officer sitting across from him.

A panicked yell from the snowcat's driver cut the officer off before he could answer. The snowcat swerved hard right, sending the officer and the soldier next to him flying into Mac and Ryan's lap. Mac thought about making a move for the soldier's pistol, but his eyes saw the reason behind the sudden maneuvering, and all thoughts of escape evaporated.

"Holy shit," said Ryan, his mouth hanging open, his eyes focused ahead through the front windshield to the mass of roiling, bubbling water near the shoreline at the inland curve of the bay.

The driver yelled something in Norwegian, looking back over his shoulder as he brought the snowcat to a complete stop. The officer, his hand on the butt of his pistol, swiveled to face the driver, yelling something back at him, but his words stopped mid-sentence as he too saw the reason for the abrupt stop.

The other snowcats had pulled to a stop alongside theirs, and Mac saw men stepping out, their faces as pale as the snow that surrounded them.

"Screw this," Mac said. He grabbed for the door handle and was outside before the officer or his men could react, Ryan right behind him, the chilled air freezing the first breath in his throat. Without even realizing it, he kept the door open, instinctively placing the meager barrier between himself and . . .

. . . the massive congealed-blood-brown bulk rising from the water of the bay, six articulated legs digging deep into the permafrost as it heaved itself from the water onto land, mist rising off it like steam. It looked like some gigantic metallic spider, a streamlined crab-shell-like body covered in bulbous protrusions, with a mass of ropelike tentacles that twisted and squirmed beneath its underbelly. The machine, finally free of the ocean, raised itself to full height, the water gushing from its body turning to ice before it hit the ground.

In two nimble leaps that belied its enormity, it positioned itself in the path of the humans, blocking the route completely.

The thought hit Mac like his proverbial namesake truck: he and his men had led the Caretakers right here to this place. Now, however many survivors there were on this rock were doomed, along with the rest of humanity, because there was no way off this island. They were trapped. They were all as good as dead.

"Ah fuck," he hissed under his breath.

The Norwegian officer was out of the snowcat and standing directly behind Mac's right shoulder. He uttered something under his breath, an expletive or a plea to whatever god he cherished, Mac did not know, but the next instant the man was yelling orders to his men. They began to take up defensive positions around the vehicles, while others scattered outward across the landscape, taking cover behind boulders or drifts of snow, all interest in Mac and his men gone in the face of this new, terrible threat.

The machine took several more steps toward them, the echo of its feet against the ground sending chunks of snowpack cascading down the face of the mountainside.

Somewhere a siren sounded, its wail echoing off the walls of the mountain.

The machine stopped, the joints on each of the sinewy legs snapping downward one by one in a controlled collapse, until the body was lowered to the ice. An opening appeared, and a ramp unfurled itself from it like a tongue. A second later, three silhouettes, two of them distinctly humanoid, began to descend the ramp.

The officer screamed a command to his men. Even though Mac could not understand the words, the intent behind them would have been obvious to any military man: *prepare to fire.*

Mac leaped from behind the door; running forward, he turned back to face the officer and his men, throwing his hands in the air.

"Don't shoot!" he yelled. "For Christ's sake, don't shoot!"

AUTHOR'S NOTE

Stories rarely write themselves. I'd like to thank a few people for their help with bringing *Genesis* to life. First, my wife, Karen, who is always at the front of the line to read each finished manuscript and always able to help whittle it into a better story.

Stefani Lowe, Kelly Graffis, and Rosemary Gaskell, for casting their eyes over the story and giving me their thoughts on what did and did not work. I shall be calling on you ladies and gent often.

Tegan Tigani, who is new to the Extinction Point series, but this writer could not ask for a better editor. Thank you for your keen eye and gentle manner. I look forward to a long and wonderful relationship with you.

All the folks at 47North for being so damn awesome.

Last, but not least, I wanted to again thank *you* for continuing to follow Emily, Thor, Rhiannon, and Mac's adventures.

PAUL JONES

ABOUT THE AUTHOR

Photo © 2011 Paul Jones

A native of Cardiff, Wales, Paul Antony Jones now resides near Las Vegas, Nevada, with his wife. He has worked as a newspaper reporter and commercial copywriter, but his passion is penning fiction. A self-described science geek, he's a voracious reader of scientific periodicals, as well as a fan of things mysterious, unknown, and on the fringe. That fascination inspired the Extinction Point series, which follows heroine Emily Baxter's journey into the bizarre new alien world our Earth has become.

ABOUT THE AUTHOR